HUNTING
GROUND

HUNTING GROUND

MEGHAN HOLLOWAY

W RLDWIDE

TORONTO • NEW YORK • LONDON
AMSTERDAM • PARIS • SYDNEY • HAMBURG
STOCKHOLM • ATHENS • TOKYO • MILAN
MADRID • WARSAW • BUDAPEST • AUCKLAND

W★RLDWIDE™

PLEASE RECYCLE
THIS PRODUCT IS RECYCLABLE

Recycling programs
for this product may
not exist in your area.

ISBN-13: 978-1-335-77394-4

Hunting Ground

First published in 2020 by Polis Books, LLC.
This edition published in 2021 with revised text.

This edition published by arrangement with Harlequin Books S.A.

For questions and comments about the quality of this book, please contact us at CustomerService@Harlequin.com.

Harlequin Enterprises ULC
22 Adelaide St. West, 40th Floor
Toronto, Ontario M5H 4E3, Canada
www.ReaderService.com

Printed in U.S.A.

HUNTING GROUND

For the women who have disappeared,
for the women who have felt their vulnerability,
for the women who have been forgotten

And for those who loved them, searched for them,
and remembered them

PART I

Detect Damaged Branches

ONE

But he that dares not grasp the thorn
Should never crave the rose.

-Anne Brontë

HECTOR

THE ANCIENT RED car was abandoned in almost the exact spot where my wife's vehicle had been found on the empty, snow-skirted road fifteen years ago.

A deep breath rattled through my lungs. I sat frozen for a moment, staring at the vast stretch of road before me, lost in memory. To my left, the Yellowstone River was a ribbon of black. A gunmetal winter sky hung low overhead, bleeding its low, heavy clouds over the crests of the deep blue mountains that hemmed the valley.

I threw the truck into park, and Frank sat up and glanced around. I rested my hand on his head. "Stay in the truck," I told him. The dog settled back into the passenger's seat with a sigh.

The wind almost slammed the door shut in my face. I dragged the jacket zipper to my chin as I walked down the shoulder of the road. It was midday, the light glaring and tepid at the same time.

As I approached the vehicle, I found myself searching for the dream catcher that had hung from my wife's rearview mirror, for the child's car seat that should have been strapped into the back. Neither were there, of course. The vehicle was unlocked, a key left in the ignition, and empty save for a cardboard box in the backseat.

My hands were red and wind-chapped by the time I got the mounts on the old Honda and the tow bar attached. I made certain the steering wheel was unlocked and the parking brake was off before I tied the warning flag to the rear windshield wiper and retreated to my truck.

I turned the heater to full blast, flipped on my hazard lights, and pulled back onto the road. The plows had been through in the early morning hours and the snow was banked on either side of the highway. The state road crossed the Yellowstone at an oxbow. The water was black with cold, ice extending from the banks to constrain its flow. Snow was collected on the surface of the boulders above the water's reach.

The woman leaning against the balustrade of the bridge straightened when I came around the curve in the road. With the bulk at her midsection, I thought she was pregnant until I saw the vines trailing alongside her legs. She cradled some kind of plant under her coat.

As soon as she saw me, she started moving, tugging a suitcase behind her. She made it to the south side of the bridge by the time I slowed to a stop next to her. When I rolled down the window, she stepped farther off the side of the highway.

Frank stood to investigate, and I leaned forward, nudging the dog's head aside so I could greet the woman.

"This your car I have hooked up?"

"It is." The woman's eyes were large behind the fogged lenses of her glasses, and her gaze was equal parts relieved and wary. Her wind-whipped hair lashed across her pale face. She looked ready to bolt at the slightest provocation. The strain on her face and the tension around her eyes were more than just a sign of exhaustion. She looked worn and so brittle I expected the wind to snap her in half, but she smiled at Frank, and the impact of the curve of those lips was a punch in the gut. "Is that a standard poodle?"

"Sure is. His name is Frank." The tip of her nose and the high arch of her cheekbones were red and wind-burned. Her hat was pulled low over her brows and ears, and her scarf was wrapped tightly about her neck. I knew she had to be chilled, even with the oversized jacket clutched about her. I had hooked her car to the tow bar over five miles back. "You've been walking a while. I can give you a ride the rest of the way into Raven's Gap."

Her gaze dropped to the side panel of the truck, where I knew she could read the logo emblazoned on the side: *Raven's Gap Police Department.* Instead of the ease those words generally instilled in people, unease pinched her brow. She clenched her jaw when her teeth started to chatter. "Thank you, but—"

"At least ride in your car. I do anything suspicious, you'll have a fair chance to jump out and make a run for it."

Her eyes flew to mine. I did not need to be a cop to see the well of secrets in this woman's eyes. She nodded eventually. "Okay."

I knew she would be leery if I helped her with her bag, so I rolled up the window and stayed in the cab. I watched in the rearview mirror as she rounded the back of our vehicles. She lifted a hand once she was settled into the driver's seat, and I put the truck in gear.

Frank bounded into the backseat. A glance in the mirror showed his nose pressed to the window as he stared at our passenger. His tail thumped against the seat. He had a better rapport with people than I.

We would have snow tonight. The sky was heavy, and the meteorologists were predicting close to a foot of accumulation. The temperature reading on the dash proclaimed it to be seventeen degrees out. The wind-chill made it even colder. I checked the mirror again but could not see the woman's face at a quick glance. I dropped my gaze.

The road curved with the river as we entered the canyon. I slowed as I entered a straight stretch and saw Ed lumbering toward me in his decrepit tow truck. He pulled to a stop beside me, and I rolled my window down.

"Jeff came by the shop and said there was a woman out here needing a tow." The man's age was as indeterminate as his tow truck's and the trapper hat perpetually perched on his head. His gaze was hard when it met mine, mouth a tight line.

Frank shoved his head between mine and the window, grinning his wide canine smile at the man who always had treats in his pocket. Ed tossed him one now, and he snapped it out of the air. At first, I had been leery of allowing Frank to eat any treats Ed offered him. But he had told me in no uncertain terms it was me he hated and wished dead, not my dog. "I got her."

He let out a low whistle. "Haven't seen a Honda that old in some time."

I had thought the same thing when I hooked it up. The car was older than its driver. "I'll drop it off at your shop."

He lifted a hand in greeting toward the car's occupant. He started to drive on, but then his brakes groaned. "Listen, Hector." He shoved the trapper hat up and scratched at his heavily lined forehead. "The cancer's back. Doc says Betty probably won't see another Christmas."

"Sorry about that." My words did not sound as sincere as I had meant them.

A muscle ticked in his jaw. "Don't want your apologies. She doesn't have long left. It would mean a lot to her if you would tell us the truth. So she could go to her grave knowin' what happened. Where Winona and Emma..." He swallowed. "What you did to them and where we could find them."

It always came back to this. In the beginning, I had been furious over the suspicious glances, the hushed gossip always exchanged just loud enough for me to hear. I had fought those rumors and raged against them for years. After a decade and a half, now I was too tired.

I sighed and stared out the windshield. The wind buffeted my truck, rocking it back and forth. An eddy of snow and grit swirled across the deserted highway. The desolate landscape echoed the hollowness within me. Emptiness had settled deep into my bones, knitting itself into the marrow, creeping to fill the crevices of my joints until nothing but a constant, bitter ache remained.

I met Ed's gaze. "I'll tell you the same thing I've been telling you for years, old man." I had said the same words thousands of times. Maybe millions. It seemed like I should just have it tattooed on my forehead. Then I would not have to taste the bitterness of them. "I didn't kill them."

TWO

There are over one hundred species of the rose.

EVELYN

THE WIND'S BADGERING was constant as I started walking, whipping my hair about my face, whispering its iciness into the recesses of my ears, fighting my grip on the handle of my duffle bag. My progress was a chilling slog.

Though the snow was banked on either side of the highway, the pavement was clear save for a crystalline dusting the wind swept across the road. Gravel drives branched off from the highway, arrowing across the narrow plain before curving into the foothills. I could not see a house or building from my viewpoint, so I did not detour and continued along the old state road. I knew my destination lay somewhere to the east, nestled against Yellowstone National Park.

At the rumble of an approaching engine, I stepped to the edge of the road, sinking up to my ankles in snow, and turned to watch for the vehicle. I slipped a hand into my pocket and wrapped my fingers around the ever-present canister of pepper spray. A Land Rover soon rounded the bend, slowing when the driver spotted me. I stepped farther off the road as the SUV pulled to a stop beside me.

The vehicle looked brand new, all sleek silver and darkly tinted glass. As the window hummed down, I saw that the man inside was as polished as his vehicle. He flashed me a disarming smile. "Need a ride?"

He was stunningly handsome, and once, years ago, before my experience with Chad Kilgore, I would have flirted with him. Now, I wondered at how he managed to get the flannel of his shirt so crisply starched and if I could outrun him if he made a move to exit his shiny vehicle. He ducked his head to meet my gaze, and I realized I had not responded to his question. "Thank you, but no."

His brows arched, and his smile dimmed a fraction. "Look, I don't blame you for being cautious. But it's freezing out. How long have you been walking?"

I tightened my grip on the duffel bag handle and shifted the philodendron on my hip. "Not long. Is there a good mechanic with a tow truck in Raven's Gap?"

"Ed's. Just hop in, and I'll take you there."

I shook my head. "I appreciate the offer. If you're headed to Raven's Gap, would you mind sending Ed this way?"

He blew out a breath. "Sure. I can do that. If you're not going to accept a ride, at least let me give you a jacket."

A gust of wind shoved against me, and I staggered, my resolve almost faltering. The man started to open his door, and my caution came rushing back. "Please don't get out. I don't want to have to run through the snow."

A startled laugh burst from him, and he pulled his door shut. He reached into the passenger's seat and tossed a jacket through the window toward me. I bobbled the house plant in my arms but caught the jacket and met the stranger's eyes. Even at this distance, I could see the startling blue of his irises. "I'll send Ed this way. Just bring the jacket by Book Ends in town."

I forced my lips to curve and return his smile. "Thank you."

He hesitated, the smile fading as he studied me. "Stay warm. You have ten miles to go."

I almost caved at that, but thankfully he rolled up the window and put his Land Rover in gear. I relaxed only when he had disappeared around the next bend. I shrugged into his jacket and shuddered at the warmth. It was heavy and dense, leather lined with shearling that smelled faintly of cologne. I turned the collar up and resumed my trudge.

I studied my surroundings as I walked. When I left Atlanta three days ago, the South was still in that purgatory between long summer heat and brief winter chill. As I had driven north and west, I left behind the balmy, green familiarity of home, and after the first long day of driving, entered that vast stretch of the windswept plains. I had never ventured out of the South, and the wide open expanse of South Dakota and eastern Montana made me feel as if I were in a small dinghy tossed upon a sparse, empty sea of white. The isolation lanced my heart, and had there been anything to return to, I would have turned back.

But then the mountains came into view, at first merely smokey smudges of hills on the horizon, growing taller the farther west I drove. The highway began to undulate in a serpentine flow parallel to the river, and the piercing sense of aloneness coalesced into wonder. The barren emptiness morphed into a stark, haunting beauty.

Even flayed by the cold, buffeted by the wind, I felt a tug of admiration for the landscape. This was the American Wild West to which the imagination still payed homage.

The road crossed the Yellowstone at a bow in the river, and I paused in the center of the bridge. Apart from the river's soft symphony and the wind's moan, the quiet was startling. No grind of industry, no cacophony of population. The hush of the wilderness was as eerie as it was soothing.

I propped the duffle bag against the concrete baluster and drew my scarf higher up over my chin. My face was numb. I could not feel my lips or the tip of my nose. The scarf's cocoon over my mouth sent condensation over my glasses. The fingers I used to grip the duffle bag's handle ached stiffly, and I tucked my hand into my armpit to warm it as I stamped feeling back into my feet.

I leaned over the edge of the bridge. The black water rushed by beneath me, and I wondered how deep it was, how quickly a cold that brutal could kill. The concrete ground against my hip bones, and I leaned a little farther, testing my own fulcrum.

A hint of movement fluttered in the corner of my vision. I dropped my boots back to the road and turned. My breath caught. At the opposite end of the bridge, an eagle perched on the baluster, a fish snared in her talons.

Her head was turned toward me, and it tilted in seeming acknowledgement as I studied her. Those golden eyes watched me for a long moment. Then in a powerful, effortless movement, she took flight, sweeping low over the water before the beat of her wings took her higher.

I leaned against the side of the bridge, this time without daring my balance, and ducked my face deeper into my scarf. I lost sight of the eagle's flight when my glasses fogged over, but I was content to stand still a little longer, blind with the quiet of the wild in my ears.

The sound of a vehicle in the distance, though, startled me from my frozen reverie. I straightened and pulled my scarf down to clear my glasses, ears pricked to determine which direction the sound was coming from. My hope for it to be the tow truck died when I realized the sound came from the north, but my shoulders slumped with relief when the vehicle came into sight. An oversized, battered pickup truck kicked up an eddy of swirling snow. It towed my little Civic in its wake.

There was movement in the passenger's side of the cab. When the truck slowed to a halt next to me and the window rolled down, a standard poodle shoved its head through the open space and grinned at me. It was hard to resist that canine smile, and I felt my own lips curve. I relinquished the grip I had automatically taken on the canister in my pocket.

Now ensconced in my car, towed in the wake of the truck, I leaned my head back against the seat rest and rubbed my aching ears with a sigh. Sitting still, the cold caught up with me. I shivered in earnest, teeth chattering. I cupped my hands around my mouth and blew a warm gust of air into my palms before rubbing a sting of feeling back into my nose and cheeks.

The road wound through a canyon, and on the opposite side of the river, I thought I could make out the faint arrowed line of what might have been an old wagon road or rail line. Clustered outposts of civilization cropped up on occasion, and on the far side of the canyon, we began to slow.

I straightened, hand gripping the door release, but when I looked ahead on the brief straight stretch of road, I saw a tow truck approaching. We stopped, and the tow truck pulled up alongside us. Both drivers conferred for a minute before the tow truck driver lifted a hand in greeting to me and we continued our route. A glance in the rearview mirror showed the tow truck making a tight three-point turn to follow us.

A few miles passed before I saw evidence of the town. A landing strip just off the side of the highway served as a minuscule airport, and within another mile we reached the outskirts of Raven's Gap.

My gaze bounced between either side of the road. I had researched the town when I first decided to follow through on the promise I had made. I had looked at Gardiner, Cody, Cooke City, Island Park, and Jackson Hole. Each had their charm; some were more remote than others; others held more tourist attractions.

The Park County Museum was located in the town that boasted less than five hundred residents. The quietness of the little town fifteen miles outside of Gardiner appealed to me. Once I had secured a position at the museum, the decision had been made. Raven's Gap, Montana was to be my new home.

Two chain hotels peppered either side of the street along with an outfitter, a bar and restaurant, a gas station, and one of the Western themed tourist shops that populated towns in this region of the country.

I rubbed my fingers along my left collarbone. I tried to drum up a sense of excitement, but that hollow weight within me was too heavy for anything so buoyant. Even the grief had faded from sharp and cutting to a dull throb.

We turned off the main road before it crossed back over the river and pulled into the mechanic's lot. I set the philodendron aside and reluctantly climbed from the warmth of my car, watching as the man unfolded his length from the truck.

He was older, around sixty, I imagined, tall and whipcord lean. His face was weathered and lines were carved deep into the skin around his mouth and eyes. I did not think they were smile lines.

He spared me a glance but remained silent as he grabbed a toolbox from the bed of his pickup and moved straight to unhooking my little car from his truck.

"Thank you," I said. "How much do I owe you?"

He glanced at me over his shoulder as he knelt at the front bumper of my car. "Nothing."

I drifted closer, tucking my hands into the pockets of my borrowed coat. "I couldn't let you do that."

He did not respond, and the rusty tow truck pulled into the lot behind us. A man who looked even older than the truck and like he had just walked out of the mountains leapt down from the cab. He was small and wiry, and he wore a trapper hat complete with earflaps. "Haven't seen a Honda that old in some time." He let out a low, appreciative whistle and tugged off a glove to run a gnarled hand over the hood.

"I take it you are Ed?"

The tension between the two men was palpable, but the smaller, older man drew his hard gaze from the taller. His gaze softened, and he smiled at me. "Ed Decker. The one and only."

"Evelyn Hutto."

"Ev'lyn, you let me, I'll take real good care of your ol' girl here and have her up and running again."

"Really? You think you can?" I could not keep the catch from my voice. The 1980 Civic had been passed down to me on my sixteenth birthday. It was the one thing I had managed to hold onto in the last months.

Ed nodded. "You come back next week, I'll have your ol' girl in the best shape she's been in for thirty years."

"Depending on the cost, I may not be able to pay you right away." The sale of the house had only covered part of the medical bills. The life insurance policy I was left with had been drained down to three thousand dollars after Medicare took its cut.

He shrugged. "Not hurtin' for money. You'll pay me when you pay me."

I swallowed. The last years had taught me that pride had very little place to reside if you wanted to survive. "Thank you." I turned to the man working on detaching my vehicle from his truck. "Thank you as well."

He did not look up from his work. "Already thanked me."

"You need one of my clunkers to get around?" Ed thrust his grizzled chin toward an ancient Chevy truck in the corner of the lot. It may have once been white or perhaps blue, but now it was red with rust. It looked like it would break apart like a dry scab if it moved even two inches.

I could practically see the town from end to end from where I stood. "I don't think I'll need it right now."

"If you change your mind, stop by anytime. If I'm not in the shop, my house is out back."

If the last months had not left me hollowed out, I

thought my eyes might have burned at his kind voice and offer. I made an effort to smile at him. "I will. I appreciate that." My entire life was packed neatly in the car, and it fit with room to spare. A backpack, a large rolling duffel bag, a cardboard box, and a philodendron that trembled to be exposed to the cold Montana air. I hefted my suitcase from the backseat and then moved to retrieve my backpack and philodendron from the front seat. "Are there any hotels in town I should avoid?"

"Stay at The River Inn," Ed said. "Faye makes the best breakfast in town for her guests. And sometimes for those of us who come begging at her door. Try her huckleberry pancakes."

The other man pointed down the side road that ran adjacent to the shop's lot. "Her place is a couple blocks down the street."

A bark drew my gaze to where the poodle was leaning out of the driver's side window of the truck staring at us. "May I?"

The clink of tools paused, and the man glanced back, his gaze sliding past me to his dog. His face was set in harsh lines, but he smiled at the poodle. "Frank'll be disappointed if you don't."

I moved to pet the tall white poodle. He stood watching me with a dark, limpid gaze that felt as if it saw straight through flesh and bone to the very heart of me. He leaned out the window and pushed his head against my hand as I reached out to comb my fingers through his topknot. Frank, the man had said. The name made me smile, and I stroked the softness of his ears.

My arm was tired from dragging the rolling duffle, but I tucked my plant into my coat once more and tightened my grip on the handle.

"Will you be in town for a while?" Ed called.

"I hope so." I hoped it would be home. There was nothing left of my previous one.

BOOK ENDS WAS located on Main Street. It was housed in a two-story brick building that looked like an old warehouse. When I stepped inside, the rich perfume of paper and glue greeted me.

The entryway opened up into a sprawl that was every book lover's dream. A counter that resembled an antique bar was situated directly across from the entry, but no one stood behind the old-fashioned register, so I wandered farther within.

The light was warm and bright, and the old plank flooring creaked and groaned underfoot. I roamed through the rows of books and into an adjoining room. There were desks and leather sofas and chairs in corners and alcoves. Lamplight created the ambiance of a study.

"Hello. I didn't hear you come in."

I turned to find a woman approaching me. "The place is gorgeous."

"Thank you," she said. "May I help you find something?"

"Actually, I came to return this." The borrowed coat was draped over my arms.

"The woman from the road. Jeff told me about you. I'm glad Ed found you. It is not exactly walking weather out there." She glanced over her shoulder, hair swinging about her chin. "I think Jeff is in the back office. I'll tell him you're here."

"Thank you." I was drawn back to perusing the shelves and pulled a coffee table book down to flip through the pages. The photographs were taken throughout the national park in varying seasons, and it showcased the wonder of Yellowstone in vivid detail. The striking hues of the hot springs, the explosive power of the geysers, the beauty of new life in spring.

A photo of a wasteland after a forest fire caught my attention. In the photograph the landscape was a charred, ashen scar, and all that remained of a large animal—perhaps an elk or a bison—was the husk of fire-bleached bones. It was a desolate scene, wrenching and poignant. But in the foreground the photographer had captured a coyote and her pup roaming between the trees. The pup had grabbed onto the tip of his mother's tail, and she was frozen mid-step, glancing over her lean shoulder at the photographer. At her paw, straining through the soot and scorched earth, a shoot of green shrub, startling against the stark gray and black landscape, forced its way into the light. It was capped with budding, bell-like pink flowers.

The floors groaned underfoot, and I caught the faint aroma of cologne before he spoke. "Striking, isn't it?"

"It is." I touched a finger to the pink of the delicate, hardy flowers. I needed this same rebirth and promise of new life and hope. I looked up at the man who stood beside me. He was even more handsome up close and now I could see more clearly just how startling the blue of his irises was. I offered him the garment draped over my arm. "Thank you for lending me your coat."

His smile was all suave, practiced charm. "I would have preferred to give you a lift."

I closed the book. "A woman cannot be too careful these days."

His gaze searched my face. "Indeed. Since we've

been introduced now, though, will you let me buy you dinner tonight?"

I arched a brow. I had assumed he and the woman who had greeted me were married. They were a perfect matching set. But a quick glance at his hands showed his fingers bore no rings. "We haven't been introduced."

"Jeff Roosevelt."

He offered me his hand and clasped mine a moment too long before releasing my fingers.

"Evelyn Hutto."

"Well?" he asked.

I tilted my head and studied him. He was perfection. The symmetry of his face made him classically handsome. His hair was thick with no hint of gray even though I put his age closer to fifty than forty. His smile was practiced, though, and the blue of his eyes was almost painful to study.

I glanced away under the pretense of placing the book back on the shelf. "Perhaps another night," I said.

"Then you'll be in Raven's Gap for some time?"

"That's the plan."

"Perfect." His perusal was as intense as mine, and when I pushed my glasses up my nose in an automatic gesture with my knuckle, something in his gaze sharpened. "I'll look forward to seeing you around," he said.

The woman at the counter looked up and smiled as I crossed to the door. I lifted a hand in acknowledgement and then pushed out into the cold.

The sun was setting, the sky stained like a fresh bruise, the last light bleeding across the sky in deep red and orange hues. I stood on the walk and took a moment to just breathe, the air so sharp and crisp in my lungs that it made me cough. I tucked my chin into my scarf and my hands into my pockets and ambled down the sidewalk.

A restaurant with a sign labeling it Maggie's stood at the corner of the street. The door opened as I strode past. The smell of food wafted out alongside the family of four exiting. My stomach tightened and protested the long hours it had been since I had last eaten. I veered inside and claimed a seat at an empty booth.

"Good evening." The woman who approached with a glass and pitcher of water smiled warmly. "Have you had a chance to look at the menu yet?"

Food had been tasteless to me for so long that I rarely even thought about what I ate any longer. It was simply sustenance to keep me going. "What's your favorite?"

"The club sandwich," she said without hesitation. "You won't find a better club sandwich than mine."

Her apron had Maggie stitched across the front, I realized. "I'll take that, then. Thank you." When she walked away, I turned to study the dinner crowd.

There was not much of one to speak of. The patrons appeared to be largely locals save for a family in the corner whose winter jackets looked like they had just clipped the tags from them and a group of young women laughing and chatting animatedly in the opposite corner. The other tables and booths were mainly occupied by older men who tucked into their dinners with the determination to fill a belly carved hollow by long days of tireless work.

I was surprised to hear my own stomach growling by the time my order was placed in front of me. The club sandwich was thick, and the fries served with it were crispy and well-salted. The smell made my mouth water, and I polished off the plate entirely. I was not certain if the food was delicious or if I was simply ravenous, but Maggie was right. I had never eaten a better club sandwich than hers.

It was fully dark when I left the diner. Night came early in the winter mountains, but the sidewalks were not empty and the old-fashioned street lights were set close together. Where one pool of light faded, another took up its vigil. I moved around a couple strolling together hand in hand and took a deep breath, the exhale like a ghostly spirit escaping my body to drift up into the night.

Raven's Gap was laid out in a grid on an incline. The state road meandered into town alongside the river and ended half a mile farther over the bridge at a campground that abutted the boundaries of the national park. The hotels and tourist stores were located off of the state road, but small local shops and businesses populated the three streets that ran parallel to the main thoroughfare.

Raven's Gap was built into the hillside with Main Street the highest point overlooking the town and the river. I turned down one of the two streets that bisected the town and descended toward the river.

Foot traffic fell away as I left Main Street, and I tilted my head back as I walked, studying the broad expanse of the sky above me. Even the street lights could not obscure the clarity of starlight here.

The scuff of a footstep behind me had me glancing over my shoulder, and I paused when I saw no one. Turning back, I studied the shadows along either side of the street. I kept walking, taking more caution to study my surroundings, and when the soft tread of footfall came again, I stopped.

I knelt on the pretense of tying the laces of my boots.

The tread immediately stopped when I did. When I snuck a glance through the screen of my hair, I saw nothing but the empty street.

Fear pierced me, splintering through the sense of peace I had struggled to rebuild in the last five years. The first time I had heard footsteps following me through the parking lot at the museum in Atlanta late in the evening, I had thought nothing of it. I had thought it unthreatening, simply a matter of innocent timing. It had proved to be anything but.

I slipped my hand into my pocket and wrapped my fingers around the canister in my pocket. I straightened, grip tight on the defensive spray, and strode purposefully down the street. Keeping my gaze from darting around was challenging, but I kept my ears pricked.

I could not make out footsteps over the sudden cacophony of my heart in my ears, but the tight, familiar sensation between my shoulders confirmed my suspicion.

Someone was watching.

THREE

JEFF

SHE WAS PERFECT. The lamplight glinted on the lenses of her glasses and gleamed on that long, straight fall of hair. The color reminded me of the fields back home. Some rich shade between brown and gold, threaded with deeper auburn as the wind stirred the wheat and the sun passed overhead like a watchful overseer.

She had reminded me of home the instant I saw her and the wind caught her hair as she turned to watch my approach. She struck a chord with me, and seeing her striding purposefully down the deserted road…so strange and yet so familiar.

That strange hunger beginning to gnaw at me was familiar as well. It had been a dull ache for so long, I had forgotten its true ravenous intensity. The claws took my breath away. It had been years since I felt it this sharply. I thought it was in remission, but now I realized it had just lain dormant, like a beast hibernating. To feel it once more was as repelling as it was delightful.

It was as if she were a sign, a good omen letting me know that this was no sickness I needed to treat by starving it into submission with only unsatisfying, periodic bites to sustain me. This was simply my nature, and it would always come back to this, no matter how long I bided my time. All men wore their civility lightly. For some, perhaps it was a ruse entirely. The realization was such a relief that I almost laughed, but I managed to refrain.

She already knew I was here, though. I could see it in the tense, cautious line of her shoulders, the quickened steps, the strategic glance over her shoulder as she turned the corner onto the state road at the bottom of the hill.

I stopped at the corner and saw her duck into the gas station across the street. It would be easy enough to find out where she was staying and meet her there. But no, there was no need to reveal everything to her. Not so soon. There was time, and the game was half of the bright joy in this. I learned in the past that drawing out the chase only heightened the satisfaction in the end.

She was different, though, and the memory of Rose once again crept from the recesses of my mind. I needed to see her. To sit in her presence and remember how it had all started.

My hands were trembling with anticipation by the time I reached the old ruins.

I had never needed much sleep. Two or three hours sustained me, and the dark of night was the best time to tend my roses. I had built the greenhouse fifteen years ago, soon after moving to Raven's Gap. Rose would have hated being left behind, but she needed a place to rest.

The combination of the geothermal springs, the rocket mass heater I had built, and the long, deep compost trench dug through the center of the structure kept my roses safe from the frigid winter just beyond the walls. The underground construction added to the year-round sustainability and to its concealment. In the winter, it was almost invisible.

Few people ventured this far into the wilderness. The ruins of the old hot springs resort were not on any map. But this was a hallowed place, a sanctuary that needed to be guarded and protected. I disarmed the electric current as I approached and deactivated the security system after I unlocked the door.

The air was thick with the scent of roses and the pungent smell of earth. I breathed more easily when I stepped inside. Dim lanterns lit the stone path through the labyrinth to the heart of the greenhouse.

I sighed as I sat on the bench I had placed close by. This could not be like the others, I decided. She would not appreciate the subtlety of my rose garden until I gained her attention. I needed her to know I had a story to tell her. And then, once she understood, she would help me write the conclusion.

I collected my pruning shears and approached, smiling when she made me bleed as I stroked her lushness. "Rose, Rose," I murmured. "Remember what I've told you. This is for your own good."

Women were so like roses. They needed to be groomed, trained, and ruthlessly pruned before their true beauty appeared. It was a promise they made to you. If you tended them, they would bloom for you. Deadheading was just a reminder she had promises to keep.

FOUR

EVELYN

I SLEPT UNEASILY, startling awake at the slightest noise. I roused again before daybreak and gave up on slumber. The clock on the bedside table blearily read 4:21. I grimaced when I toggled the switch on the lamp and pale light pierced my eyes.

The River Inn was situated on an oxbow of the Yellowstone. At first sight of the sprawling cabin of rough-hewn timber and glass yesterday, I had almost turned away and found a cheap hotel chain off the main road through town. But on second glance, I could see the first teeth of dereliction beginning to gnaw at the edges of the inn.

The place was beginning to look weathered and worn, the luster of its former glory rubbed thin in the shingles that needed replaced, the shutters and doors that needed a good sanding and refinishing, the listing bottom step leading up to the wraparound porch that needed reinforcement.

When I knocked on the door, the woman who greeted me was younger than I expected, perhaps a couple years younger than my own thirty-six. She introduced herself as Faye, and the price she named for a room was so low my skepticism must have shown on my face.

"This is the down season here," she explained, voice

soft. "You're my only boarder at the moment, so you have your pick of rooms."

The interior was a stark contrast to the exterior. The hardwood floors and exposed beams of the ceiling were polished to gleaming. The windows and skylights flooded the interior with natural light. It was bright and welcoming.

I picked the end room on the second floor with a small balcony that overlooked the river. The balcony did not look entirely trustworthy, and my impression was reiterated by Faye.

"I'm sorry, but please don't venture onto the balcony." The wrinkle in her brow was rueful as she glanced through the arched glass in the top half of the Dutch door. "It's a bit of a liability at this point."

The room was spacious with thick rugs thrown over the rolling wood floor, a queen-size bed, matching bedside tables, and a TV on an antique sideboard. An armoire stood in one corner, a chaise lounge in the opposite. The bathroom was en-suite, and I could not help but be impressed.

I placed my philodendron on the sideboard. "This is beautiful."

Her face was bright with pleasure. "Thank you. This was the first room I remodeled, and it is still my favorite. If you need a mini-fridge, I can bring one up for you, but you're welcome to put anything in the refrigerator in the kitchen. I usually serve breakfast every morning starting at seven thirty. Since you're my only guest, if you'll let me know a different time, I can accommodate you."

"Seven thirty is perfect."

Now, I had hours to spare before breakfast, and I

dragged myself from bed to stumble into the bathroom. I stood under the shower's spray with my head bent, letting the water sluice over me in a hot curtain. The heat cleared away my grogginess, and after long minutes I was roused enough to bathe. By the time I turned off the water, the bathroom was full of steam and the mirror was fogged over.

Squeezing water from my hair, I reached across the vanity and palmed away a swath of condensation. A dark shape lingered behind me in my reflection.

My heart jolted into my throat as I whirled, feet slipping on the slick tile. I caught myself before I fell, and though my heart and body were still perched for flight, my brain finally switched into gear.

It was my robe, innocent and inanimate, hung there by my own hand yesterday afternoon. I felt foolish, but my laugh was unsteady.

Last night had left me rattled. As I lingered in the gas station, watching the street from behind a display of stale snack cakes, no one had appeared around the corner. When the teen behind the counter had begun to glance at me askance, I forced myself to abandon the temporary sanctuary. My stride had been close to a jog as I hurried past darkened store fronts and across deserted side streets. My fingers were tight around the can of pepper spray, and my gaze darted over my shoulder every few steps.

The sound of a steady, surreptitious tread behind me never came again. By the time I reached the inn, I slowed to a walk, lungs burning from the high, thin air. I did not leave the curtains open to admire the moon-drenched river, instead drawing them closed as soon as I entered my room. I checked the lock on my door whenever I woke up throughout the night.

I snatched the offending robe from the hook and tied it about me, struggling to slow the pell-mell pace of my heart. I took a deep breath through my nose, held it, and let it out in a long breath through my mouth. I kept up the breathing routine as I got ready for the day.

When I donned my glasses and left the bathroom, I glanced at the clock. It was still early, so I heaved my oversized suitcase onto the end of the bed and unpacked. The contents of my life had been pared away to the bare essentials.

There was a dual tug on my emotions: bitterness at the failed system that had rendered this a necessity and a sense of relief at being so unencumbered.

The latter pierced me, especially when I carefully placed the two frames on one of the bedside tables. One photograph was over half a century old, and the portrait showed a poised young couple, she in a light blue dress with her pale hair artfully coiffed and her smile reserved, he in his Air Force uniform with a wide grin and glint of mischief in his eyes. The other was a less formal photograph taken on an old home camera decades later. A different couple stood together, unposed and caught in the moment at what appeared to be an outdoor summer party beside a lake. The woman in this photo stood in front of the man, leaning against him with her head tilted back as she laughed. His head was bent, and I could just make out the crease in his cheek that told me he smiled down at her. Their hands were interlaced and rested on her burgeoning stomach.

Memories were all I had left of one couple now; the photograph was all that remained of the other. A gamut of emotion attempted to slip through the cracks in the wall I had painstakingly constructed to keep the sorrow, loneliness, and pain at bay.

I had learned that it was not sadness that could crush you after a final loss. Instead, it was the oppressive sense of aloneness that was the heaviest burden to bear, so heavy that some mornings it was a challenge to drag myself from bed. The weight of it would crush me if I allowed it.

For months, I had given it free rein. I had allowed it to perch heavily on my chest, stuttering my breath and making each heart beat a struggle. I had allowed it to fester like a wound left to rot until all I could smell was the stench of it and all I could taste was the bitter bile of it. I allowed it to fester until I forced myself from my sour bed and found two weeks had passed without me even realizing it.

I had realized something else then. There was a reason gangrenous limbs were amputated. Left unchecked, the dead rot spread. It infiltrated your blood and poisoned your heart and head and everything else along the way. Severance was the only means of survival.

In the end, the amputation of the rest of all that was familiar and dear was forced upon me. Bitterness was even more dangerous than sorrow.

I wiped the smudges from the glass of the frames, arranged them carefully, and pushed aside the insidious, suffocating weight I had fought against for long months.

I rubbed my fingers along my left collar bone. The tattoo had long since healed. The artist had copied my grandparents' handwriting from an old birthday card. *Love always, Nana & Papa* was imprinted into my skin. I could no longer feel the raised wound of the tattoo.

But I knew the words were there, and they provided some comfort.

I would get a dog, I decided as I changed into a pair of jeans and a soft cable knit sweater. Once I was settled into the new job at the museum and had a steady income again and a place of my own, I would go to the animal shelter and adopt a dog. I thought of Frank, the dog I had met yesterday. Perhaps I could find a poodle.

I pushed aside the curtains. It was still dark and the river sighed in slumber, but I could see the pale precursor of dawn in the east. I had glimpsed a coffee bar yesterday in the great room when Faye had given me a tour.

My room was at the end of the hall. There was a door on either side before the hallway opened onto a lofted balcony over the great room. The night was beginning to lighten with the predawn, and the interior of the inn was a grid of gray and shadow as the darkness waned and retreated from the windows and skylights. I kept a hand on the railing as I descended the stairs, my footsteps hesitant in the darkness.

A massive stone fireplace dominated the center of the great room. A low banked fire glowed in the coals of the double hearth. The tour yesterday had given me the layout of the room, even though I could not distinguish anything but dim shapes now. On the opposite side of the fireplace, across the dining room, faint light bloomed through a doorway.

I followed the light and entered what would be a glorious sunroom in daylight. The doorway at the opposite end of the sunroom opened into a warmly lit kitchen.

I hovered in the threshold and watched Faye where she stood beside the deep farmhouse sink slicing bread on a cutting board. A boy stood beside her, chin perched on the countertop.

She jumped when she spotted me in the doorway, and I lifted a hand apologetically. She recovered quickly, set the knife aside, and wiped her hands on the skirt of her apron.

"Good morning. I hope you slept well."

"The room is incredibly comfortable," I offered, since my restless night had nothing to do with the accommodations. "Is this your son?"

She rested a hand on his head, ruffling his dark hair. "This is Sam." He was small and pale, his eyes too large for his face and too unblinking. I smiled at him, but he did not return the gesture. "I haven't started preparing breakfast yet, but it won't take me long to get everything ready."

A table with two chairs was tucked off to the side of the kitchen under a window. Sam scrambled into one of the chairs and snagged a piece of cheese toast from his plate, devouring half of it in one bite.

"No, no. I don't want to interrupt your breakfast. I just came down to make some coffee."

She reached into the cupboard and grabbed a mug. "You're in luck. I just finished brewing a pot. Cream? Sugar?"

"Just black." I accepted the extended mug and breathed in the fragrant steam that curled over the dark liquid.

"You're…" Faye hesitated and fixed her gaze on the countertop. "You're welcome to join us for breakfast. It's just toast."

The invitation was offered hesitantly, and I realized behind the friendly attentive guise of being an innkeeper, she might be shy. "That sounds wonderful, but I wouldn't want to impose."

"You wouldn't be." She cut off two more thick slices of bread from the loaf and dropped them into the toaster. "I can put cheese on it if you like. Or I have some home-made huckleberry jam."

"The jam, please." I retreated to the dining room and grabbed a chair.

The bread was homemade as well, soft and light and so delicious I had to bite back a moan. The coffee was hot and tasted of hazelnuts, and the simple plea-sure of enjoying a companionable breakfast made my throat tight.

My grandparents had risen like clockwork at four in the morning every day for much of my early life. Every morning, I had wandered sleepily into the kitchen to find them reading the paper at the breakfast table, a plate of still hot biscuits in the center of the table and a saucer of butter and honey waiting for me. Even before they were gone, it had been years since we had observed that unspoken ritual.

"What's brought you to Raven's Gap, especially this time of year?"

I blinked away memories and spread a layer of jam on a second slice of toast. "A job, actually. I'm the Park County Museum's new assistant collections manager."

"What does that job entail?" Genuine curiosity tinged her voice.

"They hired me to manage their Native American collections and make certain everything is in accor-dance with the NAGPRA guidelines. The Native Ameri-can Graves Protection and Repatriation Act. It's a grant position right now, but it has the possibility of turning into a permanent position."

"Graves Protections and Repatriation? So you would be making certain artifacts were returned to tribes?"

"It's mainly human remains and funerary objects, but yes. The museum apparently has a pretty sizable collection in its archives that has not been properly appraised. They've brought me in to catalogue the objects and work with the affiliated tribes to determine the disposition."

"That sounds fascinating."

"It is," I admitted. Ever since I had read about the project and applied, I had wanted to see the collection for myself. It was quiet, rewarding work, often dusty, always poignant. From past experience, I knew it would either be a treasure trove the affiliated tribe would want to reclaim possession of, or it would be mere shards of a past culture now relegated to the status of historical junk. I handled both with equal care. "I did similar work at a museum in Atlanta, but I was looking for a change of scenery."

Faye chuckled, blew a cooling breath over the rim of her coffee mug, and nodded at the window. "You've certainly got that here."

Dawn had crept over the horizon and revealed what I had not seen in the darkness. A fresh, thick layer of snow had fallen overnight.

I pressed a hand to the frosted window pane. "It's stunning. I've been thinking I would try cross-country skiing."

"I keep some outdoor gear on hand for guests. No skis, I'm afraid, but I do have snowshoes if you're interested."

I was interested, and within a couple hours it was fully light out and I made my way over the cleared and salted sidewalks toward the far end of town with the snowshoes in hand. Faye had told me there were trails branching out into the wilderness of Yellowstone from the campground at the edge of Raven's Gap.

Sunday morning was quiet in town. Wreaths and garland still festooned lampposts and doorways, the holiday decorations carried over into the new year. The only traffic—foot or vehicle—centered around a coffee shop on the corner. I stopped at the crosswalk, waiting for a vehicle to pass along the plowed, slushy street.

The light tap of a horn brought my gaze to the vehicle and I recognized the Land Rover as it slowed to a halt. The window buzzed down, and Jeff Roosevelt called a greeting to me.

I approached his vehicle and returned his greeting. "Good morning."

His gaze took in the snowshoes I carried before returning to my face. "Taking advantage of the fresh powder?"

"Hopefully," I said, hoping he would not invite himself along. I wanted peace and quiet, not the task of carrying on a conversation.

"The campground has some great trails."

"That's what I've heard."

A spit of snow landed on my glasses and slid across the lens. With an ease born of long habit, I plucked them off and polished the dampness away before shoving them back on my nose. Once Jeff's face came into crisp view again, I found that laser focus directed on me.

"Perhaps I'll see you on the trails later," he said.

It may have been the intensity of his gaze or the taut

tone of his voice, but a shiver of unease slipped up my spine. "Perhaps."

He nodded. "See you soon, Evelyn."

I stepped back onto the sidewalk and waited until he passed before crossing the street. My gaze followed his Land Rover until it turned down a side road and disappeared. *See you soon.* There was a promise implied in the words, and I wondered if he was someone I needed to be leery of.

I detoured from my trek to the campground and veered into the busy coffee shop. The place was small and local but bustling with people and conversation. I stood in line, glancing over my shoulder, peering past the people who soon fell into the queue behind me.

My breathing began to quicken. I closed my eyes, focusing on a slow breath in through my nose to a count of four. I held it, counting to seven, and then let it out in a long sigh as I counted to eight.

I concentrated on the counting, on the feel of the warm interior air of the shop, fragrant with the aroma of coffee, as I inhaled, on the movement of my chest and the ghost of air over my lips as I exhaled. Silently, I hummed the tune of "Greensleeves."

It was a challenge to resist jumping to conclusions about people's—men's—motives any longer. Even years later, my stomach shriveled into a tight, hard knot at the memories. The solicitous smile, the prolonged stare, the convenient run-ins.

I flinched when I felt a tap on my shoulder.

"You're next," the woman behind me said, and when I opened my eyes, I realized the young man behind the counter had tried to get my attention by calling "Next" several times.

"Sorry," I murmured, and stepped out of line.

I ignored any curious stares directed my way and drifted to the wall of windows. I peered both ways down the street. There was no Land Rover in sight.

I'm sorry, miss, but he hasn't done anything we can charge him with. The words had been said to me numerous times. At first patiently, but eventually with a note of exasperation and disbelief accompanied by nearly rolled eyes and snide tones.

I pressed a hand against the window. The frigid temperatures leeched through the glass and seeped into my palm, helping cut through the rising panic. This was another time and place. I was aware and on guard. I slipped my hand into my pocket and grasped the canister of pepper spray. Aware. On guard. And armed.

That knowledge bolstered me, and I stepped back into line and ordered a peppermint hot chocolate. When my name was called out minutes later, I took one of the overstuffed chairs in the corner of the shop and enjoyed my beverage. I people watched and eavesdropped, soaking in the small town atmosphere in which everyone knew one another. An hour later, I tossed my empty cup in the recycling bin and exited the coffee shop.

Raven's Gap was draped in white. The timber and brick town perched on the hillside looked like something out of a wintry fairytale. The air was so pure and clean it felt sharp in my lungs. The deep gray sky of yesterday had been replaced with a blue so pale the sun shone white, and a frail froth of scattered clouds reached like fingers over the mountains. The river was dark and lively where it was not frozen and skirted with snow.

The road through town dead-ended at the entrance to the campground on the opposite side of the river.

The gatehouse at the entrance was unmanned, and the single-lane track that meandered through the grounds was unplowed.

I stopped and knelt to secure the snowshoes to my boots. Once the bindings were tightened, I straightened and followed the narrow road into the campground.

The area was wooded, and the lodgepole pines that had been pushed back to the boundaries of the town grew in abundance here. Regular clearings marked the sites for tents and RVs, but all were empty, a smooth, unblemished stretch of white.

The sounds of civilization vanished with astonishing swiftness. Soon all I could hear was the crunch of snow under the blades of my snowshoes and the murmur of the river through the trees.

I picked my way slowly through the campground, following the curve of the road to a stretch where the trees were cleared. A bathhouse stood on the corner, closed for the season, and beyond that, a cluster of cabins sat on either side of the road. There were no vehicles parked in front of any of the ten cabins. They all appeared boarded up for the winter.

A hut sat at the end of the row of cabins. The sign for the trailhead stood beside it, the top of the wooden board iced with snow. The single-lane road came to a dead end in an empty semicircular parking area, but a curl of smoke drifted over the sharply angled roof of the hut.

The wind was still today, but the cold bit sharply down to the bone. I approached the hut and found the door cracked, a set of tracks in the snow leading within.

"Hello?" My call went unanswered, and the deserted

campground was still and quiet. It was peaceful, I assured myself, not eerie.

The woman within the hut startled me, but the widening of her eyes betrayed the fact that I had done the same to her. She reached up and pulled a bud from her ear. I could hear the tinny sound of music.

"Sorry," she said, smile wide, voice pure Texas drawl. She fumbled in her pocket and the music blaring from the earbud went silent. A set of poles leaned against the bench beside her, and when I glanced at the corner, I saw a pair of cross-country skis propped against the wall. "Come on in."

The hut was small, perhaps six feet by eight feet, and the door groaned as I pushed it closed behind me. The interior consisted of benches that ringed the walls and an old iron stove in the center of the room. The hut bordered on ramshackle, the wood unfinished and unadorned. A topographical map was nailed against the far wall, and firewood was stacked neatly under the benches.

I extended my gloved hands to the stove, sighing at the warmth that heated my fingers and wrapped around my legs.

The woman finished a granola bar and then pulled one from the backpack on her lap and extended it to me. "Want one?"

I shook my head. "Thank you, though."

She tucked it back into her backpack and took a long pull from a water bottle. She was young, late teens or early twenties, and I thought she might have been one of the women I had seen last night in the group at the diner.

She flashed that wide, guileless smile at me again and then stood and shouldered the backpack. "Enjoy the trails. They're fantastic this morning." She collected the poles and skis and slipped out the door.

My jeans began to feel overheated as the warmth seeped into my front. I turned, putting my back to the stove, and saw the coat discarded over the bench. I started to open the door and call out to the young woman, but she had been wearing a coat. When I caught the sleeve and held it up, I saw how small the coat was. It was sized for a pre-teen girl, a deep purple decorated with pink polka dots. The pattern made me smile, and I folded the garment neatly before placing it back on the bench.

Heated through front and back, I stepped outside and pulled the door closed behind me. One trail branched off from the parking lot, circling around behind the warming hut and disappearing into the woods. I studied the map etched into the trailhead sign, following the loops and fingers of the trails. Faye had assured me the trails were all clearly marked and regularly trafficked, and though I saw no one about, the ribbon of trail was already trenched with the tracks of early-rising snow-shoers and skiers. I was less than a mile from the town center, but it felt as if I were a world away in the middle of the wilderness.

I shivered, and it had nothing to do with the cold. I was a city girl, born and raised. My grandparents had taken me to museums and art galleries and the aquarium when I was a child, not hiking and camping. The closest I had been to nature was the handful of times I encountered a raccoon or possum when I lifted the lid on the outdoor garbage.

A flash of red in my periphery caught my attention. A fox darted from the cover of the forest and crept along the trail, his burnished fur stark against the smooth stream of white. My breath caught, and those keen ears twitched before the fox stopped and turned its head, staring directly at me. I held myself completely still, unwilling to frighten it into bolting.

The fox stood frozen for a moment, black-tipped ears pricked. He watched me as curiously as I watched him for several long moments before he continued padding along the trail.

I followed the fox, and stepping onto the trail was like entering a corridor. The branches of the spruce and fir trees that girded either side of the trail were heavily laden and bowed under the weight of last night's snowfall. Even broken, the trail was knee-deep with snow and shadowed by the trees. The way was harder here, each step with the snowshoes careful and deliberate. Soon I was unbuttoning my wool peacoat and loosening the scarf about my neck even as my jeans from the knees down grew icy and caked with snow.

Only once in my life had I ventured into the wilderness. The woods had been deep and stark in the last dying breaths of a Southern autumn. I still heard the moan of the trees off that forest trail in my dreams.

I sucked in a deep breath and ventured deeper into the forest along the trail. I lost sight of the fox as the track veered sharply away from its trajectory toward the river and led deeper into the forest and higher into the surrounding hills. Once I reached the curve in the trail, though, I saw the fox ahead of me. He sniffed the ground near a sagging spruce, glanced back to catch my eye when I came into view, and then continued his amble.

I dug in with my snowshoes, leaning into the climb,

and stopped when I reached the sagging spruce. I had seen a fox all of those years ago, in a different forest. I had heard the cry of a bird overhead and tilted my head back to watch a hawk's glide across the piercing blue sky. And I had known there was a possibility I would not make it out of those woods alive when I heard him approaching.

I shook off the memories. I was not the same after that. There was no way I could be. But I had survived. I had rebuilt my life after coming out of those woods. And now I was determined to follow this winding path without fear suffocating me.

The landscape as I continued along the trail was as stunning as it was otherworldly. Snow muffled the quiet of the wilderness until it was utterly silent, save for my own interloping steps and labored breath. The white was interrupted with the deep blue-green of spruce trees and the emerald of the firs. The rough, slender trunks of the pines looked as if they might shiver without any needled cloaks.

I breathed deeply. The air was sharp in my nose and at the back of my throat, pure and jaggedly cold. My thighs burned with the exaggerated high step the snowshoes required, and I stripped off my knitted beanie and stuffed it in my coat pocket. The cold had numbed my cheeks, lips, and nose, but it felt like a mother's soothing hand against my warm brow.

The trail leveled out, and I stopped, hands braced on my hips as I caught my breath. The top of the hill afforded me no vantage point view with the trees dense and tall.

The woods are lovely, dark and deep.

The line from Frost's poem came to me as I peered

into the trees, watching the fox as he moved with silent grace and stealth away from the trail. I had no promises to keep, though, so I lingered.

The winter landscape was hauntingly stark, and the beauty and wildness snagged on some latent longing within me. There was nothing to fear here. I could understand why my grandfather had been so enchanted with this land, why he had requested the promise of me. Standing watching the fox, deep in the forest's embrace, my anxiety was flayed away and, for a moment, there was only quiet, without and within.

The light trill of laughter somewhere nearby was so out of place that it was shocking, as startling as a gunshot. I jumped, took a lurching step backward, and fell when the snowshoes caught with the reverse movement. I struggled upright, dusting snow from my backside, and looked around. A low murmur of voices reached me through the trees, indistinct and distant. Ears strained, I thought the female voice might hold a slow drawl, but I could not be certain. I saw no one on the trail behind me or ahead of me.

I glanced into the trees in search of the fox, but he was gone. Irritation lanced away some of the peace that had enveloped me, and I slogged ahead.

The descent was gradual, the trail a lazy serpentine through the trees as it curved downhill. I could hear the river, but I did not realize the trail was leading me back to the water until it twisted around a copse of spruce trees and deposited me onto a stretch of path along the banks.

The river was narrow and shallow here, tumbling white over a rocky bed. Ice was crusted along the quieter water by the banks. Sunlight gilded the water and caught in crystalline fragments in the air. I gasped at the sight. The light sparkled and glinted, as if glitter had been tossed into the air.

I stripped off a glove and reached out, letting my fingers stretch and curl through the diamond dust. I imagined I could feel the tiny pinpricks of ice crystals against my skin as sunlight pooled in my palm. A smile tugged at my chilled lips, and my earlier aggravation slipped away.

And then a scream, high and full of terror, rent the air.

FIVE

About 750,000 people go missing every year.

HECTOR

I PULLED INTO the front lot of the department.

The small law enforcement outpost had been set up in the '40s when the Northern Pacific Railway had discontinued its service to nearby Gardiner and Raven's Gap had been a wild, lawless haven for those looking to live on the fringes of civilization. It was remote, the outskirts of town filled with those who still did not quite fit into society, and the canyon leading to Gardiner was impassable some years in the depths of winter.

I had joined the police department thirty years ago for a lack of anything better to do. At thirty years of age, I had a wife I was not entirely certain I wanted anymore who had been keen to move back to her hometown as soon as my career on the circuit was over. I had a new knee, hip, and shoulder courtesy of a bull. I had spent eight months relearning how to walk. I was fresh from rehab with a piss-poor attitude and a bitterness wedged deep inside my gut at the turn life had taken.

At thirty, I was young and angry and stupid. When I had seen the ad in the newspaper, I thought, *Why the hell not?* I had nothing better to do. I was mad enough at the world that I liked the idea of having a gun strapped to my hip and the authority to use it. I thought myself a real Wyatt Fucking Earp.

At thirty, I had been naive enough to expect a brotherhood. I had been met with a boys' club. Like me, had the other officers not had a badge pinned to their chests, they would likely have been on the other side of the law. The idea of fraternity was a flimsy thing when you could not be entirely certain the man next to you would not shoot you in the back.

Raven's Gap Police Department never had more than fifteen officers, including the chief, commander, detective, and three sergeants.

I had seen a number of faces come and go in the last three decades. Men and women joined the force and then moved up and on. I had never sought promotions or special assignments. I did not care enough about the job to spend more time at it than necessary. I did not want the extra assignments, extra responsibility, or extra paperwork.

I had spent half my life as a police officer. Now at the ripe age of sixty, I just wanted to get through the damn day without needing an antacid or having to put in overtime.

Frank trotted at my heels as I crossed the parking lot and entered the building that served as police department, court house, and city office space. Joan Marsden, the chief's wife, sat at the police reception desk behind an inch of bulletproof glass.

She grimaced as she reached for something on her desk, but she glanced up when I entered the lobby, and her smile was welcoming. I used my badge to gain entry down the hallway. She stood, coming slowly around the counter to greet Frank and to offer him a treat from the jar she kept at her desk. The big guy grinned up at her and leaned against her legs as he crunched the treat.

"Officer Lewis."

I nodded to her as I passed. "Mrs. Marsden."

Space was limited in our corner of the building, but seniority had its perks. I had my own office and I had my choice of shifts. I had been working the day shift for ten years now. I had done my time as a young pup on graves and swings. But as an old dog, my circadian rhythm had made itself known.

Frank joined me in the office, and the poodle took up his place on the bed beside my desk as I donned my reading glasses and booted up my computer.

Several hours later, the phone on my desk rang.

"There's a woman up front who would like to speak to someone," Joan said on the opposite end of the line. "I think everyone else is out on patrol right now."

I finished scanning the warrant application I had typed up and tossed my reading glasses on the desk. "Did she say why she wants to see someone?" I tucked the phone between my ear and shoulder.

"She thinks something may have happened at the campground." Joan spoke around the phone's mouthpiece, "Go ahead and have a seat. Officer Lewis will be up shortly." I heard a quiet murmur of response, and after a moment, she lowered her voice and said, "She must be a tourist. I've never seen her before."

"I'll be up in just a moment. I need you to notarize something for me."

"Bring it on up with you."

I printed off the warrant application and headed to the front of the building. Joan snagged the papers as I slid them across the countertop and nodded toward the waiting area on the other side of the bulletproof glass.

I pushed through the door into the lobby and paused when I saw the woman seated on the hard slats of the wooden bench. She glanced my way when she heard the door, face tight with concern.

She had been uneasy yesterday when I picked her up on the side of the road, and today dark circles still bruised the fragile skin beneath her eyes. She stood as I approached.

"It was Evelyn, wasn't it?"

"Yes, that's right." Twin flags of color were raised across her cheeks from the cold, and her jeans were soaked from the knees down. A pale pink hat was clutched between both hands. Her teeth dug into her lower lip.

I pulled a small spiral notebook and pen from my shirt pocket and flipped to a blank page. "Let's sit. Joan told me there's been an incident at the campgrounds?"

She returned to the bench, and I pulled a chair over to sit opposite her. A pair of discarded snowshoes lay at her feet. She twisted the hat between her hands, gaze on the worried knit cap, and pressed her lips tightly together before letting out of breath. "Officer Lewis, I—"

"Just Hector."

Her gaze lifted to mine. Her eyes, highlighted behind the lenses of her glasses, were so light a brown they almost matched the Macallan single malt I kept unopened in the cabinet at home.

"Hector." Her brow pinched. "I don't know that I have anything to report. I couldn't find anything—anyone—when I searched, but I...well, I wanted to make sure no one was hurt. I'm just not sure anyone is."

"Start at the beginning and tell me what happened to make you think someone might be hurt."

She told me of her morning trek, of hearing voices at one point, and of the scream that had wrenched the quiet wide open. "I ran back along the trail as quickly as I could. No one answered when I called, and I couldn't find anyone."

"You didn't see anyone on the trail or as you were leaving the campground?"

"There was a young woman, a cross-country skier, in the warming hut when I first arrived. I don't know if she went back down the trails or if she left. I never actually *saw* anything." She shrugged. "I know there's really nothing for you to go on. But..." A slight shiver coursed over her. "That scream..."

I glanced through the glass sliding doors. The day was a beautiful one, all sunshine and piercing sky and fresh powder. The only thing I hated more than sitting by the side of the road waiting for some dumbass to ignore the stop sign was sitting behind a desk in a windowless room for hours on end. A hike on the department's dime was in order. "Why don't you tell me where you were on the trail? I'll go check it out."

She slid forward to the edge of the bench, and her knee bounced. A crusting of ice followed the seam of her jeans down the side of her calf. "I was on the main trail, by the river. There's a long hill, and then the opposite side leads down to the river."

I tucked the notebook in my pocket. "I know it. The top of the hill marks where the trail enters the park and the state line."

"Does that make a difference?"

"The park more than the Wyoming line. Yellowstone

is federal jurisdiction. But I'll still check things out, see what I find." If there was anything, I would pass the information along to the rangers and be thankful I was not the one who would need to deal with the paperwork.

"Will you let me know? Please. Either way."

I studied her. She was slightly built, just shy of average height and small boned. Her features were elegant, but I thought the fine line of her jaw could probably turn stubborn in an instant. "You staying at Faye's?"

She nodded.

"I'll swing by the inn and let you know what I find." I used my badge to key my entry back into the department's inner offices. I leaned over Joan's desk and scrawled my signature across the warrant application. "Will you fax this over to the judge for me?"

"The Johnson case?"

"The very one. Everything is here, I just don't want to deal with that damn machine right now."

We both looked at the ancient fax machine. Whether it would send the fax or chew it up depended entirely on its cantankerous mood. "I'll see if I can coax it," Joan said, voice reluctant.

I strode down the hall and grabbed my coat. Frank leapt to his feet as I cued up the radio clipped to my shoulder. "Romeo 3, dispatch."

A woman's voice crackled over the radio. "Romeo 3, go ahead."

"I am en-route non-emergent to the campground." I rattled off the address. "Reports of suspicious activity."

"Romeo 3, I copy that. Do you need a second?"

"Not at this time."

Frank raced out of the building ahead of me and leapt into the cab of my truck when I held the door open for him. I drove carefully down the hill and turned onto the state road. When I crossed the bridge, I slowed as I drove into the unplowed campground. Snow shifted under my tires. There was a decent amount of foot traffic through the campground but no vehicle tracks. I parked in front of the warming hut.

Frank sniffed around the hut as I grabbed gaiters and snowshoes from the back of the truck. Once the gear was donned, I checked the interior of the hut and found it empty.

I whistled for Frank and moved into the woods. The trail was broken, but the snow was still deep. I picked my way carefully, studying the ground and surroundings with each step. There were animal tracks along and over the trail, fox and snowshoe hare.

It was only because I was searching for it that I saw a disturbance in the snow and the slight splatter. I knelt to examine the sudden depression. Six drops of blood marred the white expanse, and a curved accordion of tracks around the depression marked the culprit of the violence—an eagle. For someone unfamiliar with the wilderness and its wildlife, the scream of a dying hare would sound terrifyingly human.

I thought about turning back, but a glance at my watch showed only thirty minutes had passed. No need to hurry back.

I took my time descending the trail to the river. The trail followed the bank for a mile before it branched in two, one trail looping back to the warming hut and parking lot, the other following the river deeper into Yellowstone.

A lone cross-country ski lay sticking out of the snow to the side of the trail.

A flurry of movement was stamped into the powder, and farther off the trail I found a knit cap half buried. I whistled for Frank, and after several moments he came bounding through the woods to my side. I caught hold of his collar, positioned him so he was facing into the forest, and let him sniff the knit cap.

I pointed into the trees. "Frank, find."

The change came over him immediately, a shifting of muscles from playful, overgrown pup to a trained animal with a mission. I had started the day I brought him home from the breeder at ten weeks of age, beginning with the game of hide and seek. When he was older, I trained on different terrain, increasing the distance. I had gradually added age to the track and incorporated multiple people. He was the second dog I had trained, and he had picked it all up with ease.

He was not trained in track and trail like a bloodhound. His certification was in air scent, and he raced around the area, venturing off the trail at different points until he locked onto the scent and veered into the woods.

I followed him off trail. As I followed him off the trail, I began to spot evidence of a struggle angling into the woods. The broken branches and disturbed snow were a testament to someone's desperate resistance.

Frank found a mitten at the base of a lodgepole pine, and when I picked it up, I could imagine the circumstance that left the article here: a woman reaching out, catching hold of the tree in an attempt to anchor herself as she was dragged away.

Frank darted on, deeper into the forest, nose working the snow-covered ground and the air. I trailed him and spoke into my radio. "Romeo 3, dispatch."

There was a crackle of static and then, "Romeo 3, go ahead."

"Have there been any calls regarding this incident?"

"No, sir, dispatch has not received anything."

"I copy."

The scent trail ended at an old service road well away from the marked paths of the campground. Frank raced up and down the stretch of road, but the trail was gone. The only thing that remained was a backpack on the ground that Frank kept returning to.

I offered him a treat from my pocket, patting his side when he leaned against me. "Good boy. Well done."

I donned a pair of black nitrile gloves as I knelt beside the backpack. Frank paced by my side, whining as I unzipped the pack and searched through the contents. There were extra layers of clothing, two water bottles, several granola bars, and a first aid kit. Standard fair for someone spending a few hours on the trails.

There was no wallet, no identity tags on the pack itself, just a keychain adorned with a pink plastic cartoon puppy hanging from one of the zippers. The bag itself was from a high-end sporting brand, and one of the straps was broken.

I straightened and studied the scene. The drag marks in the snow from the woods led to a set of tracks on the service road. The tracks were spaced like the tires of a vehicle, but they had the tread of a snowmobile's tracks. They led south, deeper into Yellowstone territory.

I spoke into my radio again. "Romeo 3, dispatch."

"Romeo 3, go ahead."

"Put me in touch with the rangers in the park. Have someone call me at the station."

"Romeo 3, I copy. Is this in regards to the report of a suspicious incident at the campground?"

"It is." The suspicious incident had all the hallmarks of a kidnapping.

SIX

EVELYN

THE SCREAM RICOCHETED in my head until a sharp series of knocks cut through the echo. I jolted upright, only then realizing I had dozed off curled into the embrace of the overstuffed chair pulled close to the hearth.

The slant of light hinted at late afternoon, and Faye's son sat in a chair opposite me, his wide, curious gaze fixed on my face. I smiled at Sam as I straightened, plucking off my glasses to rub sleep from my face.

The knock came again, and when I opened the door, I found the police officer on the inn's doorstep. Hector, that was what he had told me his name was. I remembered the character from "The Iliad," bold and noble and loyal to a fault.

I imagined Homer's Hector looked much like this one. The only thing that softened his hard, square slab of jawline was the silver goatee. His thick shock of hair was the same color, though liberally streaked with white, but his dark brows gave testament to his former hair color.

His was not a face that would ever be considered handsome. His windburned features were too harshly rawboned and craggy for that. There was a remoteness and a coldness about him. But he had a face that had some indefinable arresting quality to it.

"Miss." His voice was low and rough in a way that sounded perpetually hoarse.

I glanced past him and saw a second man, this one garbed in the khaki green of a park ranger. I turned my eyes back to Hector. "You found something."

"We'd like for you to come down to the station," he said.

Dread knotted my stomach and locked my muscles. *We'd like for you to come down to the station.* I had heard that numerous times, always accompanied by solicitous, hard edged smiles. *Would you be willing to submit to a polygraph?*

I met Hector's gaze and realized I had been silent for too long. "Why?"

With the police, it was never just a conversation. It was always an interrogation, whether it was slyly casual or seated across from a detective in a small, windowless room being asked the same question over and over. With the police, it was not a matter of being innocent until proven guilty. It was always a matter of being guilty, struggling to convince them of your innocence.

"We'd like for you to give a formal witness statement and look at some things." Nothing in his voice gave him away, but from the way he studied me, I knew he saw my hesitation.

I swallowed. I did not try to smile at them as if I were completely at ease. I knew it would fall flat. "Let me just grab my coat."

The ranger was in his own vehicle. Hector gestured toward his truck, and when I opened the passenger door, I was greeted by the white standard poodle.

"Frank, get in the back," Hector ordered.

The poodle waited until I parsed my fingers through his topknot before obeying.

The ride to the police station was made in silence. It was a tense silence on my end, hands tucked under my legs and a conscious effort made to keep my knee from jostling nervously. On Hector's end, I thought it was simply because he was not a man who spoke much unless he had something to say.

When we arrived at the police department, I was braced to be led into a small, cold room and given a cup of coffee that tasted like they used toilet water and stale grounds. Instead, it was just as Hector told me. He led me down a hallway into a large room with several couches and chairs.

The room was brightly lit, and efforts had been made to make it less stark with landscapes on the wall and floral throw pillows on the couches. An office was sectioned off one side of the room, and beside the door were racks of pamphlets about domestic abuse and sexual assault. The plaque on the door read VICTIM ADVOCATE.

Hector handed me a clipboard with a stack of lined papers bearing the police watermark. I accepted the pen he offered me and took a seat. Frank hopped up on the couch beside me and curled up on the opposite end.

"Was someone hurt out there?" I asked.

"That's what we're trying to figure out," Hector said. "This is Ranger Edwards, he's with the Yellowstone Law Enforcement Services Branch. We'd like for you to write a witness statement, everything you can remember from the campground, and then we would like to go over the details with you."

I glanced back and forth between the two men. Edwards was short and stocky with a boyish face and a genial smile. "Of course."

The dread at having the police focus on me shifted into concern and the certainty that something had happened at the campground.

It took me thirty minutes to recount the morning's events in writing, and when I was finished, the two men returned to the room and pulled up chairs across from me. I handed the statement to Hector, who skimmed through it quickly before passing it to the other man.

Hector took a small notebook and a pair of reading glasses from his pocket. "What more can you tell me about the woman you saw in the warming hut? You thought she was a cross-country skier?"

I nodded. "She had those long skis and poles with her."

"Do you remember what brand of skis she had?"

"No, I'm sorry. I didn't get a good look at them, and I probably wouldn't remember even if I had."

"What else do you recall about her?"

I took my time answering as I thought through the brief exchange. "She was young. I would say late teens, early twenties. White. I think she had blond hair, but she was wearing a beanie, so I'm not entirely certain. I remember when she spoke to me that I thought she was from Texas."

"Do you remember what she was wearing?" the ranger asked.

I pondered the question, staring at the wall as I brought her to my mind's eye. "She had on one of those puffy athletic coats. It was blue. And she was carrying a backpack."

Hector wrote in his notebook as I spoke, but now he

looked up and met my gaze. "I'd like for you to take a look at something and tell me if you recognize it."

"Okay."

He left the room and came back moments later with a clear plastic bag. It looked like an oversized envelope, rectangular with a lip folded over sealing the contents within. The label on the lip was red and the word EVIDENCE was printed in bold black ink across the seal. Within the bag was a backpack. One of the straps was broken.

I stared at the backpack and then looked at the ranger before meeting Hector's gaze. "That's the backpack the young woman had. I remember that keychain on it."

"Is there anything else you can remember about her?" Hector asked.

I shook my head, scouring my brain. "No, wait. When I first saw her, I thought I might have seen her last night, eating at Maggie's with a group of girls. I'm not certain about that, though. I'm sorry. That's not much information."

"It's more than we had," the ranger said, smiling at me. "Thank you…" He glanced at the witness statement, at the section of the page where it asked for my contact information. "Miss Hutto. This was helpful."

Hector stood. "I'll give you a ride back to the inn."

The ride back was just as silent. When he pulled his truck into the semi-circular front drive of the inn, I thanked him for the ride.

Twilight had crept down the valley, and the sky burned with dying light in the west. I hesitated with my hand poised to open the door. "What did you find out there? Is that young woman I saw dead?"

He had not been looking at me. His gaze was on the

rearview mirror, but now he turned to me. He studied me for a moment. "I didn't find a body." Just as my shoulders started to relax, he said, "But I found a scene that makes me think someone was grabbed off the trail."

"Grabbed. You mean kidnapped?"

"I mean it looks like someone was ambushed on the trail and dragged through the woods to a waiting vehicle."

I flinched at his blunt words. "Jesus."

He nodded and said, "Someone from the station will be in touch if we need anything else from you."

I climbed down from his truck and stood lost in thought on the inn's front porch, watching him drive away. I thought about the young woman's guileless smile and the eerie quiet and stillness of the woods. I shivered.

I turned to the door, but a sharp sound caught my attention. I followed the porch around the corner of the inn to find Faye chopping wood. The ax bit into the wood and wedged there, resisting her efforts to see-saw the blade free.

"That looks like hard work."

She jumped at my voice, but her smile was friendly, if a bit wan, when she turned to me. She pushed her hair away from her face. "It is. I could purchase firewood. But it seems like a silly waste of money when I have plenty of trees at my disposal." She yanked the ax from the wood with such force she stumbled back a step. "I rethink that thought every winter, though."

I crossed the yard. I knelt beside the pile of raggedly chopped wood and collected a bundle in my arms.

"You don't have to do that."

I balanced the load carefully, avoiding the splinters that tugged at the sleeves of my coat. "I don't mind."

She grabbed a stack as well, and I followed her inside through a side door that led into the dining room. Sam was sitting beside the fire coloring. "Did you enjoy snowshoeing this morning?"

"The woods were beautiful but…disquieting." I did not tell her of hearing the scream in the woods, of the harrowing suspicions the police officer had just voiced to me.

She stacked her load of firewood in the rack beside the fireplace. While I followed suit, she grabbed a broom and swept aside the debris.

"When we first moved here, the quiet bothered me more than anything else," she said. "I was used to hearing traffic and people twenty-four seven."

I caught Sam staring at me. "What are you drawing there?"

He extended the piece of paper to me without saying a word, and I admired the unidentifiable pencil and crayon sketch before following Faye back outside.

"He's not being rude." Her voice was quiet as she stacked logs onto my outstretched arms. "He doesn't speak. I usually let guests know so they don't think he's being rude when he doesn't respond to them."

He had to be at least seven or eight years old. I wondered if he had never spoken or if he had stopped. But I merely said, "Thanks for letting me know. I didn't think he was rude, though. I thought perhaps he was just shy." Sorrow was etched into the lines of the other woman's brow as she collected the last of the chopped firewood, so I changed the subject. "You're not from here, then?"

Her gaze darted to mine. "What?"

"You said when you first moved here."

"Oh, yes. We moved from…back east. It was quite the adjustment." She stopped on the porch and turned in a slow circle, gaze on the darkening forest, mountains, and river. She turned back to me and smiled. "Now, though, I can't imagine being anywhere else."

I had followed the circuitous route of her gaze. "There is something about this place." I stacked the firewood in the rack and then opened the front door as she swept the debris out into the snow.

She leaned the broom against the firewood rack. "Would you like to join us for dinner?"

"I wouldn't want to be any trouble."

She glanced over her shoulder and smiled at me. "You wouldn't be. I made spaghetti. There's plenty."

"Then I gladly accept." I followed her to the kitchen, where the rich, fragrant smell of tomatoes, oregano, thyme, and rosemary beckoned me farther into the room and made my stomach growl. "What may I do to help?"

Her kitchen was state of the art and well stocked. Soon dinner was plated and the three of us were seated around the breakfast table under the window. It was quiet, there was no back and forth chatter, just the occasional clink of fork tines on a plate. But it was companionable.

Faye refused my offers to help her clean the kitchen after dinner, and I retreated to my room. Once locked within, I completed my nightly rituals quickly, humming "Greensleeves" under my breath as I readied for bed. The tune reminded me that I needed to get the box from my car, and I made a mental note to go to the auto shop in the morning.

I slipped my nightgown over my head with a sigh and

ran a brush through my hair as I moved to the window to draw the curtains. I froze, brush halfway through my hair, one hand on the heavy fabric of the curtain.

I stepped closer to the window, gaze sharpening. A fire pit with a ring of Adirondack chairs was half buried in the snow beside the curved bank of the river. A dusk to dawn light by the street cast a pale glow over the upper stretch of lawn, but the rest was in shadows.

I peered into the darkness, certain I had seen a quick shift of movement when I approached the window and a shadow in the shape of a man cast across the snow. Realizing I was clearly visible in the window, backlit by the lamps in my room, I retreated and quickly pulled the curtain across the window. I moved across the room and did the same with the other window.

I stood in the center of the room with my hands pressed to my chest, feeling that thundering pace begin anew. I knew this feeling, this stark jolt of fear. I had known it intimately six years ago.

"Alas, my love, you do me wrong."

My whispered repetition of the song was waveringly off key.

Chad Kilgore had been there at the museum in Atlanta, somewhere in my line of sight every time I looked up from my work. Then he had been there when I turned down the aisle in the grocery store. And then he had been there in front of my grandparents' home.

Six years ago now, and the memory of that fear felt as raw as if I were still standing in my old childhood bedroom.

I left the lights on, placed my glasses on the bedside table, and crawled into bed. I whispered the lines of the old song over and over, because I knew if silence fell,

I would hear that steady, heavy tread in my mind, his footfall coming ever closer to where I hid in the shadows of the museum's basement.

The sheets were crisp and cold, and I shuddered, drawing the covers up to my chin. I rolled over and stared at the gilding of silver moonlight around the edges of the curtains.

Everything had remained still as I searched the night. But I could not quell the feeling that someone had been there, just out of reach of the light, watching. I recognized the feeling. I knew it well.

SEVEN

JEFF

SHE SHUT ME OUT.

I stared at the blackened eye of her window. She felt the connection between us. She had known I lingered here, drawn by her siren's call. Rose had resisted at first as well.

I took a deep breath of the ice-bitten air and let it cool the rage that had begun simmering inside me. That strangeness within only sharpened its claws when I fed it with anger. Anger made it ravenous. And that was dangerous. Anger led to carelessness, and there was no one to tend my roses if I were caught.

This was an art. Carefully orchestrated, brilliantly composed, perfectly staged—it was a masterpiece. It could not be rushed, and it had to be done with painstaking attention to detail. Anger had no room here.

Of course she played coy. She was even more like Rose than I had thought. It only made her more perfect. She simply did not understand. Not yet. I was still gathering the pieces to tell her the story, but I would begin tonight. It would be a poetic beginning.

I had heard she was a new employee at the museum. The irony made me smile. That was poetic as well.

I took one last look at her darkened window and then turned and walked back through town to where my Land Rover was parked in front of Book Ends. It was too risky to use the service road that ran alongside the campground. Anyone in town could see me cross the bridge.

I drove out of town and pulled off the road to install the four tracks on the tires which enabled my vehicle to traverse the deep snow. I took one of the old trails that cut into that wild borderland of the national park and the Montana-Wyoming state line. It circled back toward town but then arrowed into the heart of the wilderness.

The West suited men like me, I had discovered. It was not so much a lawlessness that thrived here. I would have to venture farther from civilization for that, and a hunter would starve if there were no prey. It was the ease with which a man could slip from society into the deep wild within a matter of miles.

I crossed the river where it was wide and shallow, frozen save for the unerring trickles under the ice that kept flowing into the vast heart of Yellowstone. It was only a few more miles before I reached the old hunting cabin I had found when I first moved to Raven's Gap. Every predator had to have its den, and I had scoured the vast wilderness and found this lonely, ramshackle outpost. It was one of many.

I turned on the electric lantern on the table. My breath was a ghost of white vapor as I knelt by the pallet. I had not bothered with a fire in the old stove. Smoke drew attention, and she would not need it for long.

The woman lay where I had left her, the heavy duty, shearling lined Velcro cuffs binding her wrists behind her back and her ankles together. She had not moved in the hours since I brought her here. The cold and the sleeping pills I had forced down her throat had rendered her as limp and malleable as a doll.

I undid the cuffs, pleased that no marks had been left on her flesh by the restraints. I stripped her with brisk movements. Pale flesh gleamed in the blue-white light of the lantern.

I felt myself stir to life at the sight of all of that helplessness. Shame twisted my gut, and I was rougher than I intended when I jerked the dress I had for her over her head. It was a tight fit, and I had to smash her breasts flat to get it over her chest.

Rage began to gnaw at me again, laced with the poisoning mixture of shame at the erection that would not subside. She moaned when I brusquely yanked the dress over the curve of her hips. The seams stretched and groaned. It made me want to slice her flesh away to better the fit.

Gently, I reminded myself. It was not perfect, because she was not perfection. She was just a substitute. They had all been substitutes for Rose. Now she was a substitute for a different woman.

Unlike some who responded to that urge within, I understood my own psychology, and I did not bother to delude myself about it.

A tear slid from the corner of her eye when I drew a wipe from the packet in my coat and cleaned her face of the smudged makeup. Another tear and a whimper escaped her when I combed the tangles from her hair and fashioned two neat braids. A gasp of air left her as I cupped the back of her skull in one hand, her chin in the other, and with a quick upward twist snapped her neck.

I sat back and smoothed the dress over her knees. It was not about pain and fear. It never had been. I was pleased that there was no terror stamped on her lax features. She looked peaceful and pure.

I let out the breath I had not realized I held. The erection was gone, the shame and anger with it. Now there was only peace left for me as well. Peace and purpose.

Evelyn could resist the pull all she wanted. In the end, she would be mine. Just as Rose was. And I had the perfect way to remind her of that.

EIGHT

48% of all missing persons in the US are female.

HECTOR

I DID NOT get away from the department until four hours after my shift ended. I stopped by the diner. Maggie remembered a group of young women who had come in for dinner last night, but none of them had been local to Raven's Gap. It was likely they were visitors to Yellowstone, and I left it to the rangers to inquire about the girl's identity.

Even so, as Frank and I headed home, I cut through town. I tapped my horn as I passed the diner again, and Maggie looked up from pouring coffee. She spotted me through the window and lifted the coffee carafe in greeting. I drove through town and slowed as I passed the hardware store. The second floor was dark. I had not spotted his vehicle parked on Main Street or here along the side street.

I idled in the middle of the empty street, staring at the dark windows, until Frank rested his chin on my knee. I drew my gaze away, put a hand on his back, and drove on.

I lived between Raven's Gap and Gardiner in the rugged northern reaches of the Black Canyon of the Yellowstone. I grabbed the remote control from the cupholder and lowered the plow attached to the front of the truck as I turned off the state road onto the two mile stretch of drive that led to my place.

I had purchased fifty acres of land to suit Winona when we first moved here from Cody. She had dreams of horses and alpacas, and my dreams had been crushed on the dirt floor of the arena beneath a bull's horns and hooves. I had let my bitterness over my own loss delay fulfilling the promise to her until it had been too late to give her horses, alpacas, or the house on the ridge.

I still had not built the house, and I never planned to. My headlights illuminated the old Airstream trailer I called home. I had a tin can of a house with water, power, and sewage and a wide swath of empty, open space that reminded me I had been a selfish prick. If she had left me, I deserved it.

That had been the speculation in town in the beginning. That she had grown tired of me and finally moved on to find someone who was more deserving of her. But Winona was not one for elaborate gestures or manipulation. She was blunt and straightforward. She would have told me she was leaving me. She would have packed her bags and made no secret of the fact. I had known something was terribly wrong from the beginning.

I cut the engine and let out a ragged breath. I knew she was gone from this earth, and I knew it had been at someone else's hand. She and the baby both.

The evidence of a struggle today on the trail made my gut churn. Because I could easily imagine Winona in a similar situation. Fighting with everything she had. Desperate to save our daughter.

The headlights illuminated the remnants of the graffiti on the Airstream. I had scrubbed and scraped, but the red MURDERER scrawled across the aluminum exterior had never fully disappeared.

Vandalism had been commonplace in the first few years. It was more often than not that I came home to a ransacked trailer. The worst instance had been walking in to find the blood of some slaughtered creature smeared on the floors and walls and poured across my bed. Sometimes in the summer, I thought I could still smell that sickly sweet metallic odor.

I flicked off the headlights. It had been a relief when the people in town grew tired of trying to drive me away. I knew Jack was the main culprit, and after seven years, the man eventually developed hobbies that did not involve desecrating my home on a regular basis.

Exhaustion settled heavily over me as I exited the truck and leaned against the tailgate as Frank did a circuit around the clearing to mark his territory. A wolf howled in the distance. I wondered if it was the white wolf I had been seeing around my property lately. Its haunting, ancient call was soon joined by her brothers and sisters. Frank lifted his head and added his voice to their song.

I straightened and whistled for him, and he beat me to the front door. I scooped kibble into his food bowl, gave him fresh water, and headed into the closet of a bathroom to shower. Once out of the shower, I heated up a bowl of rabbit stew for dinner and grabbed a longneck from the refrigerator. I stood as I ate, leaning against the narrow countertop.

Frank's head came up, ears pricked, alerting me to the approaching vehicle before I heard it and before headlights cut across the interior of the trailer.

I knew who it was; I had seen the ginger way she moved earlier. I went to the fridge to grab another beer.

I opened the front door and ducked out, waiting on my cinder block front step as she parked and climbed down from her vehicle. I popped the top off the beer on the doorjamb and extended it to her as she approached. She accepted it with a sweet smile and then drained the bottle in three long gulps.

She sighed and pressed the back of her wrist to her lips. "Were you expecting me?"

"I thought you might be along tonight." I extended a hand to her, and she slipped her smaller, softer fingers into mine. "Come inside, Joan."

I led her straight to bed, peeling her fine clothes off with my rough hands, and taking her gently. Gently was always what she liked best, had been what she needed from me the last ten years. When she lay in my arms afterward, I lightly touched the dark fingerprints on her upper arm and the discoloration on the right side of her ribcage.

Wordlessly, I got up and grabbed her another beer and a painkiller from my own stash. She took both gratefully, and when I lay back down beside her, she scooted close and rested her head on my chest.

"You know I'd kill the bastard if you wanted me to." I had offered the same thing a number of times over the years.

She sighed and pressed her lips to my heartbeat. "I know you would."

Love did not leave a woman bruised. I kept that thought to myself. I had tried to make her see reason when she first started showing up on my doorstep all those years ago. Now I just gave her what she asked of me.

And what did I know about love. My first memory was of cleaning up my mother's vomit when she had returned from a bender. I had been four at the time, and in all of my memories before I left home at fourteen, I could never recall a kind word or a gentle touch from the woman.

Years later, I had been a shit husband. Winona and I met on the circuit. I had been riding bulls, and she had been chasing the cans. Truth was, it was my dick, not my heart, that took notice of her when I saw that dark banner of hair flying out behind her and watched her tits bounce when she was in the saddle barrel racing. The laughing dark eyes, high cheekbones, and full ass had sealed the deal when I saw her at the bar later and approached her.

She had loved me. I had no doubt about that. At least in the beginning. The weight of her love had left me feeling suffocated, because I had no idea how to reciprocate it. The more the years passed, the less those eyes had sparkled.

I had been even less enthused about parenthood. When she asked me to help her decide on a name, I had shrugged and said it did not matter to me. Winona had picked the name Emma after the grandmother she had been so close to as a girl.

I found the squalling infant passed into my arms more annoying than anything else. I had been ready to ask her for a divorce when she told me she was pregnant. The bald creature with a red, pinched face who cried every time I held her had seemed like a ball and chain around my neck.

But in the fifteen years that had passed since they both disappeared, I found that was my biggest regret. That I had let the only two years I had been given with Emma slip through my fingers without making her laugh or singing her to sleep or breathing in that baby smell I had been told existed but could never catch under the stench of shitty diapers and spit up.

It was her loss I felt so keenly, even though I had never bothered to be a father.

I studied the ceiling as Joan rested against me and sipped her beer, her eyes growing heavy with the aid of the pain pill. I had hung most of the material on the ceiling within the first year of their disappearance.

Maps with Winona's usual route in and out of town highlighted, memories of things she had said that might be a link scrawled on Post-It notes, receipts, photos printed from the CCTV camera footage around town in the weeks leading up to that one day. Tacks were shoved into the map at the locations she visited regularly. At the center of the web, I had pinned a photo of him.

I had not loved them well enough in life. I had not known I needed to protect them. I liked to think that if I had known, I would have been more attentive, shown more care. But I could not be sure.

I was not haunted by them now. No, it was something darker and more twisted and desperate that drove me. It was obsession.

NINE

Won't you come into the garden?
I would like my roses to see you.

-Richard Brinsley Sheridan

EVELYN

THE FOOTPRINTS ALONG the edge of the woods near the fire pit were blanketed with snow, but the indentions were still visible. The shallow hollows showed a clear path, and I followed it from the spot where I thought I had seen movement in the shadows last night up the slope to the walk. Already, it had been cleared and salted, and the trail disappeared.

I turned back to the inn, gaze drawn to the second floor and my window. I had left the curtains closed this morning. My stomach threatened to lurch into my throat. It felt as if ants prickled along my scalp at the confirmation indented in the snow.

Someone had stood in the snow, drifted through the shadows, and watched my bedroom window last night.

I pressed my hand tight against my breast to keep my heart contained. It hammered against my palm at the memories. The deep prints in the mud around my grandmother's azaleas. The cigarette butts on the ground amidst the fallen petals outside my bedroom window.

Evelyn, his voice whispered in my ear, *come out, come out, wherever you are.*

I dug the heels of my hands into my ears until all I could hear was the thundering of my own blood.

"Shut up, shut up," I said, and deafened by my own hands, I could not tell if I murmured or shouted the words. I could just feel the hissing slide of the sh against the roof of my mouth.

It's meant to be. Don't fight it.

I fought back a sob. It had taken me five years, but I thought he was out of my head as certainly as he was out of my life. Fury warred with fear in a tumult that had my stomach roiling, my chest hot, and my face damp.

I hated this. Hated that he was still there in the dark recesses of my mind. Hated that someone else had taken away my peace with a shadow slipping between the trees and a set of tracks in the snow.

A tap of a horn had me dropping my hands. I turned to find a patrol car pulled up alongside me.

"Everything okay?"

The police officer behind the wheel was not Hector. This officer looked so young I was not certain he was even of legal age himself, and his smile was too boyish to be professionally reassuring.

Nothing we can do, miss. Nothing we can do.

The memory of those words, said countless times with varying degrees of patience, stiffened my spine. "Everything's fine."

He studied me for a moment and then nodded. "Have a good day."

Once he drove away, I turned a slow circle on the

walk. The inn was at the end of the road, skirted by woods on either side, hemmed by the river at the back.

It was a quiet street. Mailboxes at the end of snow-packed lanes marked the lots on the opposite side of the road, but the houses themselves were hidden by trees. This was a lonely stretch of street, even as it was only blocks from the main thoroughfare.

I rubbed my hands along my arms to ward off a chill that had nothing to do with the temperature. My hand slipped into my pocket and clenched around the can of pepper spray as I walked the half mile to the mechanic's shop. I did not loosen my grip until I reached the auto shop.

A bell over the door rang when I entered the shop attached to the garage. The inside was spartan but clean, and the chair behind the desk was empty. "Hello?"

"Be right with you," a voice called from an open doorway behind the desk. A moment later, Ed Decker appeared nursing a cup of coffee. "Ev'lyn. What can I do for you this morning?"

The dropped syllable in my name and his welcoming smile had my shoulders relaxing. "I left a box in my car and was hoping I could grab it before you get to work on her."

"Sure, sure. I plan on getting started on her today, but she's not in the bay yet. I have her parked in the back lot." He opened a drawer in the desk and fished around for my key. He motioned for me to follow him and led me through a break room to the back door. He dropped the key into my palm. "I have to order some parts from Bozeman. You need any help with your box?"

"No, I have it. Thank you." I crossed the back lot to where my car was parked at the end of a row of vehicles.

The box held the last remnants of my life in Atlanta: a teapot from Japan that my grandmother's father had brought home after World War II; my grandfather's grandfather's pocket watch; my father's boyhood baseball glove, the leather worn to buttery softness; my mother's leather-bound collection of Jane Austen novels and an old music box.

The music box was shaped like a piano, made of etched crystal so the cogs and wheels were visible when I lifted the lid and a tinkling rendition of "Greensleeves" began to play. I smiled and let it play for a moment before tucking it inside the baseball mitt. I closed the box and lifted it from the backseat.

I moved to close the door with my hip but paused. It was the color that caught my eye. Deep purple adorned with pink polka dots.

I leaned over and lifted the coat from where it lay in the front passenger's seat. It was petite in size, designed for a teenager. Familiarity struck me, and unease walked a chilling finger up my spine.

One side seemed weighted, and when I searched the pockets, I pulled out a keychain. It was made from a thin crosscut section of tree limb, sanded but rough-hewn with the number 7 carved into the wood. A key dangled from the ring attached to one end.

I locked the door, balanced the box on my hip, and crossed the lot. Ed was at the coffee pot when I entered the break room. I handed him the key to my car and showed him the coat. "Do you know where this came from?"

He pulled his trapper hat off and scratched his head. "I can't rightly say."

"You didn't put it in my car?"

"In your car? No, never seen it before."

I made a thoughtful sound and peered out the door at my car. Something gnawed at the edges of my mind, a nudge of memory that slid out of reach as soon as I grasped for it.

"Something wrong?"

"No," I said slowly, draping the coat over my arm. "No, I don't think so. Thank you again, Ed."

"My pleasure."

Outside on the sidewalk, I started back toward the inn. I looked both ways at the intersection, but when I glanced to the left to check traffic, I froze.

I stared at the bridge. I did not know how the coat had ended up in my car, but I knew why it was familiar to me. The campground. The coat had been in the warming hut yesterday morning.

I hurried back into the auto shop. Ed was at his desk and glanced up when the bell rang.

"Actually, is the offer for a loaner vehicle still on the table?" I asked.

I was used to an old vehicle, but the Chevy predated my Civic by at least thirty years. I had to muscle the door open, and rust fell like flecks of blood onto the snow. The interior was perfectly maintained, though, the leather bench seat as smooth and supple as if it had just been driven off the showroom floor.

The truck may have been ancient, but it rumbled to life at the first turn of the key and shifted smoothly into gear. I left the lot and directed the truck across the bridge. The campground had seen more traffic since yesterday, and the snow was packed down into two ruts. I followed along the narrow lane, around the bend, and down the row of cabins.

The cabin with a 7 above the door was on the riverfront, and it looked as abandoned for the season as the others. I parked in the space allotted for the rental and darted a glance at my cell phone.

Most people had the instinct to call the police in situations in which they were uncomfortable. I had been one of those people once. I was not any longer. I pocketed my phone, collected the key and coat, and shoved out of the truck.

There was no porch at the front of the cabin. It was on the other side of the structure looking out over the river. A set of steps led directly up to the front door. Snow covered the first steps and left only one for me to climb to knock on the door. The echo of my knock sounded within. I waited and then knocked again, but there was no movement inside.

I made a slow circuit of the cabin. The windows were boarded, and when I climbed the steps onto the porch at the back of the cabin, the deck was slick under the layer of snow. I knocked on the back door and received the same greeting.

Weighing the key in my hand, I glanced around. There were two vehicles parked in the lot by the trailhead. The river tumbled by at my back. A trio of magpies eyed me from the roof of the adjacent cabin.

I turned back to the door and fit the key into the lock. It twisted easily, but snow and ice had bound the door in place. I had to shove my weight against it to break the frozen seal. The door opened with a groan, and I perched uneasily on the threshold. It was cold and dark within.

"Hello? Anyone here?"

I fished my phone from my pocket, turned on the

flashlight application, and cast the beam of light across the interior.

It was empty, even barren of furniture. The interior reminded me vaguely of the inn on a smaller scale with an open floor plan pivoting around a stone fireplace and the beams of the ceiling exposed.

It was sparse and rustic, pared down to the essentials. I imagined it was charming at the height of the season, but in its winter hibernation, it was as welcoming as a treacherous cave.

A magpie cackled raucously. I jumped, darting one last glance over my shoulder before stepping inside. I left the door open behind me and swept the light through all the corners.

Two doorways opened off of either side of the den. I approached the one on the left first. It was a bedroom with only the skeletons of two sets of bunk beds against the wall to mark it.

I crossed to the opposite doorway. When I reached the threshold and heard a scrape of sound behind me, I whirled, panning the light across the great room.

"Hello? Is someone there?" My voice sounded high and tight in my own ears.

The cabin was as empty as it had been when I first entered, but a prickling awareness of another presence raised the hair on the back of my neck. I turned quickly to the second room, expecting to see a hulking shadow in the doorway, but it remained dark and empty. I stepped cautiously across the threshold and panned my light across the room.

I froze. My phone and the coat fell from my fingers. A scream tried to crawl its way up my throat, but I was too shocked for it to escape, my vocal cords as frozen as my limbs. All that slipped from me was a muffled whimper.

The paralysis of shock released its hold, and I backed away, clamping a hand so tightly across my mouth I tasted blood. I did not stop until my shoulders hit the fireplace with a jarring thump.

My phone had fallen with the flashlight pointed toward the ceiling, the light illuminating the room in an eerie white glow. The woman's shadow was elongated on the far wall as her weight spun slowly at the end of the rope stretched from her throat to a beam above.

PART II

Remove the Stems That Grow Weaker

TEN

*There are no black roses. Those that appear black
are actually dark crimson in color.*

HECTOR

IT WAS ALL carefully staged. She wore a thin, floral sundress that was too tight in the chest and hips. It looked
as if it had been made for someone a decade younger
than the early twenties she must have been. Her hair
was caught in two braids, and her feet were bare.

The department's evidence technician, Ted Peters,
put away his kit and his camera. "I'm finished with her."

Everyone in the room looked to the detective, Martin Yates. He nodded. "Cut her down."

She was stiff, from the cold and from rigor. Ned Ashton, a young officer who had only been on the force for
a year, helped me move her to the low gurney. His face
was as colorless as the dead woman's.

Grover Westland, the county coroner, drew the sheet
over her. It slid over her ankle, exposing one bare foot.
Her toenails were painted a bright pink that looked
shocking and garish on her waxy skin. I tugged the
sheet over the small appendage.

"Do you think Frank can track which direction she
might have been brought from?" Yates asked.

I sighed. As part of the local search and rescue team,

Frank and I had found eight people too late to bring them out of the wilderness alive. I tried HRD—human remains detection—training with him, but the poodle had a strong aversion to decomposing tissue. He did not care to be around the dead, and I could not much blame him.

"I'll get him."

He was sitting in the driver's seat of my truck, and he barked when he saw me. "I'll cook you a steak for dinner tonight," I promised him as I opened the door.

I led him inside the cabin. As soon as he smelled her, his head went low, and he hunched closer to the ground.

"Get to work, Frank."

I trailed after him as he darted outside and made a circuit of the cabin, running out wide and then working back in a serpentine path.

He made it all the way around the cabin, and I was ready to call him back, thinking his search futile, when he found a scent trail. He led me down the lane toward the trailhead and then darted between the last two cabins and into the woods.

Away from where the foot traffic had heavily trampled the snow, I could see a single set of prints. The prints veered between the boarded-up cabins and trudged into the dense forest.

I scanned the ground and the surrounding trees as I followed Frank. Branches were snapped, and I cued up my radio to tell Peters where to find the trail so he could check for snagged fibers or hairs.

A quarter mile through the woods, Frank and I came upon the old service road. It was the same road he had lost the trail at yesterday, and he did so again today. The same tracks I had seen yesterday marked the deep snow, tracks set like tires with a tread like a snowmobile. The rangers had told me yesterday the service road ended at the river.

I whistled for Frank and trekked back through the woods along a different route so as not to disturb any evidence that might have been left behind. Back at the station, I left Frank in my office and headed to the equipment room.

I shrugged into one of the insulated coveralls and grabbed a helmet and my rifle before heading out on one of the snowmobiles kept in the sally port. Once in the campground, I cut through the woods to the service road and followed it into the wilderness of the Yellowstone borderlands.

The wind was sharp against my face as I rode, and I breathed deeply as the miles raced past. There was a purity to the air here, a clean scent of sky bled into earth that I had never smelled anywhere else. Winter was a hardscrabble, gritty season in this part of the country, but it had always been my favorite. The wildness was whittled to a fine blade in the winter, everything rendered sharper in the cold.

This was a land as beautiful as it was dangerous. In other seasons, the beauty could hide the danger. Pared down to bone in the winter, there was no hiding how brutal this land could be. Winter was nature at its most hard and authentic.

I rounded a curve in the old track, crested the hill, and found the river below. The rangers were correct, the old service road ended here at the summit of the hill, but the tracks I followed cut straight down to the river and then veered off to the right. The tracks headed west, following the Yellowstone River Trail.

The landscape was jagged and roughhewn. The hills were high and craggy, home to surefooted big horn sheep and stealthy cougars. Across the river, Rattlesnake Butte was blue and white in the late morning light. The way was dangerous through the steeper sections of the canyon, prone to rockslides in the summer and avalanches in the winter. I slowed the snowmobile and kept an eye on the canyon walls as I followed the curve of the river.

The tracks ran concurrent to the trail until the trail left park land and was nearing Bear Creek. The tracks angled north, all the way back to the state road that ran between Gardiner and Raven's Gap.

I killed the throttle and pulled off my helmet. I knew this stretch of road well. Around the next curve, half a mile away, was my own drive leading out to my land.

This was someone local. Someone who knew the secret passages of this stretch of wilderness. The trail I had just followed had not branched off or backtracked. Whoever had driven it knew the exact route to follow, knew the trail and the old service road.

And with the deliberate breadcrumbs laid to the scene, the careful staging of the woman in the cabin, and the expertly plotted route, I doubted this was the predator's first time hunting.

ELEVEN

*There is simply the rose; it is perfect
in every moment of its existence.*

-Ralph Waldo Emerson

EVELYN

THE SHOCK OF recognition still ricocheted through me. I
deliberately played it over in my head, refusing to flinch
from the memory of her swollen, discolored features.

It had been the woman from the warming hut.

Are you certain? the detective had asked me.

Those words had brought back other memories. Was
I certain I was interpreting his attention correctly? Was
I certain I had seen him standing on the sidewalk across
the street from my grandparents' home? Was I certain
I had not done anything to encourage him?

Yes. I was as certain now as I had been then.

I wandered along the grocery store aisles listlessly.
I could not focus on the shelves before me, though, and
I made it from one end of the market to the other with
an empty basket.

The grocery store advertised itself as locally and
family owned. It was small and neat with a surprisingly
decent selection, a deli on one side, a pharmacy on the
other. A community bulletin board stretched along the

wall between the pharmacy and the restrooms, and I paused to study the flyers.

There was a plethora of events announced and a menagerie of items for sale. One flyer caught my attention. It was a cartoon of two women in conversation. They were dressed as 1920s flappers and the caption read, *I tried to form a gang but it turned into a book club*. Amused, I stepped closer to the board and read the information emblazoned at the bottom of the flyer. It directed me to Book Ends for more information.

I placed my empty basket back in the rack and wandered across town to the bookstore. The place made me catch my breath again as I entered, and I paused in the entryway to study the bulletin board there. Many of the same community events were pinned here as well, but the cartoon ad here was of two men boxing. The caption read, *The first rule of Book Club: You do not talk about Book Club*.

The woman I had seen here the other day appeared from the depths of the shelves with a stack of books in her arms. She let out a breath of relief when she deposited the stack on the desk. She turned, smoothing her blouse, and caught sight of me in the entryway.

She recognized me immediately, and a warm smile graced her face. "Hello. I didn't hear the bell."

"I only just came in." I approached the desk. "I'm Evelyn Hutto, by the way. I didn't introduce myself the other day, but I'm new to town."

"That's what I've heard. Susan Winslow. Welcome to Raven's Gap." She was as polished and put together as she was the last time I had been here. She extended her hand to me with her greeting, and I was surprised to see that her nails were ragged and torn down to the quick. The raw, worried flesh seemed so out of place I caught myself staring.

I recovered quickly and shook her hand, hoping she had not noticed my stare. "I'm—"

I felt him behind me even before Susan's gaze moved to a point behind my left shoulder, before he said my name.

"Evelyn." The ardent tone of his voice had my shoulders hitching with tension.

I turned to face Jeff, and I knew. I *knew.*

I recognized the avid gaze as it searched my face. The too-familiar smile. The stance that edged into my personal space just enough to be uncomfortable but still look completely innocent.

I know you stood in the shadows watching me last night. I know you were there.

Are you certain? Could you be mistaken? He's really a nice guy. Completely harmless.

I felt Susan retreat. I fought the urge to call her back, to beg her not to leave me alone in his vicinity.

It was the urge to beg that forced steel into my spine and sent a jolt of anger through my veins like an electrical current. I met his stare with my own and hoped my eyes conveyed that I knew.

I knew that with men like this, nothing was by accident or chance. I had learned that last time. And this time, I would not be terrorized.

"Jeff." I did not hide the razor's edge from my voice. *I know you were there. I will not be afraid.*

He smiled that smile that hinted at a shared secret. But his words were not what I expected. "You found her." It took a moment for his words to register. He seemed to sense my confusion, because he stepped closer and breathed, "You found her."

I took a quick step back and my elbow caught the stack of books Susan had deposited on the desk. They toppled, sliding over the edge of the desk and falling to the floor in an avalanche of heavy thumps.

I stared at Jeff, breath caught in my throat, mind racing.

"Everything okay here?"

I dragged my gaze away from Jeff and found Susan approaching, her glance bouncing back and forth between us. The fallen books had crashed against my ankles and I knelt to gather them in my arms.

"I'm sorry." My voice came out shaky, and I cleared my throat. "I wasn't paying attention."

Susan knelt beside me and gathered the rest of the books. When we straightened and deposited the books on the desk, Jeff was gone.

Susan caught me glancing around. "Was Jeff able to help you find what you were looking for?"

You found her. I swallowed and scrambled to recall what had brought me through the doors. "Actually, I wanted to ask you about the book club. I saw the flyers."

Her face lit with enthusiasm. "We have three going on right now. They all meet at different times. My mystery group meets every Tuesday night. There's a popular fiction club that meets every other Thursday. I also have a romance group that gets together every third Saturday of the month. Do any of those interest you?"

You found her. "What…what are you reading in the mystery group right now?"

She rattled off the title of the latest release of a big-name author. "We usually read a book a week in that group, but don't worry if you haven't read the book. We're not tyrannical about it."

I forced a smile. "That's a relief."

"I provide wine, and everyone usually brings an appetizer or dessert, but of course it's not required. It's mainly women, and it's a small group but a fun one. We'd love to have you join us."

"What time do you meet tomorrow evening?"

"Seven. We usually break up around nine or so."

You found her. I rubbed my forehead. "I'll be here. Do you have any copies of the book in stock?"

After purchasing a copy of the novel, I hesitated on the sidewalk in front of the bookshop. My knees felt weak, and I put a hand against the exterior of the building to steady myself. I wondered if I should go to the police. But I knew what they would say. *Are you certain? Could you be mistaken? He's really a nice guy. Completely harmless.*

I took a deep breath and strode back through town, stopping into the market once more. This time, I filled my basket and left with enough staples to see me through the week.

Back at the inn, I put my groceries away on an empty shelf in the refrigerator and then retreated to the den.

A computer was set up in the corner, and Faye had told me there was internet connection if I ever needed to use it. The guest login password was written on a piece of paper and taped to the desk by the mouse. I logged in, pulled up the internet browser, and searched for *Jeff Roosevelt*.

There were social media profiles for a number of men with the same name, but I clicked through all of them and never found one that matched the too-handsome face. I searched for the bookshop's website and on the *About* page of the website, I found Susan listed as the owner with Jeff labeled as the manager and rare book dealer. There were no photos of them on the website. Just their names and occupations.

I powered down the computer and moved to the windows. The lane in front of the inn was quiet. The woods that hemmed the inn on either side were dark. But I was not certain they were empty.

You found her. As if he had known what awaited me at the cabin by the river. As if he had placed her there for me to find.

A shiver swept over me, and I placed a palm against the cold glass to steady myself.

I retreated to my room and locked the door, striving for a sense of normality as I unpacked the cardboard box and placed the keepsakes on display. I wound up the music box and hummed the lines to the old folk tune as I watered my philodendron.

I toed off my boots, grabbed the book club read I had purchased, and curled up against the pillows. I read the synopsis on the back cover and flipped to the opening scene. I did not get very far into the mystery, though, before an uneasy sleep pulled me under.

In my dreams, I crept through shadowed hallways with women swaying at the end of ropes in the yawning doorways while "Greensleeves" played haltingly somewhere in the darkness.

I WOKE EARLY the next morning, but when I came down the stairs, the sounds of quiet conversation were already filling the dining room.

Almost every table was occupied. A group of older

women sat around the table closest to the fireplace. Three men had claimed the table near the window. There were various couples and families at other tables. I recognized one face. Ed Decker and a woman wearing a knit cap sat at the table closest to the fireplace. Ed smiled when he saw me and lifted a hand in greeting.

I slipped around the tables and headed toward the kitchen. The fragrance coaxed me forward even before I reached the doorway, and when I entered, I found Faye standing at the range. Sam sat at the table methodically working his way through his breakfast.

"Is today pancake day?" I asked.

She darted a smile over her shoulder at me as she flipped the cakes sizzling on the griddle. "It is indeed. Would you like some?"

"Absolutely. I've heard about these pancakes." I glanced around. There had to be at least twenty people in the dining room, but she was alone here in the kitchen. "May I help you with anything?"

"Oh, no, you don't need to do that. It's mainly a self-service breakfast. I put out pitchers of water and carafes of coffee, I only serve one thing, and it's first come, first serve."

"That's quite a setup."

"It's simple, but it works."

She plated the steaming pancakes from the griddle, and I held out my hands for the tray. "I can take them out if you'll tell me which table."

"You don't have to do that."

"But I'm offering. With an ulterior motive. I know I'm at the end of the line, and I'm starving. This will speed things up."

She chuckled and relinquished her hold on the tray.

"Very well, then. This is for the Walshes, the family of five in the corner."

The tables were already set. Dishes of butter and gravy boats of what I was certain was homemade syrup were already on each table. With Faye staying on the griddle and me serving the plates of pancakes, we were at the last table within fifteen minutes.

Soon, she was handing me a plate piled high with four pancakes.

"Do you mind if I eat in here with you?"

She placed another pancake on Sam's plate and glanced at me, surprise evident on her face. "No, not at all. I just need to check on everyone, and then I'll be back. Don't wait for me to eat."

I sat across from Sam and added a dollop of butter to the top of my stack of pancakes before drizzling huckleberry syrup over the plate. "I keep hearing how good your mom's pancakes are." I took a bite and had to bite back a groan. "They're even better than everyone says." I glanced across the table to find the boy smiling.

Faye joined us a few minutes later. She ate quickly and then returned to the griddle. "I think a few tables are going to want seconds. Any plans for the day?"

"I have some research I need to do today for the work I'll be doing at the museum. And this evening I'm going to attend a book club."

"At Book Ends?"

"Yes, their mystery novel club."

"That sounds like a lot of fun."

There was a wistful note in her voice that made my attention sharpen. I had a feeling we shared the commonality of being alone more often than not. I did not know what her isolation was born from, but I could tell it was at least due in part to shyness.

"Come with me," I invited.

Her gaze darted to mine before it fell away and focused on the pancakes she was flipping. "Oh, I don't know…"

"I'd rather go with a friend to something like this." We were not friends, but I thought, given time, we could be.

She glanced at her son. "Sam would have to come with us, and I'm not sure—"

"It looked like they had a nice children's section." I could sense her automatic refusal wavering. "I'd feel a little awkward going by myself."

Her lips quirked, and when she met my gaze, the knowing smile in hers said she saw straight through my lie. "Okay. I'd love to go. I've seen the flyers around town and thought it looked interesting."

"Excellent."

I spent the day reading the material the museum had sent me on the tribes that lived around the Yellowstone territory. The artifacts I would be studying had unknown provenances and there were few, if any, records on the collection. I would need to reach out to tribal elders and work closely with them throughout the project. To study the artifacts I needed to first know the history of the people who had called this region home long before settlers ventured west.

Four tribes were local to the region: the Crow, the Blackfeet, the Shoshone, and the Bannocks. But it was also possible some of the artifacts I would be handling could be from the flight of Chief Joseph and the Nez Perce Indians across the Yellowstone territory in 1877.

I was keen to talk with the tribal elders and hear their versions of their own histories. I used the inn's computer to research cultural objects from each nation, and by the time the sun was sinking low and casting deep shadows through the great room, I thought I had at least a slight grasp on what each nation would have left behind in artifact form.

We arrived at Book Ends that evening just before seven. Sam paused in the entryway and stared, mouth agape. Faye put a hand between his shoulder blades to urge him forward. "I'm going to get him set up in the children's section."

I took the container of cookies from her and nodded to one of the side rooms where I could see a group of women gathering. "I think we're going to be over there."

I wandered in that direction but was waylaid when I heard my name called. I turned to find Jeff approaching. His words were still resonating in my mind, and anger flayed away my caution in that moment.

I stepped toe to toe with him when he reached me. "Did you lead me to that woman?" My voice was a harsh whisper.

His gaze roved my face, and his smile was slow, full of edge and charm. "I'm glad to know you're paying attention, Evelyn."

I took a quick step back, staring at him. The memory of the woman swaying at the end of the rope pushed into my mind, and the intensity of his gaze felt like a physical touch.

"Evelyn?" I turned to find Faye standing nearby. "I think they're about to begin."

"I'll be right there."

Jeff was already walking away, and I stared after him for a moment before moving to Faye's side.

"I'm sorry to interrupt like that," she said. "But you looked uncomfortable."

"Thank you. He—" My voice trailed away.

"He's a little…intense."

I glanced back, but he was no longer in view. *I think he killed a woman and made certain I was the one to find her.*

"Come on," she said. "Let's grab seats."

I followed her into the adjoining room, and we took seats at the fringes of the group. Faye angled her chair to be able to see the children's section across the store.

The woman sitting closest to us turned with a welcoming smile. "Hello. You're both new to the group. I'm Amanda."

Faye and I rounded out the group to thirteen women. Pleasantries and greetings were exchanged readily, and I recognized the woman who introduced herself as Joan as the receptionist at the police department. A table had been set up in the corner. When Faye added her cookies to the assortment of food, there was an exodus from the couches and chairs to the table.

This morning when I had mentioned stopping by the grocery store to pick up something to bring tonight, Faye had insisted she bake something. I had expected chocolate chip cookies. Instead, she had set about recreating the book's cover in miniature several dozen times over.

I was astonished. The woman was the very definition of artist, and with icing no less. I had argued that no one should be allowed to eat them. They should instead be framed. She had smiled and waved away my praise, her face turning pink.

"These are astonishing, Faye," Susan exclaimed. I knew I liked her when she said, "They're too lovely to eat."

"Do you think you could teach us how to do this?" the woman who had introduced herself as Amanda asked.

By the time we left the bookstore two hours later, Faye had been coaxed into teaching everyone the basics of cookie decorating. From the pleased flush on her face, I did not think she had needed much coaxing.

"How did you learn how to do that?" I asked as we walked through town. Sam walked ahead of us, his face buried in the book Faye had purchased for him. "They truly were works of art."

She smiled. "It just takes a steady hand." She went quiet, and we walked in companionable silence. "Actually," she said, "I used to own a bakery."

The reluctance in her voice told me how hesitant she had been to give me that information, so I curbed my curiosity and forestalled my questions. "That sounds really neat."

"I attended the Institute of Culinary Education, their school of pastry and baking arts."

Her state-of-the-art kitchen made much more sense now. "So you literally have a degree in baking."

She chuckled, the sound followed by a waft of fog in the cold, crystalline air. "I do." She darted a glance at me. "Are you okay? You were quiet tonight."

I had been preoccupied by watching the doorway to catch a glimpse of Jeff. When I had seen him leave an hour into the meeting, I had perched on the edge of my chair, debating whether I should follow him.

"I'm fine." I forced a smile as she unlocked the front door and Sam entered ahead of us, drifting away into the darkness.

She switched on the lamp on the table by the entrance as I followed her in and locked the door behind me.

"Thank you for inviting me," she said. "I really do appreciate it. I think I'll attend regularly."

"I'm glad you came. I'm planning to as well."

Sam came back to his mother's side and leaned against her. She rested a hand on his head and smiled at me. "I should get him to bed. Good night."

"Night."

As I climbed the steps and passed down the hall to my room, I felt like I was on uneven footing. *I'm glad to know you're paying attention, Evelyn.* I was not certain what I had thought he would say. I had expected a denial. Instead, I had received something that was not a confession, not even a warning, more along the lines of praise and encouragement.

As soon as I had seen the footprints, I thought I knew what I was dealing with, what kind of threat I faced. But this was something else entirely.

Deep in thought, I reached my door and turned the knob. The door swung open easily. Startled, I hesitated on the threshold, my hand tucked into my pocket in an automatic reach for my keys.

I groped along the wall until I found the switch and flicked on the overhead light. My room appeared exactly as I had left it, but I pulled the canister of pepper spray from my pocket as I entered. I checked the bathroom first, shoving aside the shower curtain in a swift, violent movement. No one lurked behind its cover or in the armoire.

I glanced around the room. Nothing seemed out of place. I moved to the door and locked it. I twisted the bolt back and forth several times and tried the door handle once it was locked. I turned the bedside lamp on before turning out the overhead light.

In the bathroom, I went through the motions of getting ready for bed. My gaze continually drifted to the doorway. I checked the room once more before climbing into bed, grabbing the tube of hand cream I had picked up at the supermarket on the way. I rubbed it into my hands and elbows as I combed my memory. Perhaps I had not locked my door before leaving for the book club meeting.

I replaced the cap on the tube of hand cream and placed it back on the bedside table, followed by my glasses. I leaned over to switch off the lamp and froze.

My mother's music box was missing.

TWELVE

JEFF

I PLACED MY hand against the underside of the bed frame and listened to the quickening of her breath. I smiled, imagining that I could feel the quaver of her heartbeat, the movement of her chest as she breathed, through the mattress and wood separating us.

I had gambled on the fact that she would not think to check under her bed. I was angled in such a way that I only had a glimpse of her feet, but I saw her hesitation when she opened the door.

I felt giddy with anticipation as she searched the room, imagining her kneeling to check under the bed. I would reach out and catch her wrist, feel the leap of her pulse against my fingers. The opportunity never came, and I listened to the rustle of movement as she readied for bed. I hoped she wore a nightgown, long and white and demure.

When she moved to the bedside, my fingers twitched. I longed to close the distance between us, to clasp that slim ankle, to cup the curve of her calf and feel the flex of muscle when she tried to run. I reached for her before I could check the impulse, but she moved out of reach. I felt the shift of the mattress and frame as she settled into bed.

I snatched my hand back and waited, curious to see

if she would notice. It only took her a few moments. I heard the indrawn breath, the realization, and I could not quell my smile.

Her music box played "Greensleeves," and I was tempted to open the lid on the miniature piano and allow her to hear me nearby.

Alas, my love, you do me wrong. I had not thought of the old song in years until I lifted the lid of her music box. Such a poignant song. It made anger begin to simmer in my veins.

To cast me off discourteously; And I have loved you for so long Delighting in your company. Sometimes promises were so easily forgotten. Women and roses alike needed to be reminded of their promises.

I started to lift the lid, to hum along with the tune. But it was too soon. It had been enough to leave her door unlocked so she could sense I was near. She knew. She was clever. I had known she would be. I had known she was special from the moment I saw her.

She had found my gift to her even sooner than I anticipated. I would have to be cautious and tell her the story in a way that was not rushed.

It was a challenge to keep everything hidden when we were face to face; to hear that low, husky, accented voice and not wrap my hands around her throat to feel the vibrations against my palms; to see her smile so easily at everyone who crossed her path and not place a swath of tape over her mouth so that winsome curve of her lips was only for me; to witness the way she pushed her glasses up her nose. The tension I felt in her presence was excruciating and delicious all at once.

I had forgotten the anticipation. The others, the ones I found in those forgotten corners, they had not made my blood sing with the hunt. I took them because I could. Because I needed to. Because it fed a desire within me, even as it left me hollow.

But the others were not the work of art that she would be. That Rose had been.

I had to remember her promise. A rose would bloom for you if only you tended it. She had been angry when she spoke to me tonight. I remembered Rose's reluctance at first as well, and the reminder only sweetened the pain and honed that tearing hunger within.

I had time to lay everything out for her. And right now, I had time to linger mere feet from her and bask in the tension of being so close as she slept.

THIRTEEN

Roses fall, but the thorns remain.

-Dutch proverb

HECTOR

EVELYN SAT ON the hard bench in the lobby looking as if she had not slept at all last night. I rubbed my jaw. "You know this is a serious accusation."

I could see her spine stiffen and her hackles go up. "I know," she said, voice tight.

"The police can't pursue anything based on this alone." I almost laughed at the irony of being in the position to say those words. They tasted bitter in my mouth. "Do you have proof?" Her gaze dropped, and I could see tension in every line of her body. Christ, if she had proof… I leaned toward her. "Evelyn." I heard the urgency in my own tone, and I knew she did as well when she looked up. "Do you have proof Jeff killed the woman at the campground?"

"No," she said, and I could hear the frustration in her voice. "I don't." She collected her purse and stood. "Thank you for your time."

Joan tapped on the glass, drawing my attention. She held up the phone. The automatic doors whispered shut behind Evelyn as she exited the lobby.

"You have a phone call from a Ranger Edwards," Joan said.

"Transfer the call to my desk." I hesitated, rapping a knuckle on the countertop. "I need you to call the records department in Atlanta and get them to fax over any case reports they have on Evelyn Hutto. Look at the scans attached to the campground case. Her witness statement is there, and her birthdate is on that."

"I'll get right on it," she said.

Back in my office, I picked up the phone. "Hector."

"Hector, it's Edwards. You'll want to get over here. We may have an ID on your Jane Doe."

"I'm on my way." I grabbed the folder for the case from my desk, whistled to Frank, and informed the dispatcher where I was heading as we strode outside to my truck.

Evelyn's visit to the police department weighed heavily on my mind, and when I reached my turnoff, I slowed and detoured from the state road. I left the truck running in front of the trailer, and I went straight to my bedroom.

I plucked the photograph from where it was tacked at the center of the web I had been trying to untangle for fifteen years.

Do you have any proof? they had asked me. *We can't arrest him based on your hunch alone. He passed a polygraph. Just like you did.*

There was a wealth of implications in those words. I had finally been told in no uncertain terms that if I did not stop harassing him, I would face a restraining order, charges, and dismissal. But I was as certain now as I had been then.

I needed the job, though. I needed the resources

available through the department, the cover it provided me. If I were not part of the department, they would have tried to arrest me years ago. A badge provided a man some amount of protection.

So I watched and waited and made a promise to my girls.

I tucked the photo of Jeff Roosevelt into my pocket and headed back out to my truck.

In Gardiner, I crossed the river and passed under the arch. I flashed my badge when I reached the small cabin that served as the gateway to the north entrance of the park.

The young park ranger smiled at me. "They're expecting you at park headquarters."

The five miles to Mammoth was an ascent, winding up through the hills. I came around a curve and crested the ridge. The Lower Terraces gleamed like white marble in the winter sun.

The hotel was closed for renovations this season, and this time of year was quiet in the park. There were more elk lingering on the snow-softened lawn of the hotel and wandering around the grounds than humans. Frank pressed his nose to the window, a rumble emanating from his chest.

"Enough," I warned him.

I left my truck near the Visitor Center and crossed the old fort grounds. In the years following Yellowstone's establishment as the first national park, the Army sent men from Fort Custer to protect the land. The old structures built at the turn of the century with stone quarried from the Gardner River still stood.

Edwards met me as I entered the rectangular three-story building that now served as park headquarters.

"We had a group come in today reporting their friend missing." He led me upstairs. "The friend matches the description of the Jane Doe."

The five women in the room were young, college-aged. They were all wide-eyed, concern etched into their pretty features. Four of the five women's faces brightened when Frank trotted into the room at my heels. He made his rounds greeting them as I took a seat down the table from the women.

One woman's gaze went back and forth between Edwards and me as soon as I entered the room. The concern on her face morphed into grief and shock. She knew exactly why I was here.

"Ladies, my name is Hector." I met each of their gazes, but I ended with the woman who already knew. "I'm with the police in Raven's Gap. I understand you've come in to report your friend missing."

"Her name is Sarah Clemens," the young woman said.

I drew my notebook and reading glasses from my pocket. "What can you tell me about Sarah?"

"She's a—"

The young woman who already knew cut in. "She's Caucasian, around five-foot-six-inches tall, roughly one hundred forty pounds. She was last seen on Sunday morning wearing a blue coat and a backpack." She sounded like a seasoned officer. She seemed to read the thought on my face, because she said, "My dad's a cop. Something bad has happened to Sarah, hasn't it?"

"What brought you to the area?" I asked.

She searched my face for a long moment before answering. "We're college students from Bozeman, and we decided to come down before the new semester starts. We rented a house in Gardiner for a couple of days while we explored the Mammoth area, and then on Sunday we took the snowcoach down to Old Faithful and stayed there until yesterday. Sarah stayed behind."

"Why is that?"

"She wanted to explore some more trails in this section of the park Sunday. She was planning on meeting us at the Snow Lodge on Monday."

"Why did you wait until today to report her missing?"

"Sarah…she does her own thing. We thought she must have decided to stay here, but when we arrived back yesterday afternoon, she was gone. Her stuff was still at the house. We searched all over Gardiner and Mammoth for her last night. I knew something was wrong." Her throat worked as she swallowed. "She's dead, isn't she?"

The others sucked in a breath, clearly not having seen where this was leading.

"There were reports on Sunday of an incident at the campground in Raven's Gap. It looked like a young woman had been kidnapped while cross-country skiing." The other girls began to cry, but the one who had known just watched me steadily. "On Monday, a body was found." I rested a hand on the file folder I had placed on the table before me. "I have a photograph, but—"

"Let me see," the young woman said.

I slid it across the table to her. The coroner had sent it to me yesterday. It showed the woman from the cabin from the shoulders up on a cold metal slab.

She may have known what happened to her friend as soon as I entered the room, but nothing fully prepared someone to see the dead, gray face of a friend or loved one. Her entire body flinched. Her eyes welled with tears, and her hand came up to cover her mouth.

One of her friends leaned forward and said, "Is it her?"

She slapped a hand over the photo before the other woman could catch a glimpse of the grim sight. She slid it back across the table to me and nodded. "That's Sarah."

There was nothing that sounded quite so haunting as the grief and shock of losing someone to senseless violence. I had only heard the sound four times in the last thirty years. The parents of a son who committed suicide. The sister of a woman whose husband beat her to death in a drunken rage over a burnt meatloaf. The daughter of a man who had died as a result of a hit and run. And Ed and Betty when I had shown up on their doorstep to break the news that my wife and daughter, their daughter and granddaughter, were gone. Vanished without a trace. It was a sound I would never grow used to.

The five young women huddled together with their arms wrapped around one another in their shared grief. Frank leaned against their legs, offering his support.

The one who had done most of the talking pulled away first and turned to me. "We were in Raven's Gap Saturday night. We had dinner at a restaurant in town. Maggie's. I think that was the name of it. It got great Yelp reviews."

I pulled the photograph from my pocket and extended it to her. "Have you ever seen this man before?"

Her brow wrinkled as she studied the photo. "No, I

don't think so." She passed it to her friends. "Is he the person who did that to Sarah?"

"We don't know yet." I tucked the photo back into my pocket when they had finished passing it around and confirming they could not recall seeing Jeff Roosevelt. "Do you have contact information for Sarah's parents?"

"Her brother goes to the same college. I have his number. I'll text him."

Once I had received the contact information, I called Frank to my side and exited the room. Edwards followed me, sighing heavily. "This isn't my first death notification," the younger man admitted, "but it is my first homicide."

"I hope it's your last as well."

Jeff Roosevelt had moved to town a month before Winona and Emma went missing. I had not suspected him at first.

Winona had no enemies. Those in town loved her. She was the darling of Raven's Gap. Suspicion had immediately fallen on me, but my own suspicion was directed toward tourists in the area.

Until I saw the stills from the CCTV footage. At the supermarket, the post office, the bank, the laundromat. I had poured over the photographs from every place in Raven's Gap and Gardiner Winona frequented with any regularity. CCTV footage was rarely kept for any significant length of time. Most of what I had did not predate their disappearance by more than two weeks.

I did not notice him at first. I was too caught by Winona's pensive, slight smile or her far-off gaze in the photos. When I first met her, her smile could have lit an arena. When I approached her in the bar after watching her barrel race, she had been surrounded by men.

She had smiled at them all, but she had caught my gaze and beamed.

Studying the photos, I saw the tightness of her smile, the tension around her eyes, and I wondered when she had stopped beaming. And when I had stopped noticing the dimming of that smile.

Then I had realized what I was looking at, what I was seeing in every single photograph. The same figure in the background of almost every still. Jeff Roosevelt.

He was filling up his Land Rover at the gas station as I entered Raven's Gap. I braked too quickly on the winter roads and turned in. As I pulled up to the pump beside where he was parked, he crossed in front of me to enter the gas station.

I kept an eye on him as I paid at the pump and inserted the nozzle to top off my own tank. When he disappeared from sight between the shelves, I crossed the pavement and peered into his vehicle. His windows were darkly tinted, and I had to cup my hands around my eyes and press my face against the glass to see within.

"I thought they were keeping you on a tighter leash these days."

I straightened slowly and turned to face him.

The man Susan hired at the bookstore asked me today if I would like to visit his rose garden, Winona had told me. At the time, I thought she had been attempting to make me jealous. I brushed her off before she said anything more.

Looking back, I thought I could remember the pinched tension in her face. Now I wondered if she had been trying to tell me he made her uncomfortable, if she might have been afraid of him. Now I wondered how long he had been following her and what he had done with my wife and daughter.

He stood a few feet from me with that pompous prick smile on his face.

"There are no leashes during a murder investigation," I said.

"I heard about the body found in the campground." He looked right into my eyes. "Women can never be too careful these days, can they?"

"You would know all about that."

He sighed. "I thought this might resurrect your John Wayne tendencies. This isn't the Wild West any longer, Hector. I won't hesitate to slap a restraining order on you if you start harassing me again."

A metallic thud clipped the air, signaling the pump had stopped running. "You have a complaint to make, come by the station anytime," I said as I crossed back to my vehicle. "You know where we're located."

Frank was standing in my seat when I opened the driver's side door, staring at Jeff with his lips curled back in a soundless snarl. "One day," I assured him softly.

I now knew what had made the tracks on the old service road beside the campground. I should have recognized them sooner. Until this season with their new fleet of snowcoaches, Yellowstone had used devices to convert their fifteen passenger vans into winter vehicles. They replaced the tires with a track system to allow the vehicles to drive through snow. Four similar tracks had been in the cargo space of Jeff's vehicle.

When I returned to the police department, Joan glanced up from the computer as I entered. "I left Atlanta's response about Evelyn Hutto on your desk."

I expected a page or two. A traffic ticket or the like. But I found a thick folder on my desk with a stack of printouts within. I scanned through the reports. The bulk of them were largely the same complaint filed over and over again throughout the course of 2013. The last report was different, dated from the following year. It took me several long minutes to get through the case notes, and a handwritten scrawl across the bottom of the front page caught my attention: JDLR.

I rubbed my jaw and rested my hand on the stack of papers. An idea was beginning to take shape in my mind.

I snagged the phone on my desk and dialed the number of an office in Colorado.

"It's Hector," I said when he answered on the third ring.

"Is my ma okay?" the gruff voice at the other end of the line asked.

"Maggie's fine." I rubbed the back of my neck. "I need to ask a favor of you."

"Name it," he said immediately.

When I first met William Silva, he had been five years old. His father was Brazilian, his mother African American, and it had not been easy for him growing up in a small town where he was the only black kid. He was raised by strong, hard-working parents until his father had dropped dead of a heart attack at the age of forty-three. Then he had become a strong, hard-working son who helped his mother at the diner every day before and after school. He had only joined the military after he asked me to promise to look after his mother. He had been a good kid, but he was an even better man.

"I want you to look in for someone for me, a woman

who just moved to town." I gave him all the information I knew on Evelyn. "See what you can turn up about a man by the name of Chad Kilgore, too. He was a security guard at the museum where Evelyn worked in Atlanta."

"Is there more of a connection between them that I should look for?"

"She claims he was stalking her," I said.

William let out a low whistle. "That's a connection alright."

I told him about the last report from 2014. "The officer marked it as JDLR."

"I'll see what I can find."

If anyone could find answers, it was William. He was retired Special Forces. He had done a short stint in the FBI before deciding he preferred shades of gray to black and white. The man had a sixth sense for finding people. It was why he had opened an office in Denver with a sign on the door that read *FUGITIVE RECOVERY AGENT.* The only time he had let me down was when I asked him to help me find my girls.

The phone on my desk rang as soon as I hung up the call with William, and when I answered, Joan's voice on the other end of the line was tense. "Will you come up to the front, please?"

I could hear a frantic male voice in the background.

I strode up the hall and into the lobby to find Carl Thornton pacing back and forth. He whirled around at the sound of the door.

"Hector." He rushed toward me, and the pure panic on his face had me scanning him quickly for injury. "Jesus Christ, you have to help me. Help me find her."

He looked like his legs were about to buckle, so I

caught his arm in a firm grip and led him to one of the wooden benches against the wall.

"Calm down," I ordered. "Calm down, and tell me what's wrong."

"It's Amanda."

His wife taught kindergarten at the elementary school in Gardiner. "Is she hurt?"

"No," he whispered. "She's gone."

FOURTEEN

On average, over 83,000 people are missing at any time: 50,000 adults and 33,000 children and teens.

EVELYN

"WE HAVE SET you up in Roberta's old office," Annette Zierdt said as she led me down the hall. "She was our previous image archivist, but she retired a few months ago. I thought this would be more preferable than a desk in the archive room."

"I've worked at a desk in the corner before." I stopped in the doorway, and she gestured for me to enter. It was not a large office, but it had a window and the desk was a deep L-shaped monstrosity. "This is lovely. It will be perfect." I deposited my purse and coat on the chair behind the desk.

The frustration of my meeting with Hector had worn away as the morning had been filled with the usual paperwork and human resources minutia of a new position. Annette was the archivist and collections manager of the Park County Museum, and thus far I had found her to be warm, welcoming, and excited about the work I had been brought on to do.

"I can go ahead and show you the repository and the

collection you'll be working on, unless you'd like to get your log-in credentials for our system first."

"Oh, the repository, please."

She smiled. "I had a feeling that would be your choice. It's just down the hall."

The archive room was massive, with twenty-five-foot ceilings and two parallel rows of twenty-foot mobile shelving.

"The room is badged entry. It is climate controlled, so you can prop the door open if you're coming and going. But if you're going to be in here for more than a few minutes, we ask you keep the door closed."

"Of course." I followed her down the long corridor between the shelving units, stopping beside her as she turned the rotary handle of the first rolling stack.

"I recommend moving one shelf at a time. Two at the most, unless you have superhuman strength."

I moved around her and spun the handle on the next stack.

"Thank you," she said, moving to the next. "I couldn't convince the committee to approve the added cost in the budget to add electric motors when we had these installed. As a general rule, we have paper archived material on the numerical shelves." She gestured to the row of shelves on the opposite side of the room. "And all other artifacts are stored in the alphabetical shelves."

She moved to grab the rolling set of stairs at the end of the room, but I waved her away. "I've got it."

"I'm afraid we have just had these artifacts collected under a category of 'Native' and we've been adding to it as we've been unpacking from the move into this new building." She caught hold of the leg of the rolling step ladder and positioned it next to the shelf before setting the brake. "I think you can understand that there's a lot of pressure on us to expedite this project. It should have been done two decades ago, and the project kept falling through the cracks. We didn't realize the extent of the collection until the move."

"Of course. I'll put all of my energy and focus into this project."

"I know you will, dear." She touched my arm and then carefully climbed the step ladder. "That's exactly why I hired you. Now, let me see… Yes…" She peered at each of the dozen shelves. "The paintings on the top shelf depict scenes of Native American life, but they aren't part of the collection you'll be working on. So everything but the top shelf in this section is part of the collection you'll be processing."

The space was packed with archival storage boxes, and excitement bloomed in my chest. "I'll get started on it as soon as I familiarize myself with your software program."

Annette nodded approvingly as she climbed down the ladder. "I think you'll fit in well here, Evelyn. You came highly recommended, but I always appreciate enthusiasm more than anything. Come along. I have a meeting with the head of IT. I'll take you to Rachel in that department. She'll get your log-ins set up and give you a crash course on the EMu software we use."

Rachel, I was surprised to find, was someone I already knew. She had attended the book club meeting at Book Ends. Her personality was as effusive as her abundance of curly hair. Within three hours, I had access to the computer system, felt like I could use the cataloging software competently, and was back in the repository standing at the end of the row of shelves labeled *N.* I left the push cart at the end of the row and walked slowly between the shelves, trailing my hand along the storage boxes.

It was unlikely that all of the items in the collection would fall under the NAGPRA guidelines. I would need to consult with representatives from nearby tribes once I had the artifacts catalogued, and if I found human remains stashed forlornly away in dusty boxes, I would need to bring in archaeologists and physical anthropologists. The identification process was tedious and technical and required expertise far greater than mine. But my work would be the first step in their journey home.

I pushed the rolling ladder aside, knelt next to the bottom shelf, and slid a box free. Two more boxes filled the space directly behind it. The eleven shelves were stacked four wide and three deep. I had a lot of material to catalogue, and anticipation hummed in my veins.

I loaded three boxes onto the cart and rolled them to one of the work stations at the end of the room. The boxes were all record storage boxes, and the pieces within had become jumbled together. Though none of the collection had been catalogued online, there were finding aids tucked into the front of each box, hand written in pencil.

I used the notes of my predecessors to inform my own as I studied each piece, photographed them next to a caliper, and entered information about each article into the computer system. I tucked each piece into more appropriate archival boxes and labeled the boxes.

I knew the basics of what to look for. I had read that the Crow did not practice basketry, pottery, weaving, or woodcarving, but the intricacy of their beadwork was astonishing. Their own overlay style of stitching was known as the "Crow Stitch," and they favored geometric shapes, particularly hourglass structures, and the colors blue and pink.

The Blackfoot had a unique straight-up headdress, and warriors frequently wore roaches made from porcupine hair dyed red. They used rattles and whistles in their music and wore necklaces of braided sweetgrass and teeth or claws.

The Shoshone's baskets were complexly and stunningly woven, and their bows were made from the horns of mountain sheep. Their beadwork was mainly done in white, green, blue, and cobalt, and the Shoshone rose was a recurring motif in more modern work.

The Bannock were closely affiliated with the Shoshone and were such skilled basket makers, their woven baskets could hold water. Their clothing was mainly made from sagebrush bark, and their jewelry from beads and shells.

While these were the peoples who had called the Yellowstone region home, it did not mean they were the only ones who moved through the area. With the national park's inventory of human remains, the park service had consulted with around twenty tribes in the surrounding area. I was not an expert even in the tribes immediately local to the area, so I made a notation of my guess as to the pieces' origins but knew further research would be required.

I found it in the third box. I lifted it carefully from its wrappings and sucked in a breath when I realized what I held. It was brown and mottled with age and fit neatly in my hands, curved and thin.

Someone who had never seen human bone before might mistake it for a shard of pottery, a remnant of some long-ago shattering of a vessel. In a way, the dome of the skull was just that, though the contents had once been the origins of thought and consciousness rather than grain or oil.

I set the bone aside gently and studied the other contents of the box in an attempt to determine if they were grave offerings. I kept everything from the third box together and called Annette.

A few minutes later, she hurried into the archive, face lit with excitement. "You found something?"

I held the skull fragment out to her, and she leaned over the work table. There was nothing left attached to the bone. It was nearly turned to stone, but I handled it as if it were glass. This had been a person once. A man or woman, young or old. He or she had lived a life filled with hopes and dreams, love and loss, triumph and hardship.

Now the last remnant of that life had been tucked away in a box. When Annette met my gaze, I knew she felt the import as well.

"Was there any information with it?" she asked, voice quiet.

"It was found prior to 1885 by a sheepherder near his camp outside of Jardine. It was sold several times and then donated to the museum in the 1940s." I nodded to the other items I had laid out on the table. "I don't know if these pieces were grave offerings, but they were in the box along with the skull fragment."

"I'll go ahead and contact the University of Montana. Their anthropology and archaeology departments have assisted us before." She touched my shoulder. "Good job."

"I haven't even made a dint in the collection yet," I warned her.

"And already you're doing exactly what I brought you on for." She glanced at her watch. "I need to go make that call to Missoula to give the department a head's up that we'll need some of their experts."

I placed the pieces carefully back in the box and then rolled everything back to the shelves. The box with the skull in it went on a nearby empty shelf while the others went back where I had found them. I worked methodically through two more boxes, studying each artifact, photographing it, entering into the database, and storing them in more appropriate archival boxes. I found no more bones.

Hours later, I stretched as I stood, rolling the stiffness from my neck. A sneeze crept up on me and made white stars dance before my eyes with its violence. I made a mental note to stop by the drug store on the way home and pick up some allergy medicine and nasal spray.

I rolled the boxes back down to the N section and deposited them on the shelf. A glance at my watch showed it was near the end of the day, but I pulled the next box in the row free and placed it on the floor. I removed the lid to see what items awaited my appraisal tomorrow and was surprised to find not shards and fragments of ancient pieces, but whole, unbroken pieces of pottery and artfully woven baskets.

When I searched, there was no finding aid tucked within the box. I spun the box, and on the opposite side the words *PRIVATE DONATION 2017: 1 of 4* were neatly printed in permanent marker. I found the other three interspersed with the remaining boxes I had not yet catalogued on the next shelf. Each box contained beautiful pieces of art, but all seemed modern save for the item at the bottom of the last box.

I lifted it free from the box. It was a bundle of muslin and hide, about a foot wide and almost three feet long. The bottom half was laced together with the top fashioned around a wood hoop. Bands of quillwork framed the edges that were sewn around the hoop, and at the top of the bundle was a quilled disc of red, yellow, and black.

It was a cradleboard, lovingly and skillfully crafted. I thought it must be from the nineteenth century, or perhaps earlier.

It did not fit with the rest of the private donation. There were fetishes, pottery, baskets, jewelry, a weaving, an intricately carved flute, and a number of other pieces. The colors were different with each piece, the patterns and shapes unique. But all appeared to be made by modern artisans save for the cradleboard.

Curiosity piqued, I photographed the cradleboard before I tucked it back into the box, packed everything away, and turned out the lights as I exited the repository. I grabbed my coat and purse from my office and stopped by Annette's office on my way out. She was still at her desk, gaze fixed on her computer screen. I rapped a knuckle against the doorframe, and she turned to me.

"I would say you've already had a successful first day on the job."

"The collection is fantastic," I said. "I would love to put together a display for the front with the items that aren't NAGPRA pieces."

"We have been trying to find someone to fill that role now that Roberta is gone. That was her pet project."

I had learned in my years of working with archivists and curators that the quickest way to make yourself indispensable was to enthusiastically and creatively fill any gaps. "I'll mock up some plans for you to look over. Once I complete the cataloguing, I'll have a much better idea of what we have to display, but already I have a vision for it in my mind."

Her smile was filled with approval. "I'll be happy to look over any plans you have."

"You mentioned the anthropology and archaeology departments at the university have assisted you before?"

"Yes, we've worked with both departments. Did you find something else?"

"Nothing that would fall under NAGPRA, but I did find an item that roused my curiosity. I wondered if we had any contacts who are experts on the lives of Native women and children."

Annette turned back to her computer and her fingers rushed over the keyboard. "Dr. Marilou Cobel. I just sent you her contact information in an email. She's brilliant, and if you have any questions about the historic roles of women in the Plains Indian tribes, she'll be able to answer them. If she doesn't know the answer, she'll know someone who does."

"Perfect. Thank you."

"Of course." Her phone rang, but before she picked it up, she said, "We're pleased to have you here, Evelyn."

As I left the museum, the last of the day's light faded in a wink over the rooftops, and the street lamps flickered to life. My steps felt light and buoyant as I walked out to where I had parked Ed's Chevy.

I had given up my job at the museum in Atlanta last year when it became too much to balance with caring for my grandparents. My grandmother's bedridden state and my grandfather's rapidly advancing Alzheimer's had left me drained, mentally and physically. Working the graveyard shift stocking shelves at the grocery store had been a job that kept food on our table and paid the bills.

I felt exhilarated, the gears turning in my head like they had not done since I left the museum in Atlanta, and I realized a smile lingered on my face as I drove through town. It remained on my face right up to the point that I hopped out of the truck and moved to the entrance of the supermarket.

The sign on the door read, *HAVE YOU SEEN ME? PLEASE CALL*. A phone number was listed underneath, but it was the photograph that grabbed my attention. The woman in it was grinning at the person behind the camera, her face lit with happiness.

It was a face I recognized. I knew that welcoming smile. She had directed it toward me just the other night. *Hello. You're both new to the group. I'm Amanda.*

The sign said her name was Amanda Thornton, age 41, height 5'7", weight 170 pounds, blonde hair, brown eyes. Missing since yesterday, last seen jogging on the state road headed east. My stomach twisted at seeing the vibrant, friendly woman reduced to statistics. The same signs were posted on the community bulletin boards within.

I moved straight to the pharmacy and grabbed a bottle of allergy pills and a nasal spray from the shelves. There was a checkout at the pharmacy's counter with no line, so I approached and offered the elderly woman behind the register my items.

"Need a bag for these, honey?" Her smile and voice were subdued.

"No, thank you." I glanced at the flyer taped to the back of the register. "Amanda Thornton, the woman missing…"

"Isn't it just awful?" she whispered. "Those poor babies. And Carl has been so distraught."

"Do they know…?" I let the sentence dwindle, grappling with what I wanted to ask.

She shook her head. "She just went for a run yesterday morning and never came home."

I paid and headed out to the truck. In the parking lot, I found a flyer tucked under the windshield wiper of Ed's Chevy. The paper trembled in the wind like a trapped bird, helplessly pinned, frantically fluttering. I slid it free from its moorings.

Amanda's face stared up at me from the flyer as I settled behind the wheel and pulled out of the parking lot. I glanced at her smile, and instead of turning to cut down side roads to the inn, I drove uphill to Main Street.

I parked in the public lot at the corner, angling the truck so I had a clear view down the street to Jeff's Land Rover parked in front of Book Ends. The cold began to seep in as soon as I shut the truck off, and I buttoned my coat up to my throat.

The traffic on the street was minimal as the evening slid toward night, and within thirty minutes, Jeff made an appearance on the sidewalk in front of the bookshop. He did not move toward his vehicle, though. Instead, he shoved his hands into his pockets and started down the street toward where I was parked.

I ducked out of sight below the steering wheel as he approached. The pace of my heart quickened as I strained to hear his footfall, but I could hear nothing aside from the thump of a car door being closed nearby and the sound of my own breathing as it clouded the air before my face. The temptation to look was almost overwhelming, but I made myself wait. A muffled greeting was exchanged close by, and then all was quiet again.

I lifted my head slowly and glanced around. Jeff was nowhere in sight.

I snagged the flyer and tucked it into my pocket, exiting the truck quickly and closing the door silently behind me. I hurried across the lot to the corner.

A couple strolled hand in hand down the sidewalk toward the bookstore. A glance down the cross street revealed an empty sidewalk, but when I turned and glanced behind me, I caught sight of Jeff just as he turned the corner.

I followed him, hurrying down Main Street to where it came to a dead end at the post office. I slowed as I came to the corner and peered cautiously down the cross street.

The street lights on the side street were spaced farther apart, the pools of light interrupted by shadow. Jeff walked down the opposite side of the street, stride unhurried. He began to whistle, and the tune reached me, soft and clear in the winter's night air.

I froze in place, breath caught in my throat. *Alas, my love, you do me wrong.*

I stepped back quickly, shoulder clipping the corner of the building. A startled gasp of air left me before I could contain it, but Jeff did not look back before he

turned down a lane on the opposite side of the hardware store.

I thrust my hand into my pocket, reaching past the
folded wings of the flyer to grip the canister of pepper spray. I kept an eye fixed on the spot where he had
disappeared as I crossed the street. It was not a lane so
much as a narrow alley between buildings, I realized
as I approached.

The whistle was louder issued from the tight brick
depths of the alley, mocking me with the tune, until it
was suddenly cut silent by the groan of hinges and the
heavy thump of a closing door.

When I reached the mouth, I found the alley dark
save for a sputtering light over a side entrance.

The echo of "Greensleeves" hung in the cold night
air. I started to venture down the alley, but the memory
of the dark basement, the tight space beneath the desk
I had wedged myself into, and the soft, chilling taunts
growing closer rooted my feet to the ground.

I retreated across the street, sheltering deep under the
awning of the antique shop across from the hardware
store. I studied the building. Like most of the stores in
town, it was of brick construction, square and sturdy
in that no-nonsense fashion from the early days of the
frontier. Like the bookshop, it was two stories, and after
a moment, lights illuminated the multi-paned windows
of the second floor.

I stole back through town and left the flyer on the
windshield of his Land Rover before heading to the inn.
It seemed that we both knew where one another lived
now, and the closed doorways in the shadowed corridor
felt ominous and dangerous tonight.

I hurried down the hallway, rushing to fit my key

into the lock and gain the safety of my room. Once inside, I locked the door and searched the bedroom and adjoining bathroom. It was empty, and everything remained as I had left it this morning.

I let out an unsteady breath, and before I readied for bed, I dragged the chaise lounge across the room and wedged it against the door.

FIFTEEN

Truths and roses have thorns about them.

-Henry David Thoreau

HECTOR

I SPENT THURSDAY on the search team scouring the area
for Amanda Thornton. Frank managed to follow her
trail through town to a point almost halfway to Gardiner on the state road.

She had either gotten into a car or been forced into
one. My bet was on the latter.

Still, we searched in quadrants branching out from
the road down to the river and up into the hills. Frank
and I had been on countless searches together. This act
of slogging through snow, poking through mounded
banks, combing through the undergrowth never failed
to bring back memories. Memories of a search when I
had been seeking that banner of dark hair, that certain
curve of hip. Memories of scrambling down ravines,
fording rivers, trying to find the small body with a che-
rubic face that I had been so indifferent to.

In the first days and weeks, I had been terrified I
would find them dead. But in the months and years
that followed, I had been desperate. Dread at finding
my girls had turned to despair at not finding them. And

so they lingered still, not alive but not dead, not gone but not in my arms where I should have cherished and protected them and failed to do so. They were ghosts who dogged my step, caught in this unknown purgatory with no answers.

It had been what first led me to get a dog and train him. I had done the research and spoken with breeders across the west. When I first brought Bill, Frank's predecessor, home, the dumb fucks at the police department had laughed and called the brown poodle Bob Ross. The first time I took him out into the field on a job that was not training, they had laughed when he had pranced off in the way that only a poodle can and disappeared into the woods. They had stopped laughing when we found him the next day, following the sound of his barking into the wilderness.

He had found the four-year-old girl who had wandered off from her family at the campground. She had fallen down an embankment and broken her leg. He had draped himself over her throughout the night, fending off the cold that would have killed her and the predators that would have done the same.

Every officer had shown up at the vet when I had taken Bill in to ease his way when he developed cancer at the age of ten. And no one had laughed when I brought Frank home six months later.

I called Frank back to me now and headed into town. The sun was setting, and the search would pick up tomorrow.

The search effort, made up of a handful of professionals and a number of volunteers, met at the local diner to discuss the strategy for tomorrow's search. At least half the town was packed into the space, gathered around a map spread across two tables that had been pulled together.

I stayed at the fringes of the crowd in a booth in the corner, catching Maggie Silva's eye as she passed with a pot of coffee in both hands. She stopped and topped off my mug. "I have Frank's usual coming up. You need anything?"

The poodle sat across from me, and he grinned at Maggie, tail thumping against the vinyl seat. Only one person, years ago, had ever balked at Maggie allowing the dog in the diner. She had informed the man that dogs did not try to light up a cigarette in her establishment, steal her silverware, start fights, or piss all over the bathroom floor. If he had a dog who could vouch for him, he would be welcomed back, but until then, he could eat elsewhere.

I smiled at the memory. Being here in this crowd, catching the sidelong glances thrown my way, had tension tight about my neck and shoulders. It eased slightly with Maggie standing before me, face stern, eyes warm. She had been my wife's closest friend, and, surprisingly, the only one who never doubted me. "Nah, Mags. This is fine."

"Let me know if you change your mind."

She moved away, and I listened as plans were made and quadrants were assigned for the search that would begin again at first light. The mood was somber. Men and women were angry and afraid.

"Hey, Hector," a man called. I sighed inwardly, knowing what was coming when I glanced across the room and met Winona's brother's cold glare. "You have experience hiding bodies where no one can find them. Any advice on where we should search?"

The silence that fell over the diner was deafening and filled with undercurrents.

These people had loved my wife. She was born and raised here. She had known everyone by name, worked at Thornton's Market when Carl Thornton's father still ran it, and returned home to their welcoming embrace after a short but successful career as a barrel racer. She had been their bright star, their golden girl.

I had always been the stranger she brought home with her. The one who had crushed other men's dreams of making her theirs, the one who had dampened her smile and tinged her laugh with unhappiness.

After she was gone, I was much more than that. Even the police, the very men I worked shoulder to shoulder with, thought I was responsible for her disappearance.

I held the other man's stare. I could not even drum up anger any longer. It was as the kids were saying these days: I had no fucks left to give.

A plate clunked down on the table in front of me. It was Frank's usual, three scrambled eggs with ham. I pushed it across the table to him, but his gaze was on Maggie.

"Jack, what have I told you about coming in here and spewing your hate in my diner? I don't want my food soaking up your vile bitterness. Get out."

The younger man stared at her for a moment before standing, collecting his hat and coat, and shoving through the crowd to slam out the door. A gust of frigid wind swirled inside before the door bounced closed.

"Maggie," I said, voice low and full of warning.

"Shut up and drink your coffee, Hector." She looked around the room, and heads ducked to avoid her gaze. "Anyone else who wants to voice old grievances instead of trying to find a woman who is in danger can get out right along with him."

No one moved or spoke for several long minutes until she turned away from the crowd and dropped a bowl on the table. She filled it with water from the pitcher she carried and slid it beside Frank's plate. He stared up at her, and some of the tension in her face eased as she combed her fingers through his topknot.

"Eat your eggs, baby. I added extra ham for you." He obeyed with enthusiasm, and she met my gaze. "I'm making you a burger to take home."

Her face was still pinched in anger, and I knew better than to argue with her. "Thank you."

She knew I thanked her for more than the food, and she patted my shoulder before she returned to work.

A time was set to meet tomorrow morning, and the crowd dispersed. Everyone avoided my gaze on their exodus from the diner.

Once Frank finished his eggs and Maggie slid a foil-wrapped hamburger onto the table, I tucked a twenty under the edge of the plate and headed out to my truck.

I was not surprised to find the damage. I did not need to guess at who had dug their key into the side of my truck, gouging out a groove through the paint from just over the front driver's side tire all the way around to the tail gate.

I glanced across the street and locked eyes with Jack through the windshield of his own truck. The street light illuminated the sneer on his face as he stared at me. He had adored his older sister, and when Winona introduced me to the family, he had been just a teenager. He had hated me on sight.

But since Winona and Emma had disappeared, his

MEGHAN HOLLOWAY

hatred had festered into something entirely more dangerous. I recognized obsession. I understood it. And I knew this man would try to kill me one day. He was simply biding his time until he thought he could do it and get away with it.

I lifted a hand in a mocking greeting and saw his face tighten before I opened the defaced door of my truck and motioned for Frank to load up. The poodle knew my routine, so when I turned back into town instead of heading home, he settled down in the passenger's seat with a sigh.

When I came to the intersection of Spruce Avenue and Main Street, Ed's truck in the public lot at the corner caught my eye. The shadowed figure behind the wheel had parked the rusty old vehicle to have a view down Main Street.

I turned down an alley across the street. The lane behind the shops on this side of Main was used for garbage collection, and I killed the lights as I crept down the gravel drive. I parked beside a dumpster and left the engine running with the heat on for Frank.

I crept down the dark alley between the hair salon and the laundromat. Warm gusts from the vents of the laundromat made the frigid air smell of dryer sheets. I stopped deep within the shadows.

From this angle, I could see down Main Street to the public parking lot, and I had a partial view down Canyon Lane to the hardware store. I leaned against the side of the building and waited.

I did not have to wait for long. There was a shift of movement in Ed's truck, and Evelyn's silhouette ducked out of sight. Moments later, Jeff sauntered past the lot, hands tucked into his coat pockets, strolling casually down the sidewalk. I felt tension creep up my neck just watching him.

I knew Winona's brother's intentions to try to kill me. I understood Jack's end game after years of watching and waiting, because I was plotting much the same with the man I studied now. Had I been able to get away with it, I would have snatched Jeff off the street years ago. I would have staked him out in the wilderness and slowly flayed the skin from his bones until he confessed to what he had done to my girls. Then I would have left him there for the animals to begin feasting on him before he was truly dead.

If he knew he was being watched, Jeff gave no indication. He moved in and out of the shadows cast by the buildings, a man ambling home one moment, a menacing phantom in the dark the next. Night, I had found, always revealed a man's true nature.

I turned my gaze back to the parking lot and saw movement within Ed's truck. The door opened, and Evelyn closed it silently behind her. She hurried to the corner, first peering down the street toward the bookstore, then down the cross street before turning and spotting Jeff just before he turned down Canyon Lane.

She followed him, sticking close to the sides of the buildings, footsteps careful and silent. Jeff turned the corner, and she picked up her pace, reaching the post office just as he crossed the street.

I was watching her when he suddenly began to whistle. Had I not been, I would have thought the tune was innocent and meaningless. But she acted as if she had slammed into a brick wall, staggering backward with the force of it.

She knew the tune, and he knew she was there.

He disappeared down the alley adjacent to the hardware store, and after several moments, she crept across the street. She stood there at the yawning mouth of the alley before retreating across the street and out of my line of sight.

My gaze lifted to the second floor of the old brick building, and lights soon lit the tall windows.

I lingered, and eventually Evelyn appeared around the corner, walking fast, gaze darting behind her. When she went past the parking lot, I left the shadows and moved to the mouth of my own alley to watch her.

She strode all the way to where Jeff's SUV sat in front of the bookshop and tucked something under his windshield wiper before returning to Ed's ancient Chevy and driving away.

I retreated to my own truck. I opened the door, and Frank sat up from where he was curled in my seat. He moved across the center console and I climbed within, patting his side before I put the truck in reverse and backed down the lane.

As we headed home, I realized I was smiling. Something that might have been hope unfurled in my chest.

SIXTEEN

The rose has been the national flower of the United States since 1986.

EVELYN

I DOWNLOADED THE photos I had taken of the cradleboard yesterday as soon as I arrived in my office the next morning and grabbed Dr. Cobel's contact information from the email Annette had sent me. I introduced myself and wrote that I had come across the cradleboard in a private donation and wanted to determine its origins. I attached the photos and then hit send.

In the repository, I moved the four boxes from the private donation to a separate shelf. I could not resist opening the box that held the cradleboard and lifting it from the depths.

What I loved most about my work was the unspoken stories these objects held. They did not always reveal their secrets to me. Some had been buried too far in the distant past to be anything but silent shards of abused and shattered nations. I mainly held slivers of the past. I could only guess at fragments of their stories.

This cradleboard was a story. A partial story of a child's start and a mother's heart bound safe and close. I did not know the end of their story, but the painstaking care and exquisite craftsmanship was testament to the beginning.

I left the modern pieces in the four boxes and went to the storage room at the end of the repository. The corrugated acid- and lignin-free boxes all came broken down, and I built an artifact box to fit the cradleboard. I placed it gently within, set it on the shelf, and then continued with my work.

At noon, I took a break and had lunch at my desk. My inbox showed an email had arrived from Dr. Cobel an hour ago, and I eagerly opened the message.

Ms. Hutto,

This is definitely Arapaho. The quilled disc is a traditional Arapaho design and is symbolic for protecting the brain of the baby. I would estimate it to be from the late 1800s. I am providing the contact information for Ohetica WhitePlume. She lives in Ethete on Wind River and is head of the Northern Arapaho Tribal Preservation Department. I know she will be interested in speaking with you about this item.

I grabbed the phone on my desk and dialed the number she listed at the bottom of the email.

A woman answered on the third ring. "Little Wind Casino."

I glanced at the number again. "Ah, yes, may I speak with Ohetica WhitePlume?"

"One moment."

Elevator music began playing in my ear and a minute passed before the phone was picked up again.

"Yes, this is Ohetica WhitePlume," a new voice said.

I introduced myself and explained how I had received her name and why I was calling.

"Tell me about the cradleboard," she said.

"I could email you photographs."

She chuckled. "We don't get much internet out here."

I scrolled through the photos on my desktop and described the intricate quillwork, the disc and the ladder-like bands that fringed the edges. "Also, hanging from the laces, there are some pendants. There are three of them with beads and perhaps horsehair and—"

She interrupted me. "What did you say?" Her voice was sharp. When I told her of the decoration hanging from the laces again, she was silent for a moment before she said, "May I put you on hold for a moment?"

"Of course." I tucked the phone between my ear and shoulder and finished eating the sandwich I had brought for lunch.

"Miss?"

I swallowed the last bite quickly. "Yes, I'm still here."

"I know it is a lot to ask, but is there any chance you would be willing to bring the piece here?"

I sat up straighter. "Dr. Cobel said you're in Ethete?" I spun toward my computer and pulled up a map on the internet. When the virtual pin dropped on the town, I realized Wind River was an Indian reservation in Wyoming.

"Yes. I run a small museum in the Little Wind Casino here on the rez."

The map showed a five-hour drive. Tomorrow was Saturday, and my schedule at the museum fell under regular business hours Monday through Friday. "I can be there tomorrow afternoon if that works for you."

"I'll be here to meet you," she said. There was something in her tone that quickened my heart.

I had to receive permission from Annette, and I took the cradleboard with me to her office.

"It is odd," she said, studying the cradleboard. "We are usually very careful about accessioning private collections. We receive a lot of requests, but most don't fit within the Collection Management Policy. There was no paperwork with the collection you found?"

"None, and I searched back through the records from 2017. There's no mention of this collection."

"So we can't know if there were any restrictions on the gift, and there's no record of a donor to contact. It's a beautiful piece. Such craftsmanship." She fingered the pendants hanging from the laces. "I'll approve the deaccession. Keep your receipts, and we'll reimburse you."

When I left work for the day, I carried the box containing the cradleboard with me. I stopped at Ed's mechanic shop on the way to the inn.

Ed was at his desk, and he doffed his ever-present trapper hat. "Ev'lyn. To what do we owe this pleasure?"

"My car isn't ready yet, is it?"

"I'm afraid not. She's on the lift in the shop. She'll be ready for you next week, though."

"In that case, I wondered if I might take your truck to Wind River this weekend," I said. "I'll pay you for the mileage I put on it, of course."

His brow wrinkled. "The reservation in Wyoming?"

"Yes. I thought I'd drive through Yellowstone and the Tetons."

"Can't do that this time of year," Ed said. "Roads are closed."

"Oh." The map application had not been that helpful when I had looked up directions. "I guess I'll have to take the long way, then."

"We're supposed to get more snow tomorrow afternoon," Ed said, voice hesitant. "You can take the Chevy, of course. But let me check her over and put some better snow tires on her."

"I promise I'll be careful with her, but I don't want you to have to go to any extra trouble."

"It won't be any trouble, and it's not the Chevy I would be worried about."

The statement took me aback. It had been a long time since anyone had been worried about me.

"You have a few minutes to wait while I check her over and change out the tires?" he asked.

"I do." I took a seat in the lobby after handing over the keys and dug into my purse for the next book club read. I flipped through the pages to chapter one, but before I began to read, something on the opposite wall caught my eye.

I set my book aside and crossed to it, reading the large print on one side of the banner.

HAVE YOU SEEN US?
Winona and Emma Lewis
Winona, 37 Years Old, 5'5", 140lbs
Emma, 23 Months Old, 33 inches, 24lbs
Missing since Monday, October 13th, 2003

The sign went on to list where the pair had last been seen and a $50,000 reward for any information leading to their return. There were several phone numbers and a social media site listed. Half of the banner was dedicated to a photograph.

I stepped back to study the photo. The woman clearly had American Indian heritage with the structure of her facial features, her skin tone, and the lustrous fall of dark hair around her shoulders. She stared directly into the camera with a Mona Lisa smile.

The toddler was a different matter. The woman held her on her hip, and the little girl had her mother's dark hair. The child's hair was fine and curly, though, her skin and eyes lighter. She rested her head against her mother's shoulder and grinned at the camera, one hand stretched out toward whoever had been on the other side of the lens.

The sun through the windows of the auto shop had faded the banner. The red print and the photograph both had lost their crispness of color. But the woman's gaze and the child's smile held me captive for long moments.

I returned to my book across the room, but my gaze strayed frequently to the banner.

Ed came back in with a gust of frigid air, rubbing his red, chapped hands together. "She's all set."

I tucked the book back in my purse and stood. "Thank you. I'll pay you for the extra mileage."

He waved me away. "You don't need to do that. Take one of my cards with you. It has my number on it. That drive is a lonesome one. And Wind River…it's bleak country."

I accepted the business card he handed me and recognized the number as one listed on the missing persons banner. My gaze went to the woman and child.

"Have they never been found?" I could not help but ask.

"Not yet," Ed said. "Not yet, but we don't give up hope."

When I turned back to him, his gaze was fixed on the

woman in the photograph, pain etched into his weathered features. He was a spry man from what I had seen. He had to at least be in his eighties, but he did not look it. Until this moment. Now, he looked frail to the point of breaking, withered by sorrow.

His eyes came to mine, and his smile was tremulous. "Call me if anything happens along your journey. These empty roads are dangerous ones."

I LEFT THE next morning before the sun was even up. Faye met me at the door with a thermos of coffee and a container of huckleberry muffins.

My backpack went on the floorboard, the archive box in the passenger's seat. I cranked the truck and let the engine rumble and the interior warm while I ate one of the muffins. My headlights cut over the freshly fallen snow. I put the old Chevy in gear and pulled away from the inn.

The miles passed, and I drove slowly and cautiously. Driving in the dark had always made me anxious. I had no memories of my parents, only those that had been passed down to me by my father's parents. My own parents had been killed in a car accident in early morning hours, hit by a drunk driver on their way to the hospital when my mother was in labor with me. My father's parents had been at the hospital as soon as the police informed them of the accident. I had been taken from my mother's lifeless body and placed in my grandfather's arms.

I never felt like something was missing from my life. My grandparents loved me as fiercely as if I were their own child. But I had grown up utterly doted on and rarely disciplined. I had been a spoiled little princess who turned into an absolute terror of a teenager.

My grandparents had been carefully noncommittal in their lack of reaction to the piercings, tattoos, and the phase of blue hair. When I staggered home drunk in the middle of the night, my grandmother simply bundled me into bed and left a pain reliever, a glass of water, and a waste bin beside my bed.

They had not said anything when I partied my way through the first years of college they had scraped and saved for. They had not needed to say anything. I could see the disappointment on their faces.

Then I woke up hungover one morning and saw I had a dozen missed calls from my grandfather. When I called him back, he had tearfully told me my grandmother was in the ICU. He had tried to call me the night before when she first became ill but had not been able to reach me. Within twelve hours, Guillain-Barré syndrome had rendered my grandmother a quadriplegic. The odds of her surviving were slim.

I had left that old lifestyle behind at nineteen. I dropped out of school and moved back home. It was a long, hard year of hospital stays, rehabilitation, and therapy, but my grandmother survived and regained the use of her limbs. Weakened and never quite herself physically again, but still with us.

Responsibility and discipline were things I had worked hard to learn.

Eventually, I finished my undergrad work and pursued a masters remotely. My work at the historical society museum in Atlanta had been a dream come true for six years. Then it had become a nightmare.

I shook away the memories. My white-knuckled grip

on the steering wheel eased as the sky lightened and soon was aflame with the sun's rise. Wind buffeted the truck as I drove.

I was almost the only vehicle on the two-lane road that wove amongst the hills and rocky outcroppings. A river followed my path south, and mountains hemmed my view to the west. Last night's snow had left an unmarred swath of white across the land.

It was frigid and bleak, wild and windswept. The occasional herd of elk or mule deer stood out on the stretches of white plains. I gasped when I saw a creature standing beside the road watching my passing with avid eyes and pricked ears. I was not certain if it was a wolf or a coyote.

My grandfather had loved this area of the country. He and my grandmother had taken a cross-country road trip for their honeymoon seventy years ago. They had loved Yellowstone so much they stayed a month and never completed the trek to Seattle. Every year after that until my parents died, they had made the trek to Yellowstone.

My grandfather had not known who I was in the last year of his life. Just before he slipped away from me entirely, his mind eaten by Alzheimer's, I had crawled up into the attic one day and found his Brownie 500 movie projector. The three of us had spent the day watching home films he had meticulously spliced over the years. The majority of the home movies were from their trips to Yellowstone.

The old films had brought about an increasingly rare moment of lucidity from him. *I wish we had taken you to Yellowstone*, he whispered when the film ran out and the projection on the wall stuttered.

We'll get there some day, I told him.

He had not been satisfied with that, and I could see the pensiveness on his face. He caught my hand between his own and said, *You've spent good years of your life taking care of your grandmother and me.*

Tears had pricked my eyes. He could no longer remember my name, and more often than not, he doubted the identity of the woman who had been his constant for so many decades. But in that moment, he knew me.

Didn't you do the very same for me? I asked him, squeezing those large hands that had done so much for me. I was not certain he remembered how much he had done for me.

I want you to promise me you'll live the rest of your life for yourself. I had started to protest, but he would not accept anything but a promise. *Live the rest of your life for yourself. And one day in your journeys, stop by Yellowstone and think of me.*

I had promised him. In the end, once he was gone and my grandmother followed him within months, Medicare took everything. The house, most of his life insurance policy. There had been nothing left to stay for. That Brownie 500 movie projector had been the last thing to go at the final yard sale.

I crossed into Wyoming with little ceremony, simply a brief widening of the road and a change in the color of the pavement that had thankfully been plowed and salted. I reached Cody in the late morning and stopped at a diner for an early lunch.

Two hours later, I entered the small town of Shoshoni and turned back to the west. A small green sign announced I was entering the Wind River Indian Reservation.

There was nothing to delineate the cross into reservation land. No fences, no change in the wide-open, craggy landscape. I crossed a reservoir black with cold and shined with ice. There was a sign for an RV park, but the flat, sparsely treed lot was empty. A herd of cattle were clustered together farther down the road, standing within a copse of cottonwood trees to seek relief from the wind.

It looked like any other desolate, winter-stripped space I had seen in the vast west.

I had researched Wind River last night. It was one of the most dangerous reservations in the country. A half dozen police officers patrol an area the size of Rhode Island and Delaware combined.

Life was grim here. The life expectancy was low, the unemployment and high school dropout rates high. Alcohol and drug abuse abounded. On one section of the reservation, people still had to boil their water before they drank it.

There was a long history of brutal homicides in Wind River. A two-year crime fighting initiative was enacted a few years ago at Wind River and three other reservations. People called it *the surge*. Crime was reduced at the other three reservations, but violent crime on Wind River increased by seven percent.

I stared out at the passing scenery. There was the occasional stack of hay bales covered in tarps and a blanket of snow and sporadic clusters of buildings off to the side of the road. It seemed so peaceful. Quiet and empty.

Many blamed the violence on the land being haunted. A massacre had taken place in the area in the mid-1800s.

The road seemed to stretch past the horizon. I had

been driving for almost an hour when I suddenly passed a red and cream building off to the left side of the road. I glanced at the sign as I sailed past.

I slowed, startled by its sudden appearance in the middle of nowhere. A glance in the rearview mirror confirmed the sign read *Little Wind Casino*. I performed a U-turn in the middle of the empty road.

There were a dozen vehicles parked in the lot of the windowless rectangle of a building. I parked and grabbed the box from the passenger's seat.

The wind blew me across the parking lot and to the double doors leading into the casino. It was quieter than I expected inside. The handful of people sitting at the machines were silent as they pulled levers and pushed buttons, fixated on the screens. Music played softly on a speaker overhead, and even the tinny music from the machines seemed subdued.

The young man who greeted me pointed across the room when I asked to see Ohetica WhitePlume. A restaurant occupied one part of the building, and tucked into a corner through an open doorway was a small museum and gift shop.

The woman behind the counter turned when I entered, and her gaze immediately dropped to the box in my hands.

"Ms. WhitePlume?"

"Please, call me Ohetica." She was a lovely woman, and her grip when she shook my hand was strong and warm.

"Evelyn," I said.

"Do you mind waiting here a moment? There is someone I'd like to bring in on this meeting."

"Not at all."

"He's in the restaurant," she said, gaze again dropping to the box with a tightening of sorrow around the corner of her eyes. "I won't be but a moment."

I made a slow circuit of the room while she was gone, studying the objects displayed. A drum, an eagle wing fan, a pair of moccasins with intricate quillwork, a parfleche, a pipe, and a rattle were displayed. In one glass encasement was a cradle, much like the one I carried, though there was far less quillwork decorating the one displayed.

I turned at the sound of voices, and Ohetica reentered the room with a man at her side. "Evelyn, this is Joseph Spoonhunter, the Tribal Police Chief."

Unease pierced me, and I struggled not to show the tension that suddenly gripped me. "Police?" I forced myself to shake the hand he extended to me.

His features were stern, and his gaze assessing. "Ohetica called me yesterday because she recognized the description of the cradleboard. It may be an item that was stolen from the home of a family here on the reservation eight years ago."

I placed the box on the counter and carefully unwrapped the cradleboard. "I don't know if she told you, but I work for the Park County Museum. I'm currently undertaking a project to return cultural objects to their tribes. I came across this and knew it didn't fit the rest of our collection."

Ohetica leaned over the box and lifted the cradleboard carefully from the depths as the police chief drew a pair of reading glasses and a photograph from his shirt pocket.

"This was among a collection donated to our museum about two years ago," I said. "It was never formally accessioned."

Ohetica glanced at the police chief, who studied the photograph in his hand and then the cradleboard. "What information do you have on the person who donated the collection?" he asked.

"Nothing, I'm afraid. The records just say it was a private donation." I looked back and forth between the two, taking in the grimness of his features and the tears welling in her eyes. "It *does* belong to your tribe, then?"

"It belongs to my family," Ohetica said, and a tear spilled over her cheek. "This cradle was made by my mother's great-great-great-grandmother. She only bore one child, and it was only after great struggle and much loss that she did so." She fingered the three pendants hanging from the laces. "These were to signify her thankfulness for the fulfillment of her desire to bear a child."

At the sheer emotion on her face, my own throat tightened. "I'm sorry it was taken from your family."

The police chief removed his glasses and rubbed his face. "The thing is, Miss Hutto, this is not the only thing that was taken from the WhitePlume home eight years ago."

"There are a number of other pieces in the collection. This was the only one I—"

"Marisa," Ohetica said, voice rough with pain. "My twenty-two-year-old niece. She went missing that night as well."

PART III

Remove the Stems That Cross

SEVENTEEN

There is no comprehensive data collection system regarding the number of missing and murdered women in Indian country.

HECTOR

By the time the front crept over the hills and the snow began to fall at midday, we still had found no sign of Amanda Thornton. The cell phone company informed the department that her phone was either turned off or the battery was dead. There was no activity on her joint bank account with her husband.

Thirty hours of searching. Over seventy-two hours missing. I knew the statistics involved with timing intimately. And I knew from experience that women sometimes vanished with no trace of them ever found again.

I rubbed the back of my neck and stomped the excess snow from my boots on the welcome mat before I knocked. I could hear the sound of running within moments before the door was yanked open.

Frank's tail began to wag in earnest when he took in our greeter. Amanda's youngest son stared up at me for a moment before his face crumbled and his shoulders began to shake. He left the door open when he turned and retreated into the house.

Frank began to follow him. "Stay," I said softly, and he whined in response.

I heard Carl's voice within ask if someone was at the door. Sobs were his only response.

"It's me. Frank is with me." I rapped a knuckle on the door and pushed it farther open just as Carl lifted his son into his arms. The boy buried his face in his father's neck.

"Hector." The man looked like he had not slept or eaten in three days. He rubbed his son's back. "Sorry, he thought you might be…"

"I understand."

"Come in." He set his son down and whispered something in his ear.

The young boy turned to me, face damp. "Can I play with your dog?" he asked, a quaver in his voice.

I glanced at Carl, who nodded. "Frank would love to play with you." The boy extended his hand in invitation. "Go on," I told the poodle, and he followed the boy as he darted upstairs.

"Did you find anything?" Carl asked.

I scraped my boots against the welcome mat once more before closing the door behind me. "We haven't turned up anything in the search." I glanced at the family portrait hanging in the entryway and met Amanda's smiling gaze. "They're calling off the search."

"What?" He moved to the coat rack and grabbed his jacket. "No. No. She may be lost, she may be—"

I held up a staying hand. "We've searched the area with dogs for two and a half days. With the weather moving in, it's too dangerous for the volunteers to continue."

"So you're just giving up?" His voice cracked.

"You know this town, these people. Of course we're not giving up."

He met my gaze. He and Amanda had been two of the countless volunteers who helped search for my girls even months after the organized search and rescue effort had been called off. He sagged and put a hand against the wall to steady himself. His coat hung from his elbow, and he stared down at the shell of material, expression lost.

"Have you eaten today? Have you fed the boys?"

He blinked at me for a moment before replacing his coat on the rack and scrubbing his hands over his face. "Christ, no. They must be starving."

"Let's go into the kitchen. I need to ask you some questions."

I followed him through the house. Amanda's touch was everywhere: the brightly colored throw pillows on the couch, the lesson planner open on the coffee table next to a stack of activity books, the vast collection of children's books on the shelves in the hallway, her purse sitting on the barstool at the kitchen island.

When Carl stood in front of the refrigerator staring blankly inside, I took pity on the man.

"Sit down, Carl."

He moved across the kitchen and sat at the table with his head in his hands while I took his place at the refrigerator. I collected eggs, peppers, and cheese.

"I have to ask you if you and Amanda were having any problems."

"No. No, we weren't."

"You sure about that?" I asked, keeping an eye on him as I whisked the eggs in a bowl. His head came up. "Someone's been sleeping on that couch in the living room."

He looked away. "It was just an argument. Normal married stuff."

"Like what?"

"Jesus, Hector, do I really need to dredge up our private life with you?"

I waited until he met my gaze, his angry and uncomfortable. "The sooner you answer my questions, the sooner you can be ruled out as a suspect."

His jaw went tight. "I would *never* hurt my wife."

I knew that anger, frustration, and disbelief firsthand. Knowing that a spouse was always the first suspect was far different from being on the receiving end of that suspicion.

"What was the argument about?" I asked patiently.

He held my gaze for a long, silent moment before he blew out a breath and passed a hand over his eyes. "About trying to have another baby. She had three miscarriages after David was born. She wanted to try one more time, but she… Losing those three broke her heart. I couldn't stand to see her go through that again. So this past summer, when she was at a teacher's conference and the boys were at camp, I had a vasectomy. Without telling her."

"Ah." I grabbed a skillet and let it heat on the stovetop while I chopped the peppers and grated the cheese. "Would she have gone somewhere to cool off?"

"No, not without telling me."

"Was she having any issues with anyone lately? Coworkers? Friends?"

He spread his hands, face a picture of confusion. "No. Nothing. We hosted the faculty Christmas party here. Most of her friends are fellow teachers. Everyone loves Amanda."

I whisked the peppers and grated cheese into the eggs and then poured the mixture into the skillet. "Amanda frequents Book Ends regularly, doesn't she?"

"She's there every week for one of the book club meetings. Why do you ask?"

"I just want to get a feel for her routine and the people whose paths she crossed regularly," I lied.

"Christ." Carl stood, his chair scraping across the floor, and he paced to the back door. His shoulders were tense as he stared through the glass panes. "How do you stand it, man? I'm going crazy not knowing where she is. If she's okay." His voice was raw, and when he glanced at me, I had to turn away from the emotion in his face.

I focused on the eggs. "You don't. It eats away at you. It consumes your waking moments. It haunts your sleep. It taints your food. The not knowing poisons you. After a while, you realize it has driven you past the brink of sanity." I swallowed. "But living is a hard habit to break, so you still get out of bed every damn day and do what you need to do."

He was silent. I flicked off the burner, grabbed three plates from the cupboard, and dished up the scrambled eggs between them. I left the skillet in the sink to soak and arranged the plates on the table with napkins and forks. I dropped slices of bread into the toaster. There was orange juice in the refrigerator, and I poured three glasses before I turned to Carl.

He sagged against the door, forehead pressed to the glass, eyes closed.

"Call your boys down to eat," I told him.

He lifted his head. "Can you promise me you'll find her, bring her home?"

The agony in his eyes was both painful and familiar. "I wish I could." But I knew how easily a promise like that was broken.

EIGHTEEN

JEFF

HER WINDOW REMAINED dark and shuttered throughout the day, and a clawing panic set in that she had slipped through my fingers and was gone.

My hands were beginning to tremble when my phone vibrated in my pocket. A glance at the screen showed an alert for the motion detectors being triggered at the greenhouse. I started to ignore the notification, but a moment later another alert came across the screen. The electrical current had been activated.

I glanced at Evelyn's window one more time and then strode back through the woods and into town for my vehicle.

Only once had it not been an animal that set off the security measures I had in place for my roses. A few years ago, I arrived at the greenhouse expecting to find a deer or a coyote and instead found a young man sprawled on the ground. The electrocution had not killed him, but I made short work of that.

He did not belong amidst my roses, though. Instead, I carried him to the nearby mine that had been abandoned a century ago, tore back the boards guarding the entrance into the hillside, and dragged him deep within the mine shaft.

I left the dead man there, and a week later, I heard

on the news that he was a seasonal employee at Yellowstone. He should not have trespassed near my roses.

When I arrived at the ruins, I found a snowshoe hare dead on the ground. I turned off the electric current and tossed the hare in the woods for some other predator to find. My roses were untouched, safe within the cloister of the greenhouse.

All those years ago, I thought Rose was the beginning and the end. But the hunger had lingered within me and festered until I was desperate to sate the need once more. I had resisted until I saw the beadwork on a pair of moccasins displayed at an antiquarian bookshop in Idaho. When I asked about the design, I learned it was called the Shoshone rose. It was a sign.

I had tread carefully at first. But after the fifth time, I had known. The women in those godforsaken places were easy victims. They did not sate me like Rose, but no one was the wiser when they disappeared. There were no manhunts, no nationwide press coverage. It was as simple as plucking a weed from a field.

I had found the perfect hunting ground.

I tended my roses late into the evening and stoked the rocket mass heater before I left. My hands began to tremble again when I returned to Raven's Gap.

I entered the inn the same way I had before, by picking the lock. It was a skill I had taught myself when Rose attempted to shut me out of her life. With my hands shaking, it took me two tries to tumble the pins of the front door, three times to open the door to her room.

I did not realize I held my breath until it escaped on a shaky sigh when I saw that everything was where it should be. My legs were unsteady, and I sat on the edge of her bed to collect myself. It was inconsiderate of her to leave right in the middle of the unfolding story.

Rage took over the panic, and I stood in a rush. That plant she had been carrying when I first saw her on the road sat on the sideboard, its tendrils spilling over the edge and curling down the side. It was beautiful, richly green and flourishing in health.

I crept down to the kitchen and found a container of salt. Back in her room, I poured the entirety onto the soil in the pot and carried it into the bathroom. I ran just enough water over the dirt to allow the salt to dissolve and sink in amidst the roots.

A glass bottle of perfume sat on the counter, and I held it to my nose and inhaled. It smelled fresh and crisp and just like her. I twisted off the cap and poured it down the drain. I thought to shatter the bottle and leave the glass in her bed, but no, I did not want to hurt her. I just wanted her to realize that her selfishness had consequences.

I replaced the plant on the sideboard, toed off my shoes, and climbed into her bed. The sheets were cool and smelled of her, and I found a strand of her hair on the pillow. I twined the small thread of her around my finger and placed my head in the depression in the pillow.

I stayed throughout the night until the sky began to lighten from black to gray. Before I retreated, I remade her bed, smoothing away the evidence of my presence. Being here had soothed the wound she had dealt me. Perhaps I was not speaking loudly enough to capture her attention. I had thought to whisper the story to her, to let it unfold slowly. But she did not appear to be paying close enough attention.

I had the pieces for the next chapter already gathered. I would wait and watch, and when she returned, I would ensure she fully grasped what I was trying to tell her.

NINETEEN

*The sharp thorn often
produces delicate roses.*

-Ovid

EVELYN

IT WAS SNOWING when I left the casino.

I paused in the threshold and took a deep breath. I felt adrift, and uncertainty tore at me. I had stumbled into a hunting ground. There was no doubt in my mind the disappearance here eight years ago was connected to the two in Raven's Gap.

Come out, come out, wherever you are.

Chad Kilgore's whisper brushed against the nape of my neck. I closed my eyes to block out the memory of his taunts. I had been prey once. That fear was poisonous. I wondered if these women had even known they were in a predator's sights.

I drew my hat from where it was tucked into the pocket of my coat and pulled it down over my ears before crossing the pavement to Ed's old Chevy. I stared out over the windswept, barren landscape that surrounded the casino and then pulled onto the empty road.

I retraced my route through the southeast corner of the reservation. The roads were slick, and the shroud of snow only heightened the sense of disquiet that blanketed the land. By the time I left the reservation, the snow had thickened into a white, swirling wall and my stomach was tight with nerves.

I crept along the highway, knuckles white, wipers set to the highest speed. Several vehicles sped around me, kicking up dirty snow that fell in sheets over my windshield and blinded me for terrifying seconds.

The drive to Cody took me twice as long as it had only a few hours ago. My hands were shaking and a headache beat steadily in my temples when I slid into the parking lot of the first hotel I saw.

The amenities were few, but the room I checked into was clean. I took a long, hot shower. By the time I turned off the water, the room was full of steam and my headache had abated.

I curled in bed and turned the television to a cooking channel as I ate the last two muffins Faye had packed me. I stared blindly at the screen, flicking it off after a while when I realized I had watched an entire show and had no clue what had been made over the course of the hour.

I finished my nightly routine in the bathroom and then turned the lights off and crawled back into bed. I lay awake long into the night debating about what I needed to do.

It was in the early hours before I finally fell asleep, and I slept late into the morning. When I pushed back the curtains, I was stunned to see over a foot of fresh snow on the ground. Plows had already churned up and down the street, and the sidewalks were cleared and salted. The snowfall had abated for now, but the sky was gray and heavy.

After digging the Chevy out from under the fresh snowfall, I checked out of the hotel and stopped into a drive-through before heading north. The hours passed quickly, and by the time I turned south in Livingston, it was snowing again.

I made it back to the inn as evening descended over Raven's Gap. Exhaustion weighed heavily on me. I fell onto the bed and slept straight through the night to morning, waking sprawled over the top of the covers with gritty eyes and still dressed in yesterday's clothes.

An hour later when I arrived at the museum, I went straight to Annette's office. "Who else would accept a private donation into the collection?"

She glanced up from her computer, and her forehead creased at the tone of my voice. "What's wrong?" She gestured for me to take a seat. "Did it not belong to the Northern Arapaho on Wind River?"

"It did. It was stolen a few years back."

"Stolen?" She looked stunned. "From the museum?"

"No, from a family's home." And a young woman was stolen away with it.

Her face creased in thought. "Roberta could have accepted it. She only handled donations occasionally, but I'm positive I didn't accept that donation."

"You said she retired? Is there a way I can get a hold of her?"

"Yes, she moved down to Florida for the warm weather and to be closer to her grandchildren. I have her phone number. I'll get it for you." She had an old Rolodex on her desk, and she flipped through it. She found the card she was looking for and snagged a sticky note to jot down the number. She held onto the piece of paper when I reached for it, though, and her gaze was troubled when it met mine. "What is the likelihood of more items in that donation having been stolen?"

"I don't know," I said honestly. What was more pressing on my mind was the likelihood that more missing women were associated with the pieces in the collection. "But I intend to find out."

"Please do."

Once I reached my office, I tossed my coat over my chair and called the number Annette had given me. After a few rings, I was directed to a cheerful greeting that invited me to leave a message.

"Hello, Roberta," I said after the tone. "My name is Evelyn Hutto. I'm working at the Park County Museum, and I have a question about a private collection that was accessioned by the museum in 2017. I wondered if you might be able to shed some light on the donor, because I can't find any records filed for the collection." I gave her my cell phone number before ending the call.

I went straight to the shelf where I had stored the four boxes of the private collection and carried them to the work table. I unpacked each box, laying out the pieces in neat rows on the long table. With so many different objects, the patterns, colors, and shapes unique, they had to be from numerous tribes.

I counted the pieces and dropped into the closest chair when my knees weakened. The cradle board had made for twenty-seven pieces in this anonymous private donation. I had the sinking feeling that the remaining pieces had twenty-six more missing women linked to them.

I spent the first half of the day pouring over the private donation. By noon, my research had shed at least some light on a handful of the pieces. The fetishes—small carvings of a wolf and a bear—were Zuni, three of the baskets were Tohono O'odham, and a bracelet was Diné. It was not much, but it was a start.

I turned the bracelet over in my hands. It was thin and small, a cuff made for a fine-boned wrist, and the silver needed polishing. It left my fingers smelling like old pennies as I handled it. A scene was depicted on the surface of the bracelet, highlighted in gold. Etched into one end of the cuff were the words NAVAJO A. JAMES.

I took the bracelet to my desk with me as I sat down to eat lunch and powered up the computer. A quick internet search showed A. James to be Andrew James, a silversmith in Canyon de Chelly in Arizona. The piece of his jewelry I had before me was a storyteller bracelet depicting a scene from daily life in the canyon: a traditional hogan and water wagon, the sun and clouds, a cottonwood tree, Spider Rock and the White House Ruins. It was beautiful and unique, skillfully and artfully rendered.

I could not help but wonder who the woman was who had once worn it.

I checked my cell phone, but there were no messages or missed calls from Roberta. I drummed my fingers on my desk and then scanned Andrew James's social media page and found a phone number. I dialed the number. After a few rings, a man answered.

"May I speak with Andrew James, please?" I asked.

"Speaking."

"Mr. James, my name is Evelyn Hutto. I work at the Park County Museum in Montana outside of Yellowstone. I recently came across one of your storyteller bracelets, and I wondered if you keep sales records."

"I'm afraid I don't, Miss Hutto," he said, voice low and quiet. "Most of my sales are cash, purchased by visitors here at the canyon."

I pushed my glasses up onto my forehead and rubbed my eyes. "If I were to send you some photographs of the bracelet I have in my possession, is there any way you could look at it and give me any information about it? Perhaps when you made it?"

"I can certainly take a look and see." He gave me an email address and then said, "May I ask what this is about?"

I rubbed my thumb along the tarnished silver. The work was three dimensional, and I could feel the meticulous detail of the bracelet. "I found it at the museum, and I'm hoping to return it to its owner."

After I ended the call, I took photographs of the bracelet from several different angles and then loaded them onto the computer and attached them to an email.

The latter half of the day was dedicated to the NAGPRA collection, but my mind continually strayed to the private donation.

Before leaving work for the day, I photographed the contents of the private donation, capturing close-up details on each piece, studying them from all angles. I emailed the pictures to my personal account, and as soon as I reached the inn, I powered up the computer in the den and clicked through each photo numerous times.

I uploaded the photos into an image search on the internet to see if any results came back. There were suggestions of tribes for some pieces, and I jotted down the information. Nothing came back as an exact match.

A touch on my shoulder startled me, and when I turned from the computer screen, I realized it was fully dark. The glare from the screen throbbed harsh and white against the back of my eyes and blinded me in the dim room.

"Sorry," Faye said. "I didn't mean to startle you. I wondered if you'd like to join us for dinner. I made meatloaf."

My stomach growled in response but I said, "I wouldn't want to be any trouble."

"You wouldn't be. There's plenty."

I forced my mind away from the private donation for the next couple of hours as I ate dinner with Faye and Sam. When the meal was polished off and the kitchen cleaned, Faye hesitantly invited me to play cards with them. I readily said yes.

This little family roused my curiosity. The pair smiled at one another often. Sam would lean against his mother in an armless hug whenever nearby, and she would comb his hair back from his forehead. But Sam remained silent, and it seemed that Faye had largely followed suit.

There was no ring on her hand to indicate the presence of a man in their lives. When she invited me into her home in the adjacent wing of the house, I could see no hint that the family consisted of anyone but the two of them.

Their private domain was down the hall from the

kitchen, past the laundry room. It was tidy and clean and decorated with the same rustic elegance as the rest of the inn.

We sat on the floor around a coffee table in the living room and played a card game akin to rummy. The pair I played with were not grim, but they were straight forward, matter of fact, and quiet as they played their hands.

I had grown up playing bridge every Friday night with my grandparents and their friends. I was used to a livelier scene. I groaned when Sam laid down two sets of three before I could. I let out an appreciative whistle when Faye laid down a set of three and a straight run of seven. I gave a victorious fist pump when I was able to lay down a full run of ten a few rounds later.

Faye and Sam glanced at one another, lips quirked. A hand later, Sam whistled a trilling note when Faye was able to lay down all of her cards at once. She looked at him in surprise. Only because I was looking did I see the tremor that shook her smile.

She cleared her throat as she shuffled. "Two more rounds." She hesitated and then said, "Good luck beating me. I'm trouncing the two of you."

Sam's gaze flew to her and his head tilted as he studied her expression. A smile spread slowly across his face until it split into a grin. It was the most animation I had seen on his face, and from the hitch in her breathing, I knew it surprised Faye as well.

He ended up going out first the last two rounds, and when Faye tallied the points and announced he had won, he mimicked my victorious fist pump in the air above his head.

I chuckled and extended my hand across the coffee table. "High five."

His smile was shy as he reached over and tapped his palm to mine.

Faye put the cards away. "Time for bed, Sam. Go brush your teeth, please."

He scrambled to his feet and disappeared into his bedroom. I stood and followed Faye back down the hall into the main section of the inn.

It had been a long time since I had anything that could be considered a social life. There had been a time when partying had been the main focus of my life and I had been constantly surrounded by those I considered friends. After the call had come and I had dropped out of college to return home, those friends had disappeared. None called, none stopped by to visit. Finishing my bachelors and getting my masters online had not facilitated any connections with my peers outside of a few email exchanges that had dwindled as the years passed.

When I had first started at the museum, I had tried to make room for friendship.

Evelyn, his voice whispered in my ear, *come out, come out, wherever you are.*

I shuddered and shoved the memory away. I had been ostracized quickly after the first time I had complained about Chad.

I missed companionship, I realized, the sheer pleasure of sharing connection and conversation.

"Thank you."

Faye turned from checking the locks on the windows and the deadbolts on the doors. She studied me for a long moment. "You're welcome. Thank you for..." She glanced away and I remembered the look on her face when Sam had whistled. "Thank you."

Once in my room, I headed into the bathroom to brush my teeth and wash my face. When I reached blindly for my face cream as I patted my face dry, my hand knocked over the bottle of perfume on the counter. I heard the cap bounce to the floor and roll. I smoothed the cream into my damp skin and then donned my glasses and knelt to search for the cap. I found it in the corner behind the door.

I straightened and moved to replace the cap only to find the bottle empty. Brow furrowed, I felt along the countertop, wondering if the bottle had cracked and spilled when I knocked it over, but the vanity was dry. The bottle had been almost full when I left for Wind River Saturday morning.

My gaze strayed to the closed shower curtain, and fear crept with prickling tension over me. I wondered if the sudden rough saw of breath was my own sounding raggedly in my ears or someone else's, waiting for me to turn out the light before they sprung from their hiding spot.

I lunged for the shower curtain and shoved it aside so forcefully I yanked half of the curtain from its moorings on the bar above.

The shower was empty.

I whirled around, expecting to find someone behind me, but the bathroom was empty. I searched the room hurriedly as anxiety unfurled its sharp, thorny tendrils in my chest. No one lurked in the armoire or under the bed.

My heart was lurching painfully behind my breast

bone as I dragged the chaise in front of the door, and when I sank onto the end of the bed, I tucked my hands under my legs to quell their trembling.

He had been here again, stealing into my sanctuary, violating my space. Not even "Greensleeves" was a comfort, for when I hummed the old tune, I remembered how he had whistled the tune as I followed him home.

I left the bathroom light on as I crawled into bed and drew the covers tightly around me, forcing myself to breathe deeply and slowly. I stared at the shadows on the ceiling, gaze darting to the door when I thought I caught a faint creak of movement outside my room. I rolled over so I could watch the door, waiting to see if the knob was jostled, but it remained still.

Sleep was a long time coming.

I woke the next morning exhausted and nauseated from the light snatches of sleep. Lying in bed shivering at the coolness of the sheets, I pulled the covers closer about me as I swallowed against the sourness in my stomach. A headache pounded in my temples. When I did manage to drag myself from bed, I moved immediately to the dresser to slip on a thick pair of socks and to pull a sweater on over my nightgown.

I switched the lamp on and paused. My philodendron was turning brown from the stems up, wilting and listless. I felt the soil in the pot, but it was still damp from being watered before I left for Wind River. Frowning, I fingered the leaves. They were dry and brittle.

A pang of sorrow struck me, and I wondered if the cold had been too much for the plant. I picked up the dying greenery and moved the pot closer to the window, hoping a bit of light would help.

I crossed to the window and dragged the curtains aside, glancing back to make sure the philodendron would receive the full advantage of the light through the day.

Some slight sense of movement drew my gaze back to the window, and I searched the tree line. In the early morning hours, the light was low, the shadows gray. The sky was pink with the sun's rise, and frost laced the edges of my window.

The movement came again and snagged my gaze. The slight sway, the flutter of the dress hem. I stood frozen, and my heart seemed to stutter in my chest before the pace lurched into a heavy, hot thrum. I heard the choked sound of my own breath in my throat. The first fingers of the dawn sun crept through the trees and touched her bare feet.

Galvanized, I shoved the chaise away from the door and bolted from my room. I took the stairs three at a time and did not realize I was yelling for Faye until she skidded through the doorway into the dining room as I flung open the front door. "Call 9-1-1!"

I did not wait to see if she responded. I leapt off the front porch and ran. My socked feet slid on ice and snow, and I fell as I reached the bottom of the sloped yard. I scrambled back to my feet and raced first to the tree. I grappled with the knot, tearing at the sinews, ripping two nails down to the quick, but the rope was tied too tightly around the rough trunk.

I wrapped my arms around her calves and braced her against me, struggling to lift her to ease the tautness of the rope wrapped around her neck.

It was too late. Creating slack in the rope would do

her no good. She was stiff, limbs rigid, and with my cheek pressed against her thighs, I could feel the coldness of her skin against my face even through the soft floral print cotton of her dress.

My arms shook with the effort of holding her up. I tightened my hold on Amanda's body, unable to release her and allow her to swing heavily at the end of the rope from which she hung.

TWENTY

The National Crime Information Center reports that, in 2016, there were 5,712 reports of missing American Indian and Alaska Native women. The US Department of Justice's federal missing persons database only logged 116 cases.

HECTOR

"Frank," I called. "Get to work."

The poodle ignored me, circling a tree with a keen expression fixed upwards. Something was hiding from him in the branches above, but this was not why I had brought him into the woods this morning.

It was our weekly ritual now. I knew there was no scent of Winona and Emma lingering in the woods surrounding Raven's Gap, even if they had been dragged into this wilderness. But still I searched.

The not knowing made their disappearance a wound that never healed. The lack of answers kept worrying the ragged edges of rawness, kept the bitter ache constant, kept the blood weeping at the surface. There was no scab, no scar. It was as fresh and tender now as it had been fifteen years ago.

I had spoken the truth to Carl Thornton. The not knowing drove you past the brink of sanity. Years passed, and the madness became a constant companion. You took it to bed with you at night and opened your eyes in its embrace in the morning.

"Frank!"

I realized my voice held more snap than I intended when his tail stopped wagging and his head drooped as he trotted through the snow toward me. I dropped into a crouch and extended my hand to him.

He rushed to close the distance between us, and I pressed my forehead to his, resting my hand on his neck. "I'm sorry. You're right. We've had enough for the day." He leaned against me. Forgiveness was something dogs gave far too easily.

To make amends, when we got back to the truck, I fetched his tennis ball from the cupholder and threw it for him. He bounded gleefully after it. All was right in his world again.

My phone buzzed in my pocket, and when I answered, Joan was on the other end of the line. "It's bad, Hector."

When I made it into town fifteen minutes later, the scene beside the inn was an echo of the one at the campground cabin. The dress, the braided hair, even the pink polish on her toes were the same as Sarah Clemens, the young woman found at the campground. The scene was staged in the same careful manner as the cabin.

I glanced up the hill to where Martin Yates, the detective, was taking Evelyn's statement.

"Isn't that the woman who found the girl at the cabin?" Ted Peters asked as he finished photographing the scene.

She had. My mind churned with the implications.

The county coroner's van parked in front of the inn, and Grover Westland carefully picked his way down the embankment. He studied the scene before walking a slow circuit around Amanda's body.

He came to a halt beside me. "Shit." He let out a breath. "Let's get her down from there."

A commotion drew my gaze to the top of the hill. "Fuck," I breathed. "I'll handle this."

I climbed the embankment in ground-eating strides and caught Carl Thornton's arm as he scrambled down the slope.

"Amanda? Oh Christ. Is it Amanda?"

I jerked him around and dragged him away from the scene, not relinquishing my grip on his arm until we were across the street and the woman hanging from the tree was no longer in sight.

"It's Amanda, isn't it? I heard the sirens and thought maybe… But then I saw the coroner's van." He turned in a circle, hands fisted in his hair.

I waited until he met my gaze. "It is Amanda."

He moaned and staggered under the weight of my words. "No. God, no. I have to see her."

"Don't." I put a hand to his shoulder when he would have pushed past me and held him in place when he tried to shake me off. "Don't let that be the image of her that sticks in your mind and visits you every time you close your eyes."

His shoulders began to shake under my hand, and he sagged against me.

I looked across the street and found Evelyn standing on the porch of the inn, staring at the scene unfolding at the tree line. Her arms were wrapped tightly around herself, and she leaned against the railing for support.

Sensing she was being watched, she dragged her attention from the work of the coroner and the other officers. Her eyes found me, and I held her gaze across the distance separating us.

"I couldn't promise you I would find Amanda and bring her back to you," I said quietly to the man whose world had just been destroyed. "But I can promise you I will find who did this to her."

TWENTY-ONE

JEFF

I HAD NOT been able to resist staying deep within the tree line to ensure she understood what I was telling her. I had almost gone to her when she came running outside, and my heart sank when she touched her. She should not have sullied herself like that. I wanted to go to her and yank her away, but then the other woman, the innkeeper, had arrived, and the moment to approach her had been lost.

Just as well. It was not time yet. I still had much to tell her. At the moment, I had one more part of the story to leave with her.

This one held sentimental value, and it was hard to part with it. It had been a gift to Rose in our childhood. It had been the gift of one child to another, but she had kept it with her, even when it became worn and frayed. She had understood the sanctity of my gifts. At least in the beginning.

In the beginning, we had shared everything. We were inseparable. Rose had promised we always would be, that she would always love me more than all else.

But over the years I had seen the changes come over her. She no longer looked at me the same way. She no longer wanted to share herself with me. She had forgotten her promises, and she had ignored me when I tried to remind her of them.

Anger began to burn in my heart, and I strove to calm myself. Evelyn would understand. Evelyn would know the sanctity of a promise.

I waited until the police were finished, until they cut down that whore, bagged her, and carried her away like the garbage she was. Dissatisfaction gnawed at me. There was a difference between dining and feeding only to sustain oneself. That was all she and the others were. Sustenance. Not what I truly needed, not what I desperately craved. Rose had been the only one who truly sated me. Rose, and now Evelyn.

Once they were gone, I crept into the inn and into Evelyn's room. I tucked my gift into her bed and smiled over the picture of innocence it made. I wanted to linger, but I had to be cautious now.

The boy startled me when I left Evelyn's room and entered the hall. He stood like a small specter, and I eyed him carefully as I closed the door. He did not move when I turned to face him fully, did not bat an eyelash. He left me in a precarious position.

I had no qualms with snapping this child's neck. However, he was not part of the script in my head, and it would end everything before I was ready to write the resolution. The convenient thing about children was that they were absurdly easy to frighten and manipulate.

He took a quick step back as I approached him, and his shoulders thumped against the wall. His eyes were wide, the whites stark in the shadows, as I knelt before him until our gazes were level. I searched his face. There was a solemnity and seriousness to the young features. His breath quickened when I smiled at him.

"If you tell anyone you saw me here, I will come back and slit your mother's throat in the middle of the night while she sleeps." He paled even further and flinched as if I had struck him. "Do we understand one another?" His chin wobbled, but he nodded. "Good." I patted his shoulder as I straightened, and he cringed away from me with a gasping whimper of noise.

I had to stop myself from whistling a merry tune as I slipped from the inn.

TWENTY-TWO

A rose's rarest essence lives in the thorn.

-Rumi

EVELYN

I MADE IT to work in a daze by midmorning.

"Are you certain you don't need to take the day off?" Annette asked when I apologized for my tardiness. She had already heard the news.

"I'm certain," I said. A headache pounded behind my eyes.

I immersed myself in the NAGPRA collection. I had found no other human remains thus far in processing the collection, but the history and culture contained in these boxes was rich. As I catalogued the pieces, I sketched out several ideas for displays for the museum.

An email from Andrew James landed in my inbox in the middle of the afternoon.

Miss Hutto, I'm afraid I do not have any information about when I made this bracelet or who purchased it. I am sure your effort to return it to its owner is appreciated. -A James.

I pulled up the internet browser on my computer and searched for "women missing in Canyon de Chelly." The only article that was returned was from several years ago about a body being found after a local woman was swept away in a flash flood.

I performed another query, this one a broader search for "missing Native American women." A number of articles populated for the search, and I pulled up a recent case study from the Urban Indian Health Institute. I sucked in a breath as I studied the data.

My horror grew as I read article after article. The statistics were staggering. Native women living on tribal lands in America were murdered at an extremely high rate—in some communities, more than ten times the national average. The Center for Disease Control and Prevention reported that murder was the third-leading cause of death among American Indian and Alaska Native women.

No comprehensive data collection system existed regarding the number of missing and murdered women in Indian country. In 2016, the National Crime Information Center reported that there were 5,712 reports of missing American Indian and Alaska Native women and girls, though the US Department of Justice's federal missing persons database only logged one hundred sixteen cases. American Indian women not only went missing, but they were also allowed to fall through the cracks, disappearing not just from life but from the data as well.

I did the math. The numbers equated to fifteen women going missing every day over the course of a year with no record of their disappearance in the federal databases.

It was an epidemic of violence and abduction I had no clue existed. A harrowing normality of mothers, daughters, sisters, and friends being gone one day, never to be seen again. No resources put to use to find them, no widespread media coverage, and no remembrance of those lives in the data.

For a predator, was there a more perfect prey?

I felt sick as I returned to the repository. I pulled the private collection from the shelf. Between the cradle-board, the Zuni fetishes, the Tohono O'odham baskets, and the bracelet, I had a collection divided between four tribes and three states—Wyoming, Arizona, and New Mexico.

That was only a small part of the collection. There was so much potential for loss and tragedy in these pieces. I wondered how many secrets this collection held, if each piece was linked to a woman who had vanished without a trace.

Troubled, I returned to my work. By the time I left for the day, the sharp headache had faded to a dull, ragged throb. When I reached the inn, my gaze was drawn to the woods that hemmed the west side of the property. All remnants of what I had found this morning were gone save for the trampling of snow around the area that revealed the rough, dead flotsam of past seasons beneath the white.

"Are you out there?" I called into the darkness. The moaning of the trees in the wind was the only response I received.

I retreated from the light spilling across the front porch of the inn, climbed back into my borrowed truck, and drove across town. I left the Chevy in the lot at the corner of Main Street and darted a glance over my shoulder as I locked the door. Jeff's Land Rover was still parked in front of Book Ends.

I pulled two bobby pins from my hair as I hurried down the sidewalk. I made my pick first, bending one of the pins open to about ninety degrees. I put the end in my mouth, catching the bit of rubber with the edge of my teeth and prying it off. I spit it out and bent the end slightly before folding the opposite end into a loop for a makeshift handle.

I glanced back as I reached the corner. The street lamps flickered. Jeff's vehicle remained parked. I crossed the street and worked the second bobby pin into the lever, forcing the looped end of the pin over at another ninety-degree bend.

In the alley beside the hardware store, the light over the side entrance sputtered and whined. The alley ended at a dumpster. I looked around as I approached the door. The area had been cleared and salted, so I would not be leaving tracks in the snow to give away my presence. I tested the door, startling when the handle turned easily.

The door groaned as I pulled it open, and I shot one last look over my shoulder before I stepped inside. I stood at the base of a set of stairs. Aside from an umbrella leaning in the corner, the entryway was empty. I kept a hand on the door as it closed so it would not slam shut, and then I crept up the stairs.

My heartbeat was a ricochet. Heat swept over my chest and up my throat. When I reached the landing, my palm was slick as I tested the handle. This door was locked.

I knelt on the landing and wiped my hands on my jeans. A tremor tried to work its way through my hands, but I tightened my fingers into a fist and sucked in a deep breath. I needed steadiness.

I inserted the lever into the lower side of the keyhole and put a turning pressure on the barrel of the lock. I slipped the pick into the upper side of the keyhole, feeling carefully for the seized pins. I kept pressure on the lever as I worked, closing my eyes and leaning my forehead against the cool surface of the door. The first two pins moved up and down freely, but the third was harder to move. Slowly and carefully, I forced the pin upward until I heard an audible click.

I let out the breath I had not realized I was holding. I repeated the process, feeling for the next seized pin until all five were aligned and the lock opened. I straightened and pocketed the makeshift lock picks as I pushed open the door.

It was dark within Jeff's home. My hand went automatically to the wall to feel for a switch before I stayed the impulse. I closed the door behind me and locked it before pulling my phone out and swiping the screen to turn on the flashlight application.

A quick pan of the space with the small beam of light revealed a loft apartment, one large open space with exposed ducts and copper pipes, brick walls, and plank flooring. I directed the flashlight at the floor and moved quickly through the large space. I had limited time, and I did not know exactly what I was searching for.

His kitchen was state of the art. There was not a dish in the sink or a crumb on the countertop. I caught a glimpse of movement from the corner of my eye and spun, almost leaping out of my skin before I realized it was my own gray reflection peering back at me in the mirror hanging on the wall.

His bathroom was as immaculate as the rest of his home, his bed large and crisply made, and the far wall housed bookshelves from floor to ceiling, complete with a rolling ladder. The shelves were laden with leather-bound tomes and gardening manuals.

Displayed amidst the books were pieces of art. Baskets and pottery, carvings and jewelry, turquoise and silver and beadwork.

It was a vast collection, displayed with pride on the shelves. The pieces were intricate, unique, and all Native American in origin.

Any number of people collected Native American art. It was no confession, no proverbial smoking gun.

As I stared at the wall of shelves, I recalled Jeff's pleased smile and intense gaze. *I'm glad to know you're paying attention, Evelyn.* The two women I had found dead at the end of a rope.

Serial killer. I allowed myself to think the words for the first time. It drove a tremor through me.

But it was the groan and thump of the alleyway door closing downstairs that shot terror into my veins, as potent and lethal as any drug. I fumbled and almost dropped my phone as I scrambled to turn the flashlight off. Heavy footfall ascended the stairs, and I stood frozen and frantic.

The pause at the top of the stairs galvanized me. I bolted across the room, dropped to my stomach on the floor, and scrambled beneath the bed. The door opened, and light flooded the place. I pressed my hands so tightly against my mouth I tasted blood.

The splatter of keys on a surface, footsteps, and then the rush of water reached me where I hid. I breathed shallowly through my nose and wondered if he could hear the clatter of my bones against the floor as I trembled. I was certain he could at least hear the thud of my heart on the floor.

Long moments passed, and I kept my eyes on the sliver of space I could see. My ears were pricked to every rustle of movement, every footstep. He began to whistle suddenly, and the familiar tune was like a knife in the gut.

Alas, my love, you do me wrong.

Footsteps approached. I was afraid that a whimper had escaped me when I saw his shoes come closer. I closed my eyes when they stopped at the foot of the bed.

There was silence and stillness for so long I grew uneasy. I opened my eyes and lurched in shock. A scream almost escaped me when I met his gaze where he knelt and peered under the bed.

His smile was perfect and terrifying. "Boo."

TWENTY-THREE

It will never rain roses: when we want
to have more roses we must plant more trees.

-George Eliot

HECTOR

FROM MY VANTAGE point in the alley between the hair salon and the laundromat, I spotted her the moment she pulled Ed's old Chevy into the parking lot. My attention sharpened as she hurried down the sidewalk, working something in her hands, darting glances over her shoulder.

"What the hell are you doing, Evelyn?" I whispered.

She slipped down the alley adjacent to the hardware store, and when she did not return, I directed my gaze to the second-floor windows. After several minutes, there was a brief sweep of light across the glass. She was inside.

Not five minutes had passed when movement from the opposite end of Main Street caught my eye. Jeff's Land Rover backed out of its parking spot in front of Book Ends. I stepped farther back into the cover of the shadows. He drove slowly down Main, turned at the corner, and then did a tight turn and reverse into the alley.

I watched the windows on the second floor. They were soon flooded with light.

I pulled the GPS tracker from my pocket. Last year when a group of local teens started stealing cars around town, the department had purchased a dozen of these gadgets. They were so small they went unnoticed and had rechargeable batteries that lasted for two weeks. They could be tracked in real-time and were programmable to send location alerts by email or text.

I secured the tracker in the waterproof magnetic case and glanced at the windows once more before leaving my hiding place. I stayed close to the building, sticking to the shadows until I was out of sight from the second-floor vantage point.

The sudden sound of screaming from the apartment above raised the hair at the nape of my neck.

If he killed Evelyn tonight, I needed to ensure she was found in his apartment or in his vehicle. If he transported her body somewhere, I needed to find where he kept the women he killed. I needed to know if what remained of my girls was there as well.

He had pulled the Land Rover deep into the alley close to the side entrance. I knelt at the front bumper and reached under the vehicle to snap the magnetic box in place.

The sound of a police siren brought my head up. I jogged out of the alley and back up the road to the shadows between the laundromat and the hair salon. My gaze darted to the windows above the hardware store just as two squad cars pulled up, lights flashing. Cooper and Ashton hurried down the alley, hands on their weapons.

I retreated to where I had left my truck. Frank greeted

me when I opened the door and moved accommodatingly into the passenger's seat. I did not flip my headlights on until I pulled onto Main Street. I headed straight for the station.

Thirty minutes later, when Cooper and Ashton came in through the sally port escorting a deathly pale Evelyn, I met them in the hall. Cooper led Evelyn into an interview room.

"What're you doing here at this hour?" Ashton asked.

"Paperwork," I lied. "What's going on here?"

"Dispatch got a call from Jeff Roosevelt saying there was a burglar in his home."

What the hell? I had assumed it was Evelyn who had called 911 as soon as she realized she had company. I had been certain Jeff would kill her upon discovering her. Those blood-chilling screams had been a confirmation of that.

I stood there staring blankly at Ashton for too long as my mind raced.

"Everything okay?" he asked.

"Mind if I sit in on the interview?"

"No. Cooper is going to handle it while I get started on the case report."

I retreated down the hall and collected the file folder from my desk drawer. Frank lifted his head from his bed beside my desk.

"Stay here," I told him, and then retreated to the break room. I filled a paper cup with coffee, laced it liberally with cream and sugar, and headed to the interview room.

Cooper was seated across from her when I entered. Evelyn's gaze met mine as I quietly closed the door behind me and took the chair at a right angle to her. I

placed the cup of coffee before her. Her face was colorless save for the shadows that smudged the skin beneath
her eyes and a livid red mark across her left cheek that
was already beginning to bruise. Her fingers trembled
as she wrapped her hands around the cup.

Blake Cooper was a burly man who had been with
the department for ten years now. He was no-nonsense
and gruff but unfailingly polite.

"Why don't you tell me what you were doing in Mr.
Roosevelt's home tonight, Miss Hutto," he said. "You
do realize breaking and entering is a felony charge."

"I wasn't there to steal anything," Evelyn said. "I
was looking for proof."

"Proof." Cooper leaned back in his chair. "Proof of
what?"

Evelyn glanced at me and then met Cooper's gaze
evenly. "Proof that Jeff Roosevelt is a serial killer."

Cooper's brows winged over his forehead. I had to
quell the urge to smile. "And did you find proof?" he
asked.

"I think so."

I leaned forward and felt Cooper's gaze swing to me.
Christ, if she truly had proof…

"Are you going to share that information with the
police?" Cooper asked. I heard the hint of disbelief in
his tone.

Evelyn must have as well. "Not at the moment, no.
You wouldn't believe me."

"Alright," he said slowly, scrambling to regroup.
"Why don't you tell me why you think Jeff Roosevelt
is a serial killer?"

The two women she had found dead in town were
not news to us. But she told us of her suspicion that

someone had been coming and going from her room at the inn. When she recounted the brief, odd conversations she had had with Jeff, a chill went through me remembering Winona's attempt to tell me how uneasy the man had made her.

Cooper and I sat quietly. When she finished, he folded his hands on the tabletop and leaned toward Evelyn.

"Here is the issue, Miss Hutto. Jeff says that *you* have been stalking *him*."

She shook her head. "I—"

"He says you've shown up where he works."

"He works at a *bookstore*," she snapped. "I read. Of course I've shown up there."

"He says you've followed him home." Evelyn looked away, and Cooper continued, "And tonight, he found you *in* his home. Can you see why I'm having a hard time putting much stock in what you say?"

"You *need* to believe me." Her voice was vehement. She slid to the edge of her seat, face as earnest as her voice. "Two women are dead. I think there are many, many more. I'm being stalked, and—"

I placed the folder on the table, slid it across to her, and flipped it open. She met my gaze before glancing down at the contents. Her entire body flinched.

"This isn't the first time you've made claims of being stalked. You filed…" I flipped through the papers and counted aloud as I did so. "One, two, three—"

Evelyn reached out and slapped a hand over the fan of reports. "Thirty-seven." I could see her throat work as she swallowed. "You don't need to count them. I filed thirty-seven."

She pushed the pile of reports back across the table.

Cooper caught the file and began to scan through the pages.

"You filed thirty-seven complaints against a co-worker at the museum in Atlanta," I said. "Against Chad Kilgore, a security guard at the museum."

She shoved her glasses up her forehead and rubbed her eyes. "And not one of them did me any good."

"Did Mr. Kilgore ever issue any verbal threats?"

"No."

"Did he ever assault you?"

"No."

"Did—"

"He watched me, all the time. Showing up in the area where I was working and just standing there staring at me. That was in the beginning." Her words were rushed and heated. "But then it became more. He would show up on the same aisle in the grocery store. In the parking lot at the post office. I would turn around at the movie theater and he would be in the row behind me. I would look out my bedroom window and see him on the sidewalk in front of my house. He didn't *do* anything, he didn't *say* anything. Just being there, being *everywhere* was enough."

Cooper had flipped through to the final pages of the stack of papers as she spoke. "This last report you filed says he locked you in the basement of the museum overnight and 'hunted' you," he said. "That is the word you used, Miss Hutto."

Underneath the table, her knee started bouncing up and down. "I know what word I used." Her voice was a mere whisper.

I pushed the last report across the table to her. "And then five years ago, a year after you started filing complaints against him, everything stopped. Chad Kilgore went missing."

"I know."

"And do you know what JDLR stands for?" I pointed to the scrawled letters at the bottom of the report. Evelyn shook her head. "Just doesn't look right. That's what it means. You're listed as a person of interest in this case, do you know that?"

"The police spoke with me several times after he went missing," Evelyn said. She glanced at me again and then met Cooper's gaze squarely. "I'll tell you exactly what I told them. Am I sorry he disappeared? No. I've never been so relieved in my life." She sucked in a breath. "But I didn't have anything to do with him going missing. The police came to the same conclusion."

"The police could never charge you," I corrected. I did not miss the irony of saying that to someone else when I had once been in the same position and, to many in town, still was.

Her face was blank. "Are you charging me with anything now?"

Cooper leaned back in his chair. "No. Jeff isn't pressing any charges. As I told you when we started this interview, you're not under arrest."

"Then I've been through this process enough to know I'm free to go." She pushed back from the table and stood. She swayed for an instant, and I instinctively stood, but she caught the back of her chair. Once she had steadied herself, she turned and walked to the door, standing with a rigid back, gaze straight ahead as Cooper moved to open the door for her.

"Stay away from Jeff Roosevelt," he warned as he led her from the room.

I leaned back in my chair and steepled my fingers against my chin. I did not know what the hell Jeff was up to, what game he was playing. But I knew that it did not matter if Evelyn was the cat or the mouse. She could help me bring him down either way.

TWENTY-FOUR

In the last twenty years, there have been approx-imately 24,000 unidentified persons files in the United States as listed by the NCIC.

EVELYN

INNOCENT PEOPLE ARE INDIGNANT, Evelyn. Remember that. My grandfather's words echoed in my head.

Once I reached the inn, I headed to my room and went straight to the bathroom. I stripped out of my clothes and left them in a pile on the tiled floor before stepping into the shower. I did not bother giving the water time to heat. I turned on the shower, and an icy blast hit me directly in the face, stinging my skin for several long moments before heat began to temper the chill.

I had been terrorized for a year. I did not need to feign anger. No one had done anything about Chad Kilgore. Not for a year of being frightened every time I turned around. Not until I had tried to leave work and found myself trapped in the bowels of the museum.

I stood under the spray with my face tilted up. I could not hear anything through the rush of the water cascad-ing over me. When the tears came, I did not bother to stem them.

Come out, come out, wherever you are.

My knees weakened at the remembered terror that had filled me as I hid beneath a desk and listened to his voice and footsteps come ever-closer. I leaned against the cold tile of the shower and slid to the floor, knees caught to my chest, wet hair a curtain around me.

It had been my grandfather who voiced the truth I had realized hiding in the dark.

My grandfather had reached across the kitchen table when I finally made it home, something I had doubted would happen in those hours I had spent cramped and shaking in my hiding place, and clasped my hand in his. He had been the one to call the police and send them to the museum when I failed to return home from work. His hand swallowed mine, blunt fingers rough with callouses.

"He is going to kill you, Evelyn."

I had covered my eyes with my free hand and sucked in a shuddering breath.

"He is going to hurt you, and then he is going to kill you." He caught the hand covering my eyes and pulled it away from my face. His hold on my hands was tight, anchoring. "But not if we take care of him first."

I had blinked at him, struggling to process what he had said. Shock had me attempting to pull away, but he kept his grip on my hands. "Papa—"

"Listen to me," he whispered. "*Listen to me*. Men like that won't be stopped. Not by words, not by a piece of paper, not by a slap on the wrist by the police."

"We can't—"

"And I will not lose you when I could have prevented it. I will *not*." He squeezed my hands. "Do you hear me?"

I had searched his face, so dear to me, the only father

figure I had ever known. He had had a heart attack six months ago, and it had taken a toll on him. Time and illness had carved deep into his face, but his eyes were steady on mine, sharp and calm.

He spoke the truth. We both knew it. I wondered when it had become a truth I had accepted like a bitter pill without argument.

I swallowed and nodded. "I hear you."

"Your grandmother will never know. No one will. A simple plan is the best."

And he was right. Simple was best. We had left no evidence. There was no trace of him in our home or in our vehicles. His own car was scrapped and compacted in a junk yard at the opposite end of the state, and his body was in a well-dug grave deep in the mountains northeast of Hiawassee near the state line well away from any trails.

Tonight, I thought I would die. When I opened my eyes and met Jeff's gaze, I scrambled to slide deeper into the tight recess of space. But he was fast, and his reach was long. He caught my wrist and dragged me from beneath the bed.

There was nothing beneath the bed I could latch onto, but I caught the leg of the frame as he yanked me from my hiding place. I clung to it so desperately the bed scraped across the floor with a screeching groan.

I did not realize I was screaming until Jeff's knee came down between my shoulder blades and cut off my breath. His weight on my spine crushed me into the floor as he leaned over me and pried my hand from its grip around the leg of the bed.

"Screaming only excites me, Evelyn," he breathed

before he caught the collar of my coat and pulled me across the floor.

I did not bother crying out. I swiped at his ankles. He stumbled before twisting his fist so tightly in my collar it began to cut off my air. He wrenched me upright and my collar formed a tight noose around my throat. I almost blacked out. Then a hard shove sent me careening forward.

I tripped and fell. My cheek glanced off the curved edge of the toilet. Pain burst across my face, and as I lay on the cold tiles of the bathroom, I heard the door slam behind me.

It took a moment for the stars swimming across my vision to fade. My face was hot. My cheek throbbed. I could not catch my breath around the terrified hitch in my chest, but I scrambled to my feet.

The bathroom door did not lock from the inside. It was jammed closed. I could hear Jeff's voice on the other side, but I could not make out his words.

I flung open the cabinets in his oversized vanity. There had to be something I could use as a weapon.

When the door opened minutes later, I was armed with a razor blade and a cleaning solvent in a spray bottle. It was not Jeff who greeted me, though, but two police officers with their weapons drawn.

Now I allowed myself the release of weeping until I was wrung dry. I staggered to my feet and let the tumult of emotions swirl down the drain along with the soap. By the time the water was cooling, I felt calmer, steadier.

Once out of the shower and my nightly ritual complete, I pulled my gown over my head and retreated into my room. I paused as I approached the bed.

Leaning against my pillow with the coverlet drawn over its legs as if it were tucked in for the night sat a teddy bear. It was ragged and worn, the picture of innocence. Unease sliced through me.

I dragged on leggings and a thick pair of socks and pulled on a sweater before I grabbed the bear. The inn was dark, but I was familiar with the place now and made my way down the hall and stairs with sure feet. I paused in the den, drawn to the wide swath of windows that looked out over the river.

The figure standing on the deck startled me with a violence that felt as if my bones were trying to flee the confines of my skin. I placed a hand on the icy glass and leaned against it while my heart thundered and jolted back into place.

A snowman smiled benignly back at me, oblivious to the fright it had given me. I shivered. Such a lighthearted thing took on a macabre edge in the moonlight.

I straightened from where I sagged against the window and crossed through the den and dining room. The sunroom was flooded with moonlight, all pearl blue and swan white. The dishwasher hummed in the kitchen, and at the end of the adjoining hallway, light bled from under the door leading into Faye's personal wing.

She opened within moments of my knock. "Evelyn, come on in."

I stopped just within the threshold. "I won't stay. I know it's late, and I don't want to bother you."

Her eyes widened. "What happened to your face?"

I ignored her question and held the teddy bear out to her. "Is this Sam's?"

Her brow furrowed. She stared at the stuffed animal,

making no move to take it from me. "No. Sam doesn't have a bear like that. Where did you find it?"

It was as if a current ran through me, shock and fear as blinding as a bolt of electricity. The bear fell from my fingers. Faye watched it fall and bounce gently on the floor.

"It was in my room," I whispered. Her gaze flew to mine. "It was in my bed."

Faye caught my arm, pulled me all the way inside, and closed the door. The lock tumbled into place.

"Someone's been here. Inside the inn." Inside my locked room, tucking something for me to find in my bed. A tremor worked its way through my limbs.

"They might still be here," Faye said.

"We can't call the police."

"We don't need the police."

Something in her voice cut through my horror. Her face was set, voice brisk as she called for Sam. He appeared in his bedroom doorway and hurried to his mother's side when she held out her hand.

I followed her into her bedroom and then into her walk-in closet. She shoved aside the few articles of clothing and revealed a half door in the wall. It was metal with a key in the lock and a handle shaped like a Y that Faye spun to open. An electric lantern, stack of blankets, and case of bottled water lay within.

She handed Sam the key to the door. "Just like we've practiced, remember?"

He clung to her hand for a moment and then ducked within the room and turned the lantern on. Faye pushed the door closed after him and spun the handle, and I could hear a series of locks turn inside.

She moved to kneel in front of a safe tucked into the

corner of the closet. It was fingerprint entry. I sucked in a breath when she opened it to reveal a small collection of guns and ammunition.

I glanced back and forth between the door in the wall and Faye, and it struck me then that this woman and her son's isolation and quiet were deliberate. Whatever secrets she had were dangerous ones, and she handled the pistol she lifted from the safe with the confidence and ease of an expert. The magazine she slid into the base of the pistol was already loaded. She pulled the slide to chamber a round.

"Do you know how to handle a gun?"

My grandfather had insisted on being the one to pull the trigger. He had used a German pistol his uncle brought home from the European front after World War II. I had wiped the gun clean and buried it and the shell casing in a creek bed miles from where we had buried Chad Kilgore's body. She grabbed two more loaded magazines from the safe and tucked them into the waistband of her yoga pants.

I waited too long to respond. When she straightened, she offered me the baseball bat that was leaning against the dresser. "I'm sure whoever was here is long gone. But I'm not willing to bet on that."

Gone was the quiet, reserved innkeeper. Standing in her place was a hard-eyed stranger who held a handgun as if it were an extension of her arm.

I did not know this woman, but I took the bat from her. "I'll be right behind you."

We searched the inn systematically, turning on lights as we went until the whole place probably stood out on the curve of the river as a beacon. My heart lurched every time we shoved a curtain aside and dropped to our knees to check the space under a bed.

I fully expected to encounter Jeff's smile and hear him say *Boo*. My breath quickened with each closet door we threw open and each shadowed corner we explored.

No windows or doors were ajar. No one hid tucked away in the unused rooms. Nothing lurked in the shadows at the back of the closets or under the beds.

"Someone has been in here," I said quietly when we finished our search and stood in my room. "And this isn't the first time."

Her brows shot up. "Why didn't you tell me?"

"I wasn't positive at first." I looked around my room and wondered what else he had touched while he was here. "You'll probably hear about it in town, and I would rather you hear it from me. I was almost arrested tonight. For breaking into Jeff Roosevelt's apartment over the hardware store."

"Why did you do break into his home?"

"Because I think he's a serial killer." I shivered as I said it aloud. "I'm certain he's the one who has broken into the inn and into my room."

She studied me for a long moment, gaze searching. She did not ask for proof, and she demanded no explanation. Instead, she simply said, "I think you should stay with us tonight. I have a security system in my section of the inn."

"Are you sure?" I did not want to impose, but I also had no desire to sleep in this room tonight.

She nodded. "You can have Sam's bed. He can sleep with me."

I grabbed the items I would need to get ready for work in the morning and locked the door behind me. I followed close at Faye's heels as she led the way back through the inn. We shut off lights as we went.

I had to quell the urge to glance behind me. My scalp prickled, and I kept expecting to be yanked back into the darkness.

She went to a cabinet in the kitchen and pulled out a shot glass and a bottle of whiskey. She poured a liberal amount and offered it to me. "You look like you need it."

I tossed it back in one fiery swallow. The whiskey hit my stomach, and warmth spread through my midsection. I pressed the back of my wrist to my mouth to contain a cough and handed Faye the shot glass. "Thanks," I wheezed when I had breath again.

She moved to the freezer and offered me a bag of frozen peas. "For your face."

When we were safely ensconced in Faye's apartment and her security system was armed, I noticed the profusion of locks on her door.

She extended her hand for the baseball bat I still clutched, and I had to pry my fingers loose to relinquish my grip.

"Let me put these away." She searched my face. "I'll get Sam settled into my bed, and I'll put fresh sheets on his bed for you."

I sank onto her couch before my knees gave way and held the bag of frozen peas against my throbbing cheek. When Faye returned, she did not ask questions. She wordlessly took up a spot on the opposite end of her couch and turned the TV on to a documentary about whale sharks.

I did not think I would be able to sleep at all, but the warmth of the whiskey spread throughout my body and the quiet deep blue imagery of the documentary was lulling. Within an hour, I slipped between the fresh superhero sheets Faye had put on her son's bed and fell into a dreamless sleep.

When I arrived at work the next morning, I went straight to the private collection. It was becoming an obsession, I realized, as I laid out the pieces on the work table in the repository. I had jotted down information on slips of paper for each piece that I had discovered a tribal provenance for. I set those aside and studied the remaining pieces.

The one my attention kept returning to was unique in the collection. It was a carving about eight inches tall, colorful and intricate. The carved figure was full bodied, rendered with human arms, legs, and torso, but the head looked like an animal mask. It stood on a round wooden base, but when I turned the carving over, there was no artist signature to be found.

I took a photo of it and then ejected the camera's memory card, collected the carving, and headed back to my office. At my desk, I loaded the photograph on my computer. I placed the carving beside my keyboard and eyed it as I dragged the photo into an internet image search.

Hopi katsina figures, also known as kachina dolls, immediately came up as the search results. They were carved by the Hopi people, mainly located in Arizona, to instruct young girls and new brides on the immortal beings the Hopi believed controlled the natural world and acted as messengers from the spirit world.

None of the images pulled up in the search results showed this exact kachina doll, but a number of trading posts and Native American art and jewelry companies came up in the results. I grabbed the contact information from half a dozen trading posts and companies and compiled an email, asking for information on this particular carving and the artist. I attached the photographs, hit send, and then returned to the repository and the NAGPRA collection.

On my lunch break a few hours later, a response from one of the art and jewelry companies waited in my inbox.

Miss Hutto, this is a Badger Hopi Kachina doll. It is considered the Chief Kachina during certain ceremonies. The doll you are in possession of may have been carved by Awenasa Tewaquaptewa. It bears some of her trademark work. I will attach her contact information.

I grabbed the phone on my desk and dialed the number listed in the email. A woman answered.

I read her name in the email again. "Hello, may I speak with Mrs. Tewaquaptewa, please?"

"This is she." The voice on the other end of the line was as worn and cracked as old leather. "Who's speaking?"

"This is Evelyn Hutto, ma'am. I work at the Park County Museum in Montana. I'm calling because I found a kachina doll in a private donation that was gifted to the museum, and I am trying to track down the original owner."

"Is it one of mine?" the woman on the other end of the line asked.

"I think it may be. I contacted a Native American art and jewelry company. They gave me your number and said that the carving resembled your craftsmanship."

"But my name isn't on the bottom?" A dry cough on the other end of the line punctuated her question. "I sign all of my work."

"No, there's no signature on the base. The company said they thought it was a badger kachina, and I—"

"That little bitch," she wheezed.

"I… I'm sorry?"

"Text me a picture of the katsina."

"Of course. Is this a cell phone number?"

"It is," she said. "I'll stay on the line. My grand-daughter showed me how to look at texts while still on the phone."

I grabbed my own cell phone, snapped several pictures of the doll, and sent them in a text to her number. I could hear her emphysemic breathing through the line as she waited for the photos to come through.

Her voice was even rougher than it had been when she spoke again. "In our culture, the badger katsina is believed to have the power to heal the sick. I made this for my sister, gave it to her when she was diagnosed with cancer."

"If it is your sister's, I'll be happy to return it to her."

"My sister is dead," she said bluntly. "She died three months after this katsina was stolen from her."

"I'm sorry to hear that." I hesitated and grappled for a way to phrase my next question. "Do you… Did anything else go missing when the kachina doll was stolen?"

"She took three hundred dollars in cash and my sister's prescription pain pills as well."

"She?"

"My sister's granddaughter. She stole from my sister seven years ago. We haven't heard from her since."

"I…see."

"Did she try to sell you the katsina?"

"No, nothing like that," I said. "If you would like, I can return this doll to you."

"No," she said, voice abrupt. "No, I do not care to have it back. Thank you for reaching out to me. Do with the katsina what you will." She hung up before I could get another word in, and I reluctantly returned the phone to the cradle.

I wondered what the likelihood was that the grand-daughter had been as much a victim as the grandmother.

I grabbed my wallet from my purse, pushed back from my desk, and made my way to Annette's office. "I'm going to run a quick errand while I'm on my lunch break," I said after rapping my knuckles on the open door of her office. "Do you need anything while I'm out?"

She glanced up from her computer, expression harried. "No, thank you, though." She did a double take when she saw the bruise across my cheek. "Are you okay?"

"I will be."

I drove across town to Book Ends and was relieved to see Susan at the front desk.

Her automatic smile was welcoming, but it cooled slightly when she saw me, even as her brows pinched when she glanced at my cheek. "Evelyn. How are you today?"

"I'm well, thank you. Do you have a map collection?"

"We do." Despite what Jeff may have told her, she was the consummate professional. She rounded the counter, motioning for me to follow her. "It's mainly local maps. Are you looking for something specific?" She led me past the nonfiction section in an adjoining room.

"Do you have anything that shows just the western United States?"

"Hm…it doesn't look like I have anything specific to the region as a whole. It looks like I have Montana, Idaho, Wyoming, Yellowstone, and then some local maps. I can see about special ordering you something, though."

"What about just a map of the US in general?"

Susan crouched to look at a lower shelf and snagged a folded map. She straightened and held it out to me. "Here you are."

"Thank you." I traced the folded edge of the map and pondered how I wanted to phrase my question. "You have a significant rare books collection here, don't you?"

"We do. Book Ends started as an antiquarian book-shop. It was my father's passion, and it was why…' She hesitated and glanced at me. "It was why I brought Jeff on when I took over the shop."

"Do you travel often to maintain your rare book collection?"

"I don't, no." She did not say that Jeff did, but I sensed that was the other half of her unspoken response. Her smile was polite, but the friendliness she had shown me in past interactions was missing. She nodded to the map. "Are you sure I can't order you something more specific?"

I followed her back to the front of the store. "No, this should be fine." I handed over cash when she rang it up on the old-fashioned register.

"We didn't have our book club meeting last night," she said. "But we're having a meeting tonight. More of a vigil to honor Amanda, really, and a community meeting. You and Faye are welcome to come."

"I'll be here," I said. "I'll invite Faye as well."

When I made it back to the museum, I raided the supply closet and found a box of push-pins. In my office, I unfolded the map and pinned the full spread to the wall opposite my desk. Going down my list I had begun to compile, I added a pin to where Raven's Gap would be if it showed up on the map, to the Wind River Indian Reservation in Wyoming, to the Navajo and Hopi reservations in the northeastern corner of Arizona, to the Zuni Pueblo in New Mexico, and to the Tohono O'odham lands southwest of Tucson along the Mexican border.

I stepped back and studied the map. The pins were sprawled across the west and southwest with no discernible pattern between the four states aside from the fact that they were all pushed into the sections on the map labeled as reservation land.

I remembered the statistics I had read about missing and murdered Indigenous women and girls. Native women living on tribal lands in America were murdered at an extremely high rate—in some communities, more than ten times the national average.

Five reservations and two women missing. I knew there were more, but I was not certain I would be able to find them. At the epicenter of it all, two women dead.

I pulled up the internet browser on my computer and searched for the website of The Antiquarian Booksellers' Association of America. I searched their member directory by state, studying the map as I did so. An hour later, I pushed pins into Tucson and Phoenix, Arizona; into Albuquerque and Santa Fe, New Mexico; into Pueblo and Denver, Colorado; into Moab and Salt

Lake City, Utah; into Pocatello, Idaho; and into Livingston, Montana. All cities with antiquarian booksellers, all cities with easy access to Indian reservations. I jotted down the names of the booksellers and their contact information.

I grabbed my phone and dialed Roberta's number. It rang through to voicemail again. I hung up without leaving a second message.

I stared at the map for a long moment and then shook myself and returned to the repository and my work.

THE ATMOSPHERE AT the book club meeting was tense. Husbands arrived with their wives. The women of Raven's Gap were afraid.

Amanda had two boys, ages ten and six, I was informed. There were already coordinated efforts from the women in town to aid Amanda's husband with getting the boys to and from their extracurricular activities.

Because this was what women did in the face of tragedy. We rallied. We grouped together and coordinated efforts to provide normality. We doled out comfort with compassion and practicality. There was already a calendar going around town with people signing up to prepare a meal for the family.

I added my name to the calendar to take a meal to the Thorntons in three weeks' time. The calendar was filled until the end of February. Faye had not been able to make it to the meeting tonight. Sam was not feeling well, and she had stayed home to put him to bed early. She had asked me to add her name to the list, so I marked her down in the following slot.

The conversation never strayed into book territory. Shock was the emotion that pervaded the group's discussion. The women discussed the possibility of neighborhood watches, nightly patrols, and putting a buddy system in place.

I sat quietly and listened to the book club strategize. Jeff was nowhere in sight this evening. Tension hummed through me. When I stood, Susan glanced at me.

"Bathroom," I mouthed.

The sign for the restroom hung over an open doorway at the far back corner of the shop. The restrooms were down a hallway, and I veered past the labeled entrance and wandered farther down the hall. Four more doorways led off from the corridor.

I looked over my shoulder and tried the handle on the next door. It opened into a dark storage closet. The next two were locked. I turned to the door across the hall. Light bled from under the door, and the handle turned easily under hand.

I pushed the door open cautiously and glanced within. I knew immediately the office was Jeff's. His jacket hung from a coatrack in the corner. A faint hint of his cologne hung in the air, and the room was as immaculate as his apartment. I slipped inside and closed the door soundlessly behind me.

Like in his home, laden shelves filled one wall of his office, but there was no Native American art interspersed with the tomes. I moved to his desk and tapped the space bar on the keyboard to wake his computer. A login screen blinked to life asking for a password. I abandoned the computer to search the desk drawers.

I darted a glance at the door as I searched. The drawers contained the usual miscellaneous items. Nothing out of the ordinary. Nothing that hinted at whom he really was.

The day planner on his desk was a fresh one for the new year. When I flipped through it, I found the pages empty. Frustrated, I straightened from my crouch and moved around his desk.

A vase sat at the corner of his desk. A single rose stood in the glass. The flower was stunning, full and lush, the petals a deep crimson. I reached for it without thinking.

The sharp prick made me jerk my hand back, and the rose fell to the floor. A bead of deep red blood welled from the pad of my thumb, accompanied by a sharp throb.

"The rose has thorns only for those who would gather it."

I started violently and spun.

"That's a Chinese proverb," Jeff said. He pushed the door farther open and leaned against the jamb. "You should come see my roses. I grow over a dozen different varieties in my greenhouse."

I eyed him warily. His smile was amiable, but his eyes fell to the rose on the floor. His face moved, and when he looked up and met my gaze, every hair at the nape of my neck stood on end.

Careful, a small internal voice warned. I imagined an animal had a moment of a heightened sense of self-preservation when they recognized they were in a predator's sites, a quiet moment of realization before every instinct to run leapt to the surface. I imagined that moment felt exactly like this one.

"I was looking for the bathroom," I said, and was amazed at how steady my voice sounded.

He shook his head and chuckled. "Ah, Evelyn." He

straightened and stepped within the office, closing the door behind him and tumbling the lock into place.

I backed around his desk. "Susan will miss me in the meeting."

He smiled. "Susan is oblivious, completely wrapped up in herself and this store." He moved deeper into the office, and I backed away in equal measure. "You're in my office, searching through my desk. Do you want the password for my computer? It's 'rose.' All lowercase." He gestured to the chair behind his desk as he took the seat across from it. "Go ahead, sit down."

He lounged casually, sinking back into the chair, crossing an ankle over his knee and lacing his fingers behind his head. For all his relaxation, he reminded me of a snake poised to strike.

"I'm fine standing."

He sighed. I watched every flex of movement and shift of expression, expecting him to lunge across his desk at any moment. "You should be careful," he said. "The police already think you're stalking me."

The short distance to the door felt like a yawning chasm. His desk between us was a flimsy barrier keeping a predator at bay. "You and I both know I'm not the dangerous party here."

He smiled. "Do I? Don't all women have their dangers?"

"Is that why you kill them?"

He tilted his head and studied me, expression benign, eyes sharp. The silence grew between us, jagged and tense. I only let my gaze move from him to glance at the locked door.

"I think you need more time," he said.

He stood suddenly, plucking up the fallen rose as he

did so. I took a quick step back. He did not approach me, though. He placed the rose carefully back in its vase and retreated to the door, flipped the lock, and swung it wide.

I remained frozen in place, not trusting the gesture.

"It's time for you to leave now before I change my mind," he said.

I wanted to flee, but I forced my feet to move in a measured pace. I approached him like I would a cobra, reluctantly and with slow, carefully placed steps, adrenalin thrumming through my veins. He stood in the doorway.

When I moved to edge past him, he struck, swift as a snake.

He grabbed my face, palm over my mouth, fingers and thumb digging into my cheeks. A startled cry caught in my throat, and my hands flew to his wrist. I flinched when he reached toward my face with his other hand, but all he did was push my glasses up the bridge of my nose, settling them back into place.

"You delight me," he whispered, and I could feel his breath on my forehead. "You remind me so much of her."

Then his hand was gone from my face. I lurched into the hallway. This time, I did not quell the urge to run. I raced down the hall and into the brightly lit sanctum of the bookstore. I staggered, fear turning my knees to water. I put a hand against a shelf.

My heart was in my throat and rushing in my ears, but I glanced back. Jeff still stood highlighted against the shadows of the hallway in the doorway to his office.

I straightened and swallowed around the dry tightness of my throat. "I want my music box back," I said, voice hard and steady.

I turned and moved between the books. I heard a low chuckle behind me, and then the whistled tune of "Greensleeves" followed me around the shelves.

TWENTY-FIVE

JEFF

ROSE HAD GROWN sharp with me as well in the end. A rose would always have thorns. I accepted that as her nature, and I never whittled away those barbs. I took the blood with the blooms.

It took patience to tend to roses. They did not bloom for you immediately. Roses required time and effort, diligence and tenderness. They could not be rushed.

Evelyn was not ready. Not yet. I had to be patient. Giving her Rose's gift had been the right decision. I had another gift for her, but the timing had to be perfect.

Rose had mistaken this gift. I had slipped into her room in the middle of the night and left it on her pillow. She thought it had been from another man. I would not make that same mistake with Evelyn. She would know. There would be no misunderstanding between us.

I had been tempted tonight. I saw the way she watched me so avidly. She felt the pull between us. But anticipation would make everything sweeter. I could hold out and savor the unfolding of our story.

In the meantime, though, I had to at least curb that gnawing within me to have the patience to wait for Evelyn. I prowled after the woman when she left the book club meeting. She was the last to leave. She always was. She was always alone. She wore clothes that displayed the fleshy mounds of her breasts and the deep crevice between them that always looked warm and damp. Her makeup was always done with too heavy a hand, and she laughed too loudly at everything I said.

I could not recall her name as I dogged her steps in the darkness. She kept glancing around, the jerkiness of the movement betraying her nerves. She was right to be nervous, but I found it curious that she could sense me in the shadows stalking her. She always struck me as a complete idiot.

She did not live far away. I would have to be careful to ensure I was not seen. Her house was down the same road as The River Inn. So close to Evelyn. I wondered if my choice had been a subconscious one born of proximity to what I truly wanted.

Caught for a moment by my thoughts of Evelyn, I did not realize the woman had stopped in the middle of the street suddenly and turned. She stood in a wide round pool of light under a street lamp. She scanned the shadows beyond the light where I lurked.

Rachel. That was her name. A harsh, ugly name for a harsh, ugly woman.

I strolled casually into the light. She lurched in surprise but then relaxed when she recognized me.

"Oh, Jeff." She tittered with that laugh that scraped annoyingly along my nerves. "It's only you. You startled me."

I drew closer and watched as she patted her frizzy mop of hair and undid a couple buttons on her coat so that deep cleavage was on display again. My stomach lurched in disgust, and I almost turned away. But no, whores like this one deserved to die. The world did not miss the garbage when you collected it off the streets and put it in the trash.

I smiled at her. I must have miscalculated my smile and let too much of my intention slip into the curve of my lips, for her eyes went wide. She took a quick step back, and I heard her indrawn breath.

"Yes," I agreed. "Only me."

TWENTY-SIX

*Native women living on tribal lands are murdered
at an extremely high rate—in some communities,
more than 10 times the national average.*

EVELYN

I SLEPT IN my rented room, dragging the chaise over to block the door once more. I woke at every creak as the inn settled for the night, at every moan of the wind in the trees outside, but I refused to be driven into hiding.

In the morning, my thumb throbbed, a hot, steady pulse from the wound the rose in Jeff's office had dealt me. The entire digit was stiff and swollen.

On the way to work, I stopped by Ed's garage.

"Ev'lyn," he greeted warmly when I entered the shop. "Just the lady I was hoping to see today." He grabbed a set of keys from his desk drawer and extended them to me.

"She's ready?" I asked, unable to keep the excitement from my voice.

"I just finished with her yesterday. She should be good as new now and last you another thirty years."

I chuckled. "How much do I owe you for this?"

He gave me the price, and we discussed a payment plan. I wrote him a check for the first installment, gave him the keys to the ancient Chevy, and headed out into the back parking lot.

I hesitated before sliding into the driver's seat and peered through the windows to see if anything had been left behind for me to find.

There were no purple coats with pink polka dots in the seats. The interior of my car was empty and clean. I let out a breath and slid into the driver's seat. The engine turned over smoothly at the first turn of the key, rumbling quietly without a cough or hiccup.

I rubbed a mittened hand along the dash. "It's good to have you back, old girl."

I shifted into gear and headed across town to the museum. I detoured by my office to drop off my coat and purse, tossing my badge on my desk, and then headed into the break room to leave my lunch in the refrigerator.

Annette swung past the open doorway of the break room and paused when she caught sight of me. "Evelyn, you haven't seen Rachel this morning, have you?"

"No, but I just arrived."

"I'm having an issue I need her help with. She's usually already in her office by now, but I can't find her anywhere."

"I'll let her know you're looking for her if I see her," I said as I headed back down the hall to my office.

My badge was missing from where I had tossed it, and I knelt to search under my desk. I retraced my steps to the break room to no avail. When I wandered down the hall and turned the corner, I found the repository door ajar.

I pushed the door open and glanced around. I was not the only person with access to the room. Others were in and out throughout the day. A badge on the work table caught my attention, and when I crossed to the table and flipped it over, I found that it was my own.

Brow furrowed, I pinned the badge to the lapel of my blouse and wondered who would have borrowed it from my desk. I had been leaving my office unlocked throughout the day, but now I pondered the wisdom of that. I hurried down the hall to my office and locked the door before returning to the repository.

I went to the private collection first. It called to me like a siren's song, and like those sailors of lore, I could not resist its enchantment. As in legend, I had a feeling that the secrets these pieces kept were just as deadly. I touched one of the boxes, and then grabbed the ladder to roll it farther down the shelf. After setting the brakes, I climbed to reach the shelves overhead.

It began so quietly that I thought at first I imagined it. But the soft sound grew, and I froze when I realized it was not in my head. It was a tinny little echo that traveled through the cool air to reach me. I knew the tune. Hearing it here sent a jolt through me.

I tucked my pencil into my hair and hurried down the ladder so quickly my foot slipped off the last rung. I staggered, a sharp twinge radiating through my ankle, and limped to the end of the row to peer down the corridor between the shelving units.

"Hello? Is someone there?"

The tune played faintly in a constant loop, the sound coming from deeper in the archives. I followed the lilting sound, glancing down each row as I passed. By the time I reached the far end of the room, the tune was beginning to hesitate and stutter as the cogs and wheels slowed.

A scuff of footfall sounded behind me. I whirled around but saw no one.

"Who's there?" I demanded. "Jeff?"

Alas, my love, you do me wrong. I could hear the lyrics clearly in my head. My breath wheezed in my tightening chest.

It was coming from the farthest corner, deep into the last accordion shelving unit. The shelf had not been rolled fully open. The space between the wall and the unit was just narrow enough for me to walk through.

And there on the very last shelf sat my mother's music box.

I stared at it, every hair on my arms raised, as "Greensleeves" faded. The music box went silent. I reached for it, and one last sporadic note twanged through the air. I started violently and picked up the music box in a rush.

Everything went dark.

I almost dropped the music box as the lights went out. I clutched it to my chest and stood rigidly. In the distance, at the front of the room, I heard the door open and close.

The darkness was absolute. I could not even see the shelf I knew was less than a foot from my face. The oppressive feeling of being crushed by the darkness all around me began to tighten my chest. The archives room was a yawning black cavern that had swallowed me whole.

Come out, come out, wherever you are, Evelyn.

Pain ricocheted through my knees as I hit the floor, and I realized my legs had given out.

I don't have much patience for these games of yours any longer.

A whimper threatened to escape, and I bit my lips until I tasted blood. I stayed hunched and small, knees tucked to my chest, the music box digging into my breastbone, praying he would not find me.

Don't make this more painful than it needs to be.

My heart was galloping away from me, my stomach a hard knot that churned sourly in my belly. My eyes searched the darkness for any sense of movement. I was terrified he could hear my teeth clattering together, the tremor that jostled through me. I pressed myself into a smaller ball, edging deeper under the desk, pushing aside boxes and—

The thump of archival boxes falling to the floor yanked me back to the present. A sob as weak as a whisper escaped me.

I was not hiding under a desk in a basement in Atlanta. I had burrowed into the lowest shelf, pressing myself flat, shoving boxes aside to fit.

Chad Kilgore was not stalking me in the darkness, whispering taunts that seemed to draw closer and closer. That tormentor was dead, and I had helped bury him in a deep grave no one but the most desperate coyotes might ever find.

I pressed my forehead against the cold metal shelf beneath me. My face was hot and damp. Chad Kilgore was long gone, but Jeff Roosevelt was a very real and current threat. He would kill me eventually. He would continue to kill innocent women whose only wrongdoing was stumbling across his path.

A simple plan is the best. My grandfather's words echoed in my head.

I crawled out from where I was curled on the shelf, joints protesting the cramped position as I staggered to my feet. I shuffled in small steps along the wall, putting a hand against the shelves to guide me to the end of the row. The metal was smooth underhand, and I followed it to its end. The gap between the shelves seemed like a chasm. I placed one foot in front of the other, hand out, fumbling for the next anchor in the dark.

My knuckles cracked against the next set of shelves, and I repeated the process all the way down the line of shelves. The cool air felt rough against my over-sensitized skin. My ears strained to hear anything—anyone—else in the darkness. Every sense was pricked and alert, every nerve in my body vibrated with awareness.

My progress was slow and painstaking through the room. Each time I ventured between shelves, I felt as if I were stepping into a vast void. I did not realize I had passed the last shelving unit until I had floundered into the emptiness, hand reaching out and searching futilely.

I froze when I realized I would not find another shelf and struggled to recall the orientation of the space around me. I ventured forward hesitantly, and soon my foot connected with something. The work table, I realized. Hand on the surface to guide me, I moved around the long table. At the corner, I followed the turn of the table, and at the next corner, I paused.

I strained to see. The tall double doors were some-where nearby, but the seals on the seams of this climate controlled room meant there was not even a faint glow to delineate the edges of the door. I took a deep breath and stepped away from the table, hand outstretched.

Within ten steps, my hand connected with the wall. I shuffled to the right, hand sweeping along the smooth surface, and soon I reached the door. When I found the handle, I shoved the door open and stumbled into the hall.

The overhead lights blinded me. I closed my eyes and bent double, struggling to draw air into my constricted lungs. I staggered down the hall and shoved into the women's restroom.

I set the music box aside and propped my elbows on the edge of the sink, letting the cold water run over my hands and wrists. I met my own gaze in the mirror. My face was pale save for the livid bruise on my cheek. My pupils almost swallowed the color of my irises. A smear of blood stained my lips. I dampened a paper towel and wiped the blood away.

The likelihood that I could get away with it a second time was slim to none. I did not fool myself into thinking that I could. I had two options: make it look like self-defense or disappear after I had done it. With the doubt already stacked against me with the police, the latter was my safest option.

But then I thought of the women tied to the objects in the boxes in the repository. I thought of those thousands of American Indian women who had disappeared from their homes and been forgotten by the system. Gone without a trace, their families left without answers. They deserved a name, a face, a testament to what had happened to them. I thought of the woman in the cabin and of Amanda.

I dampened another paper towel and bathed my neck and chest in the coolness. I would need a gun.

I stopped in the hallway and drank deeply from the water fountain. When I straightened and wiped the dampness from my lips, I felt more human and less like an animal trapped in a flight response.

I moved down the hall to Annette's office. She glanced up when I stopped in her doorway, and her gaze sharpened on my face. "Is everything alright?"

"Yes." My voice sounded rough. I cleared my throat. "Yes, I was just wondering if we have any security cameras in the building."

"Only on the main floor, and they're all directed at the displays."

I nodded. "Did you happen to see anyone come down the hall recently?"

Her brow wrinkled. "No, but I only just got back to my office a few minutes ago. Rachel hasn't shown up for work yet, so I was over in the IT department. Are you sure you're okay?"

I forced a smile. "I am."

My office door was still locked. When I entered, I placed the music box on my desk and stared at it warily. This remnant of my mother had been sitting next to my bedside, playing its haunting tune nightly, from the time I was in a cradle. I knew every line and curve, every scratch and chip, every note. But staring at it now was like staring at something unfamiliar and sinister.

I left it on my desk and found the flashlight I always had tucked in my purse before grabbing my pepper spray from my coat pocket and heading back to the repository. I hit the series of switches, and the lights staggered on one after the other down the entire room. Flashlight tucked into my pocket, pepper spray in hand, I walked down shelves, checking cautiously along each row.

The room was empty. Jeff was long gone, his trick played, harmless and menacing all at once. I kept the flashlight and defensive spray close at hand for the rest of the day.

It was late afternoon when I found it in the bottom of a piece of pottery with a broken lip. I caught my breath when I turned the vessel over and let it slip into my hand. It was half of a lower jaw, a single molar still embedded in the bone. Excitement humming in my veins, I handled it with care and took copious notes about the objects within the box.

The hours raced by, and I did not realize how late it was until I glanced at the clock on the wall. It was over an hour past the museum's closing time.

I packed away what I had been working on and returned it to the shelves, turning out the lights in the repository before I left the room. The lights in the corridor were turned off, and I worried I had been locked inside the building until I saw the light spilling from Annette's office at the end of the hall.

I grabbed my coat and bag from my office, locked it behind me, and stopped in Annette's doorway as I shrugged into my coat. She jumped when she glanced up and spotted me.

"You scared me. You're still here as well?" she asked.

"I lost track of time." I could not keep the smile off of my face. "I found another bit of bone."

Her face lit with excitement. "A second fragment?"

I nodded. "It's a piece of a jaw bone. There's a molar still attached. I've set everything aside that could be related to it. I think there may be some funerary objects with this one."

"I'll make a note to let the university know we have another bone for their experts to analyze." She glanced up from writing. "I've been incredibly pleased with your work thus far, Evelyn. I've discussed it with the board, and next week, I'd like to talk to you a bit about some projects that would keep you on in a permanent position."

Bittersweet elation burst through me. This was exactly what I had been hoping for, and I may yet have to abandon it. "I would love that. The collection is incredible, and I would like nothing more than to continue working here in a more permanent capacity."

"Good. Why don't we talk more Monday morning, then?"

"That sounds great. I'll come by your office as soon as I get to work." My steps were slow as I walked through the shadowed museum. The overhead lights were dimmed, and only the display lights remained lit. I knew the front doors would be locked, so I veered to the side entrance for employees.

The parking lot was dark, the dusk to dawn light buzzing futilely. A sharp wind cut across the pavement and blew ice crystals into my face. I ducked my head, clutched my coat about me, and hurried to my car, fishing my keys from my pocket.

A prickle of awareness brought my head up as I reached my Civic. A shadow moved in the reflection of the car window, and there was a rush of movement behind me. I scrambled for my canister of pepper spray, but he was on me before I could whirl around. His body slammed into mine and a grunt wafted across my ear when my elbow collided with his midsection. I heard the defensive spray clatter to the pavement and roll away.

I fought wildly, reaching back over my head to try to claw at his face, but he eluded my fingers. My frantic struggles knocked us off balance, though, and we careened into the side of my car.

The sharp scream that erupted from me sounded no louder than a whisper. It cut off as his arms wrapped so tightly around me that I thought my ribcage would crack. I gave up trying to reach his face and clawed at his arms. His grip was unbreakable, though, and my ragged breath sounded like a sob.

When he began to drag me backward, away from my car, away from the sputtering light near the side entrance of the museum, I scrabbled to gain purchase on the ground, fighting to dig my heels into the slick surface of the parking lot. His breathing was rough and hot against the side of my head.

The crushing pressure around my midsection eased suddenly. I screamed, high and desperate and piercing. I lurched forward, trying to take advantage of his relinquished grip, but his arm whipped around my throat. His fist clipped my chin, and he yanked me back against his chest.

His arm tightened around my throat, cutting off my scream. I fought against the compression of my windpipe and struggled to drag air into my lungs. I felt myself grow heavy and limp, and the edges of my vision began to darken.

"Evelyn?" I heard a voice call. *Annette*.

I tried to make a sound, felt my throat move against the arm that bound it, and then everything went black.

TWENTY-SEVEN

The largest rose bush spreads over an arbor that covers over 9,000 square feet.

HECTOR

MY CELL PHONE rang as I parked in the driveway of Rachel Vickers's house.

"I think the odds of your girl being involved in her stalker's disappearance are high," William Silva said as soon as I answered.

"What have you found?" I asked.

"Nothing," he said. "Chad Kilgore got in his vehicle one day, drove away, and never came home. No activity on his credit cards, no posts on social media. His car was never found. The man vanished."

"It looked like Evelyn was a person of interest from the beginning," I said, recalling the notes in the police report.

"She was, and she repeatedly declined requests to take a polygraph. The police put a tail on her after Kilgore disappeared and came up with nothing. They even searched the house. Evelyn's grandfather gave police permission without a warrant. They combed the house and yard and didn't find a thing. The case is cold."

I remembered how she had hesitated when she saw

the police emblem on my truck the day I found her car abandoned on the side of the road. "Did you uncover anything about her that raised a red flag?"

"You mean that made me think she could make a man who was terrorizing her disappear?" William asked, voice wry. "No. She was raised by her grandparents. Had a few run-ins with the law when she was a kid, but normal teen antics. Underage drinking, being at parties that were busted for drugs. As an adult, though, she's been a model citizen."

"Any clue as to why she left Atlanta?"

"Both grandparents died in the last year. They'd been ill for a while, and Medicare pretty much took everything," William said. "Raven's Gap is quite a change from Atlanta, though."

"It is," I agreed.

"Why the interest in her?" he asked. "You don't usually don't call me just because you're curious."

"Jeff Roosevelt is fixated on her."

The silence on the other end of the line was palpable. William knew my suspicions. He had been the first person I called when I began noticing Jeff's constant presence in the background of Winona's last few weeks alive. He had dug up everything he could find on the man, which amounted to nothing that could back up my suspicions.

"She's the key," I said.

"Shit," William muttered on the other end of the line. "Does she know she's your sacrificial lamb?"

I ignored his question. "Let me know if you find anything else." I hung up the phone before he could comment further. I glanced at Frank in the passenger's seat. "I'll be back."

My knock on Rachel Vickers's door went unanswered, but I could hear her little dog barking frantically within. I moved back from the front stoop and studied the exterior of the house. The blinds were closed, the lights were off, and her car was not parked in the drive.

I forded through the snow around to the back of the house and cupped my hands around my eyes to peer through the glass of the door leading onto the deck. I could see the living room, dining room, and kitchen from my vantage point. The interior of the house remained shadowed and still.

"She doesn't have any family in the area," Annette Zierdt had said earlier on the phone. "As far as I know, she's not in a serious relationship. It's not at all like her to not come into work without giving word that she needs time off. I'm concerned, especially…" She left the sentence hanging.

She did not need to clarify. No woman in Raven's Gap felt safe at the moment.

I knocked out the pane of glass closest to the handle and reached within to flip the deadbolt. Louie, Rachel's Bichon Frise, came running through the house at the sound of glass breaking, but when I opened the door and stepped within, he cowered away from me and scampered off to hide.

"Rachel?" I called. Only silence answered me.

Her home was lived in but neat aside from the puddles of piss and piles of shit on the tiles in the kitchen. Louie's water and food bowl were empty. There were no signs of struggle anywhere, nothing that hinted she had been attacked in her home.

I cued up the radio on my shoulder. "Romeo 3, Dispatch."

A crackle, and then a woman responded. "Romeo 3, go ahead."

"I am clearing from the check well-being call. I need an Attempt to Locate put out on this individual. Rachel Vickers, mid-thirties, her birthday and description are on the teletype of her DL you sent me. I want an ATL on the vehicle registered to her as well. It should be a silver Honda Accord."

"Romeo 3, I copy. I will send out an ATL on both Rachel Vickers and her vehicle."

"Thank you. I will follow up with the individual who requested the check well-being."

The house was small, two bedrooms, one bath. I ventured farther down the hallway to the back bedroom the little dog had disappeared into.

"Louie," I called. "Here, Lou." I whistled for him but received no response.

The back bedroom served as an office space. Louie was hiding under the desk. He began to tremble as I approached. He did not growl when I knelt, though, and when I held my hand out to him, he did not snap at my fingers.

"Everything is going to be okay," I said. "I bet you're hungry and thirsty." I kept my voice low and soft as I spoke to him, and after several minutes he crept from his hiding place to nose at my fingers.

Moving slowly so as not to startle him, I stroked a hand down his back. His tail was tucked tightly under him. He panted heavily, but remained docile as I lifted him into my arms.

He buried his head against my chest as I carried him to my truck. Frank greeted me as soon as I opened the door. "Don't frighten him, now," I said as he sniffed the small bundle in my arms. Louie's head came up, the whites showing around his dark eyes, but when I placed him in the passenger's seat next to Frank, he curled against the poodle's side. Frank glanced at me, expression equal parts appalled and intrigued.

There were only a handful of customers, leftovers from the dinner crowd, at the diner when we arrived. Maggie lifted a hand in greeting when she saw me.

"Why do you have Louie? Where's Rachel?" she asked as she approached, brow wrinkled in concern.

I dipped my head toward the hallway and followed her as she preceded me down the corridor. She pushed open the swinging doors into the kitchen and called out an order to Chuck, one of her cooks, before opening the door to her office.

Frank trotted in like he owned the place. I knelt to place Louie on the floor. He hunched close to the ground and shook. Maggie crouched beside him, looping an arm around Frank's neck, and stroked the Bichon, murmuring soothingly.

"I don't know where Rachel is," I said. "That's what I'm trying to find out."

Maggie looked up at me, eyes wide. "Oh Christ, Hec. Another one?"

I blew out a breath and nodded to the trembling lump of fur on the floor. "We all know how much she loved that dog. She would never go off and leave him. Not voluntarily."

"The poor darling." Louie tentatively licked Maggie's hand. I did not know if she spoke of the dog or the woman. Knowing Maggie, her benediction included both. She cupped the little dog's face in her hands. "You need some food."

I followed her into the kitchen, waving a greeting to Chuck, and filled a bowl with water. Back in Maggie's office, I sat on the worn sofa against the wall and watched Frank stand over Louie as the little dog gulped the water.

When he had his fill, I carried him outside and let him do his business. Maggie was back in her office when we returned. Louie went directly to the plate she placed on the floor for him. He ate with more gusto than Frank, who polished off his eggs and ham delicately, keeping an eye on the smaller dog the entire time.

"You're going to take him home, aren't you?" Maggie asked from where she sat on the floor between the dogs, leaning back against her desk.

Louie finally stopped trembling. His tail wagged as he ate. "He's frightened and confused. He would be miserable at the shelter."

When Maggie did not respond, I glanced at her and found her lips quirked in a smile.

My radio toned. Louie started violently and began to bark.

"All units available, we have a report of a kidnapping in progress."

Maggie scooped Louie into her lap and put a hand on Frank's shoulder. "Go. I'll watch them."

I ran to my truck and let dispatch know I was en route emergent along with the other officer on duty. It took me less than a minute to make it to the museum. I threw the truck into park and had the door open before it had fully rocked to a stop.

"Here!" a female voice called, waving frantically. She knelt on the ground next to another woman who lay prone.

I ran to them and knelt beside the pair. Evelyn lay unconscious on the icy pavement.

"What happened?" I tucked my fingers under the collar of Evelyn's coat. Her pulse was strong and steady against my fingertips.

Sirens sounded behind us and another vehicle squealed into the lot. Running feet approached.

"Romeo 4, Romeo 3 and I are on scene," Cooper said into the radio.

"Romeo 4, I copy."

I tuned out the rest of his exchange with dispatch.

"I don't know," Annette Zierdt said, voice shaken. "I was in my office. Evelyn worked late and stopped by my office on her way out. A few minutes after she left, I heard a scream. I was coming to the front of the museum to look out the window when I heard another scream, and I called 9-1-1 as I ran outside. There was a man dragging her across the parking lot, but he let her go as soon as I started yelling at him."

"Which way did he go?" Cooper asked.

"I'll show you."

I did not look to see where Annette directed Cooper. Evelyn looked small and fragile and wounded.

For a moment, guilt pierced me. She was a pawn to me. But seeing her lying on the cold ground, wounded and helpless, I saw her as a woman. As someone who deserved protection from a man I knew was dangerous. I put my hand to her cheek and wondered when my humanity had slipped away.

Evelyn's eyelashes began to flutter. She came to with a violent start, lashing out at me with fists clenched. She struggled wildly, caught in the grip of terror, unhearing when I called her name until I caught her by the elbows.

"You're safe," I said. "It's Hector."

She blinked and her gaze finally focused on me. She sagged in my grip, and her clenched fists reached out to grasp the front of my coat. "Hector," she breathed, voice hoarse. "He's still here?"

I pulled her into me, stroking her hair back from her face. "You're safe. He's gone. You're safe now." She trembled in my arms.

Four hours later, she was released from the clinic, and Evelyn sat across from me in the empty diner.

Maggie slid a mug of tea in front of her. "Chamomile, and I added extra honey to sooth your throat."

Evelyn smiled wanly at her. "Thank you." Her voice was a near-soundless whisper.

She was more composed now, but her face was pale and I caught the tremor of her fingers as she wrapped her hands around the mug.

I pulled my notebook from my pocket but waited until she had taken a careful sip of the steaming tea before I spoke. "It's easier to go over the details while they are still fresh in your mind." She nodded. "Did you see who grabbed you?"

"No." Her voice was raw, and she touched her throat gingerly. "Someone came up behind me when I was unlocking my car. I never had a chance to see…his face."

"But you think you know who it was."

She hesitated, meeting my gaze and then glancing away. "You wouldn't believe me." Her gaze dropped to her tea, and she took another sip of the pale liquid.

The guilt that pierced me earlier crept in. Jeff was fixated on her. When she became his next victim, I would be there to finally bring him down. My sacrificial lamb, as William had put it.

For Winona and Emma, I reminded myself, pushing aside the nudge of guilt. This woman was the key. "Let's say that I did."

Something in my voice brought her eyes up, and they narrowed on my face.

I leaned forward, braced my elbows on the table, and lowered my voice. "Let's say that I've been trying to catch the bastard for a long, long time and have never been able to pin anything on him."

She stared at me for a long moment. I did not know what she saw in my face. But when she finally spoke, Evelyn told me of the private collection at the museum, how she had linked two items to missing Native American women, how she knew there were more but she could not make the connection. She recounted the incident in the bookstore and the eerie way her music box had been returned to her.

"He told me I reminded him of someone," she said. "I reminded him of *her*. I don't know how many women he has killed, but I know it's more than two."

I leaned back, bracing myself against the support of the bench seat behind me. Native American. I closed my eyes and could almost feel the silk of Winona's long, dark banner of hair. I could almost see the curve of those high, rounded cheekbones when she smiled. I blinked and found Evelyn watching me.

"That meant something to you."

I cleared my throat. "Winona, my wife, was Hunkpapa Lakota. She and my daughter went missing fifteen years ago."

Her brow furrowed and then cleared. "Winona and Emma Lewis."

I nodded. "Ed won't take that sign down until they come home."

If they could have come home, they would have by now. Not for me, but for Ed and Betty, for Jack, for everyone in this town who loved them and searched for them and missed them.

"And you think Jeff took them?"

"I know he did. I just can't prove it."

A tap of a horn outside drew both of our gazes out the window as one of the EMTs pulled Evelyn's old Honda into the parking lot.

I slid from the booth. "Let me take care of this, and then I'll follow you home." I pushed through the front door of the diner and lifted a hand. "Bob. Thanks for bringing her car around."

He tossed me the keys. "No problem. I found her purse in the parking lot and put it in the passenger's seat."

"Need a lift?"

"Nah. Thanks, though."

As the man strode across the empty lot, I glanced back through the wide windows into the brightly lit interior of the diner. Maggie stood at the table. Evelyn was turned away from the window to speak to her.

I pulled the tracking device from my pocket, checked to make certain it was secure in its case, and then knelt to attach it to the undercarriage of Evelyn's vehicle. As I straightened, I made certain Evelyn was still turned away from the window.

She was, but Maggie watched me through narrowed eyes.

I reentered the diner and placed Evelyn's keys on the table. "Give me a moment, and I'll follow you to the inn."

Maggie followed me down the hall to her office. "You're up to no good."

I ignored her as I took in Frank sprawled on his side on Maggie's sofa, with Louie curled up on top of him using the large dog as a bed.

Maggie closed the door behind us and sighed. "William called me. Don't get that woman hurt in your quest for vengeance, Hector."

That guilt nipped at me again. I arched an eyebrow at her. "You've been watching too many westerns again."

"Don't patronize me," she snapped. "I know you. Others may think you've finally let it go, but I know better." Her voice softened. "Honey, Winona wouldn't want this for you. She—"

"You know what Winona wanted?" I interjected. "She wanted me to pick up the cake she had ordered from the bakery for Emma's birthday party. I forgot. It slipped my mind until I was almost home, and by then, I didn't feel like coming back for it." Frank's tail thumped in concern at the tone of my voice. "And when she asked me to go back into town for it, I told her I was too tired, she would have to go instead. That's all she wanted. For me to pick up a fucking cake." I let out a breath that felt raw in my throat. "You can't ask me to let it go, Mags." I met her gaze and saw her eyes were bright and damp. "This is all I'm able to give my girls."

TWENTY-EIGHT

I was born with the devil in me. I could not help the fact that I was a murderer, no more than the poet can help the inspiration to sing.

-H.H. Holmes

JEFF

FEELING HER STRUGGLE against me had been one of the most arousing things I had ever felt. It reminded me so much of Rose. The urge had come over me there in the parking lot. With her wild struggles and her scream ricocheting inside of me, I had come close to snapping her neck. Only the press of her last gift in my palm had stayed the urge.

Even now, watching her climb the steps to the inn and disappear within, I ached and trembled with the force of it. Only Rose had brought me such painful euphoria before. I considered waiting and slipping into the inn, going to her when she was asleep in her bed, but the last time I had given in to this high, it had cost me Rose.

I moved through the woods and back into town to where my Land Rover was still parked at Book Ends. I drove the winding stretch of road to Gardiner and parked down the street from where I had left Rachel's car.

Of course I had found that old dog of a police officer's tracking device. No one knew about the cameras I had hidden within the alley, the stairwell, and my apartment. I left his device untouched.

He had been a thorn in my side for fifteen years now. I knew he watched me; I knew what he suspected. He would have been amusing had his harassment not drawn so much attention to me that for fifteen years I had to hunt far from my own familiar territory.

Now it was my turn to make things difficult for him. I owed the bastard that much.

I retrieved Rachel's car and then turned off the state road onto Jardine Road and followed it up into the craggy canyon. I took the road all the way through the tiny town five miles up into the mountains and turned off onto a narrow tract of trail on the far side of town. The way was rough, and it came to a sudden dead end several miles later when wilderness overtook the trail.

I went the rest of the way on foot. The moon was new tonight, and the darkness suited me. A wolf's distant howl was a thread of sound in the dense forest, soon followed by a chorus of its brethren, all weaving together to form a haunting tapestry that blanketed the night.

I was not afraid. I was tempted to throw back my head and echo their mournful call. Predator knew predator and left the other alone to its hunt.

On nights like this, when the darkness was at its deepest and the predator restlessly paced its confines within me, I felt more animal than human. And like an animal, I knew the wisdom of having more than a single den. There were plenty to choose from in these mountains. Caves and defunct mines, old hunting shacks and long-abandoned homesteads.

I approached the latter now, the cluster of buildings

listing on their crumbling foundations. I ducked through the low entrance into the pitch black interior. I found the electric lantern just inside the door and turned it on. It was barren. The floor was dirt, cold, and littered with the debris of the woods. In the corner were the skeletal remains of some animal a mountain lion had dragged inside last spring.

The woman lay covered with a thick wool blanket, inert on the floor where I had left her. I tossed the blanket aside as I knelt next to her. The chill in the air had cooled my arousal, but now it bubbled to the surface once more at seeing her bound and helpless. This woman lying in the refuse of the forest was not the one that I wanted, though, and my movements were brusque. I took less care than usual as I yanked off the cuffs.

Perhaps had I not been so consumed with the throbbing in my pants, I would have recognized the signs of her wakefulness before she reared up and swung at me. Caught off guard, I could not defend myself against the first blow. How she was conscious, let alone able to function after the pills I had forced down her throat, I did not know.

That first blow knocked me back, and in those moments while I was stunned, she scrambled to her feet and ran. I caught her at the edge of the meadow. Her head thumped against the frozen ground like a melon when I tackled her. A scream burst out of her, piercing in the quiet of the night, ringing in my ears.

She struggled frantically, wriggling under me like a squealing, mewling pig trying to escape slaughter. I felt myself stir to life again against her.

She felt it, too, for she froze. She turned her face to the side and took a deep, quavering breath.

"Please don't hurt me," she whispered, voice breaking. "I… I'll do anything." She moved against me, and this time her movements were as sinuous as a snake rather than frantic. "I'll do a-anything you want. Just p-please, don't hurt me."

I dug my groin into the fat swell of her ass. I heard her breath catch in a sob before she pushed back against me. I reared back, revulsion bringing bile rising to the back of my throat, and I gagged.

I did not realize my hand was on the rock until my fingers closed around it. I did not realize I had raised it until I brought the edge down on the side of her skull in a swift, violent blow.

I raised the rock again, and this time, I did not bother to quell my rage. I let it boil over unchecked.

TWENTY-NINE

The Center for Disease Control and Prevention has reported that murder is the third-leading cause of death among American Indian and Alaska Native women.

EVELYN

THE GLINT OF gold against the hollow of my throat winked in the light as I drew my sweater over my head. I froze, arms stretched above me, hair still caught in the garment, and stared at my reflection in the bathroom mirror. A fine filigree gold chain lay against my skin with a heart-shaped locket nestled against my breast bone.

I let my sweater fall to the floor and scrabbled to find the clasp of the necklace. My fingers shook too badly to work the clasp free. I gave up struggling with the clasp, caught the chain in my fist, and yanked.

The necklace dug into my throat for a moment, grating and burning against my skin, and then with a snap, it broke. I dropped it as if it had singed me. It landed on the tiles of the bathroom floor with a soft chime.

My heart began a heavy, laden thud again as I stared down at the necklace. I knelt and reached slowly for the piece of jewelry. It was small and delicate.

I plucked it off the tiles and straightened. There

were no photographs within the locket, but an elegantly scripted R was engraved on the front.

I placed it on the counter and backed away until my shoulders thumped against the wall.

Come out, come out, wherever you are.

I closed my eyes and sucked in an uneven breath.

In the basement of the museum in Atlanta, I had been lucky. I thought being locked in was an accident at first. When the lights had gone out, I assured myself there was nothing to be concerned about. But as soon as I heard that soft, steady footfall, I had known. I had known before I heard his voice that seemed to come from all directions in the dark.

We're going to play a game, Evelyn. You like playing games, don't you?

What game are you playing at, Evelyn? a coworker had asked me after I made the first complaint about him. *Chad is the nicest guy.*

He certainly gave that appearance. Clean cut, handsome, personable. He had a beautiful wife and two young daughters. As a security guard, he instilled trust in others.

But he had also stopped by my desk several weeks after he began working at the museum. As he exchanged pleasantries with me, he reached out and caught a lock of my hair. *You have beautiful hair,* he said, rubbing my hair between his thumb and forefinger. When I tried to move away, his fingers tightened. When I told him to take his hands out of my hair, he held my gaze and pulled until I felt the tear at my scalp.

He had walked away with strands of my hair tangled around his fingers. As he had walked away, I had known I was dealing with someone who was not what he seemed on the surface. It was only the beginning.

I knew my way around the basement of the museum. It was the only thing that saved me. In the dark, struggling to be silent, I fled through the labyrinth. His voice and footsteps trailed after me. In one of the storage rooms filled with old office furniture, I crawled beneath a desk. My cell phone had no service in the depths of the museum. I was alone and helpless, and the man who had terrorized me for a year was whispering my name in the darkness.

Now, locked safely in my room at the inn with Chad Kilgore dead and buried in the wilderness two thousand miles away, I moved to the toilet and vomited.

Being grabbed tonight had been exactly what I expected to happen at any moment hiding under the desk in the museum's basement.

I averted my eyes from the necklace as I brushed my teeth. My thumb where the rose's thorn had pierced me was red and warm to the touch. My throat was sore, my neck stiff. A bruise was developing on my chin to match the one on my cheek. I needed to act. It was no longer merely about me and about the fear of how far Jeff would escalate.

I had recognized the little white dog Hector carried in the crook of one arm. I had seen photos of him on her desk at work.

"Rachel is missing, isn't she?" I had asked.

He met my gaze, and it was all the answer I needed.

Another woman was missing. Unease gripped Raven's Gap.

Hector believed me. I was not certain he was truly

an ally, but he knew what kind of predator lurked in his town.

I slept in fits and starts, and by morning, I had a plan. *A simple plan is best*, my grandfather had said.

I called Annette and asked for the day off.

"Of course," she said. "Take all the time you need, and please let me know if I can do anything for you."

"Any plans for the day?" Faye asked when I came into the kitchen.

"I'd like to purchase a gun," I said, voice hoarse. My throat was swollen and tender today, but the warm shower and the pain reliever I had taken were already easing the ache.

She placed a mug on the table before me. "Hot water with honey, lemon, cinnamon, and whiskey." She studied me for a long moment. "Do you want to obtain one legally or…?" She let the sentence hang.

It was my turn to study her. Her words reminded me of the easy, confident skill with which she had handled the pistol the other night, how calm she had been at the prospect of someone hiding somewhere in the inn. Her words reminded me of the hidden saferoom in her closet, the numerous locks on the door.

I needed a paper trail. "Legally."

"There's a place in Livingston with a range as well. If you don't mind company, I could go with you after breakfast. I just need to run Sam to school first."

"I don't mind company at all."

The hot toddy went a long way toward easing the soreness in my throat, and the cream of wheat Faye made for breakfast was warm and easy to swallow.

After helping her clean up the breakfast dishes, I changed into jeans and a sweatshirt and met her back downstairs after she returned from taking Sam to school.

"Is he feeling better?" I asked.

"He hasn't been himself for a few days now. He keeps insisting on sleeping with me, which isn't normal behavior for him. I've woken up several times in the middle night to find him wide awake sitting up in bed. I don't know what has triggered this, and he can't tell me." She sighed. "Or won't."

"Is…" I did not know how to phrase the question. "Has he always not spoken?"

Her smile was sad when she turned from the door. "He was like a little magpie as a toddler. Always talking, always asking questions. He stopped speaking five years ago."

The guarded look in her face, the protective way she held herself, and the closed off tone of voice forestalled any questions about what had spurred his mutism.

"We can take my car," I said.

The drive to Livingston rolled by quickly, and in an hour and a half we were pulling into the parking lot of our destination.

One of the men behind the counter at the gun range readily answered my questions and had a recommendation for me.

He reached into the case to retrieve a pistol and placed it on the counter before me. "This is a Heckler & Koch VP9. I consistently recommend this handgun to women."

"Why?"

"The slide pull. This is one of the easiest I've found, easy on the hands. It's a reliable piece. But my advice is to test out a few before deciding for yourself. Check for comfort, weight, how the grip feels in your hand."

"I'd like to test this one. And maybe something smaller."

"You can try my Glock 43," Faye said.

Within twenty minutes, we had rented a lane and purchased paper targets. We donned the hard plastic ear muffs. My own glasses would suffice for eye protection.

Faye fastened a target to the carrier system and used the automated pulley system to position it at the ten-yard mark. "You don't want to let someone too close to you. If they are within arm's reach, they can over-power you. But you also want them close enough that your shots are true, because believe me, your aim is not going to be as good in a tense situation as it is standing here shooting at a paper target."

She moved around our small corner of the range with ease and familiarity. She did not even flinch at the loud reports of nearby gunfire.

"How long have you been doing this?"

"Shooting? Five years now."

Five years since she had learned how to handle a gun. Five years since her son had stopped talking. The same son who crawled into a hidden safe room in their home as if it was something he had done any number of times before. I wondered what had sparked the fear and silence that governed the two of them.

She must have mistaken my own silence, for when she glanced at me, she paused in drawing a gun case from her bag. "It's all about knowing the gun and learn-ing how to handle it safely. Even Sam knows how to shoot. I would never leave him alone with access to a gun. But in an emergency, he knows how to use one."

"My grandfather taught me how to shoot," I admitted.

Though not when I was a young girl. As a child, I had not even known about the old Browning hidden on the top shelf of his closet. We had gone to a nearby shooting range the first time I had opened my curtains one morning and found cigarette butts on the exterior windowsill and footprints amidst my grandmother's azaleas. My grandfather had insisted on me sleeping with the old Browning on my bedside table after that.

I had not known about the German pistol his uncle brought home from World War II until he retrieved it from a shoebox tucked at the back of a drawer and told me the plan.

I fed ammo into the magazines and remembered my grandfather's instructions. The way he had shown me how to hold the gun, firmly but not squeezing, pushing with my right hand, pulling with my left. Straight arms, but no locked elbows. Relaxed shoulders. Balanced stance. Do not pull the trigger; squeeze it.

After we had buried Chad Kilgore, neither of us had gone to the range again. I had not touched a gun since that day.

I pushed the loaded magazine into the butt of the Heckler & Koch and took a deep breath as I pulled the slide until it lurched forward and locked into place. I placed the pistol on the high table with the barrel facing downrange and took a step back.

"Want me to go first?" Faye asked.

She could not know what made me hesitate. She did not remember the way Chad Kilgore's head had been thrown back with the blow from the bullet. She did not recall the fine mist of blood, how heavy he had been, or how long it had taken to dig his grave.

She had not felt the horror. Or the relief.

I swallowed. "Sure."

She stepped forward, stance like a boxer's, shoulders squared, and fired at the paper target in quick succession until the magazine was empty. She held the pistol with such ease, it seemed like an extension of her arms, natural and deadly.

This shy, reserved woman was shockingly and composedly lethal. I stared as she ejected the magazine and laid it and the pistol aside. She hit a button beside the booth. The target carrier system whined into motion and towed the paper toward us in a ghostly waft. Faye pulled down her target, placed another on the carrier, and sent it back across the room.

I gaped at the target she had used, a traditional bull's eye. The pockmarks from the bullets were not all dead center, but the ones that were not were a tight cluster around it.

We traded places, and I flexed my fingers before I picked up the HK. I fit my hands around the butt as my grandfather had once instructed and sighted down the barrel.

I closed my left eye so I could see the sights better, adjusted my aim to the center of the target and fired. The noise and jump in my hands startled me, and the shot went wide, not even touching the target. I focused on the target once again. I took a deep breath and, as I let it out, I forced my shoulders to fall and loosen. When I fired this time, I hit the center of the silhouette.

Aim for the center of mass, my grandfather had told me.

After shooting through several magazines with the HK and with Faye's Glock, my shoulders burned and my arms felt weighty. The HK was my preference, but the subcompact Glock would fit in my pocket. I needed something small and easily concealed.

I purchased a Glock 43 when we finished in the range. The process was disconcertingly easy and swift, and soon I was walking out of the place with a gun in a hard plastic case and a box of 9mm hollow-point ammunition.

It was midday, and we stopped at a nearby restaurant for lunch. After we ordered, I glanced at the chain supercenter across the street.

I leaned across the table. "Do you mind if I run across the street really quickly while we wait for our food? It's getting to be that time of month."

"No, not at all," Faye said.

"I won't be but a minute."

In the store, I swung through the pharmacy section and grabbed a pack of sanitary napkins and a box of gloves and then headed straight to the electronics. I found a slim, pocket-sized digital camera. I grabbed an extra memory card, duct tape, and a remote shutter release as well.

After paying, I stopped into the bathroom and opened the pack of sanitary pads, tucking the camera box, memory card, and remote within, hidden from sight. I had paid with cash, and I flushed the receipt down the toilet.

Back at the restaurant, I slid into the booth just as the waitress arrived with our food. The meal was hot and filling. Once we polished off our plates, we headed home.

School was letting out as we drove through Gardiner, and upon Faye's request, I pulled into the carline. Sam was all quiet smiles when he climbed into the backseat.

When we arrived back at the inn, I was the first to spot her. It was the ruffle of the wind in the hem of her floral print dress that caught my attention. She sat slumped on the front porch swing.

I put my car into reverse and quickly backed out of the drive. Faye glanced at me, startled, and then her gaze swept the area and locked on the woman on the porch. "Oh Christ."

I pulled down the street and parked out of sight from the inn. "Just stay in the car. Sam can't see this."

I ran back to the inn, slowing when I reached the front walk. My eyes went automatically to the woods on either side of the inn.

Someone was watching. I could feel it with absolute certainty. Not even a magpie cackled in the trees.

"Miss?" She did not respond to my call, and I hesitated with my foot on the bottom step of the porch. "Miss, are you alright?" I swallowed and climbed the remaining steps as dread grew heavier and heavier in my chest.

Her dress was sleeveless. Her feet were bare. And her face was gone.

My stomach lurched into my throat. I rushed to lean over the railing before I lost my lunch. I vomited until there was nothing left and I was reduced to dry heaves. Once I had stopped gagging, I straightened and shakily wiped my mouth with the back of my hand. I forced myself to turn back to her.

Her face and one side of her head were completely caved in, reduced to a matted pulp of shards of bones, blackened blood, and exposed brain matter. The violence was like nothing I had ever seen before.

A tremor worked its way through me. Had her head

not been attached to her body, I would not have known I was looking at the remnants of a woman, of someone who had once been capable of smiling and laughing.

My stomach heaved again, and I clamped a hand over my mouth. With my free hand, I fumbled into my pocket. I almost dropped my phone several times before I managed to dial 911.

"Please state your emergency," a voice on the other end of the line said when the call was picked up.

"I…" I had to clear my throat. "I think I just found Rachel Vickers."

PART IV

Cut Above the Bud

THIRTY

*A bit of fragrance always clings
to the hand that gives you roses.*

-Chinese proverb

HECTOR

EVEN THE DETECTIVE's face was pale as he joined us on scene. Sarah Clemens, Amanda Thornton, and now Rachel Vickers.

DNA tests or a fingerprint analysis would have to confirm her identity. She was beaten beyond recognition with more brutality and rage meted out to her than I had ever witnessed. It was a gut-wrenching sight, the horror of it impossible to stomach.

The cause of death was evident and vastly different from the previous two women. But the stained dress she wore matched the pattern the two other women had been found in. Her toenails were painted the same pink. The hair attached to the one section of skull that had not been caved in was fashioned into a rough braid matted with blood and brain matter.

My cell phone rang in my pocket, and it was a relief to turn away from the scene. The number displayed on the screen was the station. "Hello?"

"Officer Lewis," Joan said, "an officer with the Gardiner PD just called. He saw your ATL. Rachel's car was found parked behind a gas station."

"Send me the address and tell him I'll be there in twenty."

The officer was waiting for me when I arrived. He was built like a tank, almost as wide as he was tall, with a face like a pit bull. He introduced himself as Davis.

"It's around back. Some kids noticed it was unlocked with the keys still in the ignition and thought they'd take it for a joy ride. Until they noticed the backseat. Spooked them."

I could see why. The lower half of the exterior was splattered with mud and dirty snow. One side of the backseat was saturated in blood with pieces of Rachel's shattered skull and the gray pulp of her brain matter left behind.

"Has anyone else touched it?" I asked.

"Not since I came on the scene."

I pulled out my cell and called Ted Peters. He had another scene to process after he finished at the inn.

When I hung up the phone, I directed my gaze upward and searched the eaves of the building.

I pointed to the surveillance camera. It faced away from where we stood, directed to look out over the side entrance into the gas station's lot. "I need to see that footage."

The clerk in the store readily agreed and led us into a cramped office space. She pulled the feed up on the desktop and then toggled through several computer screens to the archived data and began to rewind.

Davis's eyes were quicker than mine. After a few minutes, he said, "There," and pointed to the vehicle pulling into the station from the left side of the screen.

The vehicle was only in view for several seconds on the far side of the screen as it pulled around the building, but it was unmistakably Rachel's car. The headlights were off, and it was too dark to make out any details of the figure sitting in the driver's seat. The time stamp on the camera read 04:27.

"Let it play forward," I said, pulling my reading glasses from my pocket and leaning over the clerk's shoulder.

The screen showed nothing but the still night for several long moments. Whoever drove the vehicle to the spot and abandoned it did not walk through the camera's field of vision upon their departure. But when the timestamp read 04:39, headlights cut a swath across the surveillance tape. No vehicle came into view. The headlights were extinguished for two minutes before they suddenly lit the screen again and veered off.

I straightened. "Pause that a moment," I said as I fished my phone from my coat and swiped through the home screen.

I logged into the tracking app. I selected the date range and data points from the drop-down menus in the app and pulled up the travel log report on the device I had attached to Jeff's vehicle. A map view slowly loaded on my screen.

"I'll be damned," I breathed. "Rewind the feed."

The clerk toggled the mouse across the screen, and the footage rolled backward. And then there it was. At 21:07 the night before, Rachel's vehicle could be seen driving past the gas station, starting in the upper right hand corner of the screen and a moment later disappearing in the upper left hand corner.

"That's headed up to Jardine," Davis said.

"I need copies of that footage dating back to Wednesday evening." The last time Rachel had been seen alive was at the community meeting at the bookstore that night. "I'll be back for them." I turned to Davis. "I need that vehicle to remain exactly how you found it until my evidence tech shows up."

He nodded, and I strode out of the gas station. I stopped in the parking lot, peering at my cell phone screen before glancing at the crossroads. On foot, I traced the path marked in blue on my screen.

I crossed the street, followed the route back down to 89. I walked along the highway and crossed the river. The road became 2nd Street on the south side of the bridge, and I followed the route two blocks and turned left. The blue line on the map ended here. I pocketed my phone and turned in a slow circle, studying the area.

A cluster of hotels and inns past their prime lined either side of street. Cars were parked in front of each one. It would be an ideal spot to leave a vehicle for a couple of days without raising suspicion.

The laundry stood out on the street, a small brown building with red trim and a bright yellow sign. I approached the building and stopped under the awning.

I studied the dome of the surveillance camera. "I hope you smiled for the camera, you son of a bitch."

THIRTY-ONE

Man is harder than iron,
stronger than stone and
more fragile than a rose.

-Turkish proverb

EVELYN

I SET TO work as soon as the police left and the coroner drove away with Rachel's remains. I donned a pair of gloves before I extricated the digital camera from its case. The small remote shutter control was easy to program.

The sun was setting when I stepped outside. I avoided looking at the taped off section of the front porch and hurried down the street. There was no one about, no vehicles driving past, no pedestrians passing on the walk.

I veered into the woods, quickly losing sight of the road as I slipped down the ravine into the dense coverage of trees. I had not gone more than twenty yards from the inn, but the trek through the thicket of forest, heavily laden with snow and underbrush, felt farther.

I stopped when I was still within the cover of trees downhill from the inn. From this vantage point, I had a clear view of my window. I had purposefully left the curtains pulled back and the light on.

I drew off my mittens. I still wore the rubber surgical gloves beneath. I pulled the camera from my pocket and snapped dozens of photos of the inn and my lit window.

I tugged the roll of duct tape from my pocket and quickly mounted the camera on a tree. I adjusted the angle so the lens had an unobstructed view of the front drive of the inn, the porch, and the front door.

I exited the woods the way I had entered them, waiting in the shadow of the trees until I was certain no one was passed on the road. On the street, I walked slowly, gloved hands tucked into my pockets, fingers wrapped around the remote shutter control. As soon as I thought I was in the camera's viewfinder, I clicked the button on the remote control over and over as I traversed the front walk of the inn, climbed the porch, and opened the front door.

The last of the day's light winked out as I retraced my circuitous route and retrieved the camera. I was tempted to leave it there overnight. The less back and forth I did, the less likely I would be seen. But the battery light was already beginning to blink in the cold.

Once back in my room, I checked the photos and was pleased with the result. I looked unsuspecting, innocently returning home, unaware that someone watched and photographed me. I kept the gloves on the entire time I handled the camera, only taking them off after I plugged it in to charge.

I readied for bed and lay sleepless until the sky began to lighten. I dressed quickly, donned another pair of gloves, grabbed the camera and roll of duct tape, and headed back into the woods. I snapped photos again of the inn and of my window before mounting the camera on the tree and heading back inside.

This time, I waited until I had dressed, eaten breakfast, and was leaving before I activated the remote shutter control and captured my exit from the inn on camera.

My original plan had been to capture my comings
and goings over several days, but I was running out of
time. I needed to act quickly.

I retrieved the camera from the woods and made my
way through the early morning quiet of Raven's Gap.
A small herd of elk lay on the library's front lawn, and
only a couple of cars were parked on the street in front
of the coffee shop.

Main Street was still empty. I veered through the
public parking lot into the alley that ran behind the
diner and the bookstore. I saw no security cameras in
the alley. When I reached the back door of Book Ends,
I donned another pair of surgical gloves and extracted
two pins from my pocket that I had already shaped into
a pick and lever.

Within minutes, I was inside the dark bookstore. I
closed the door silently behind me and tumbled the lock
back into place. I stood still and silent, listening. My vision adjusted slowly, and I realized I was in the hallway
at the back of the building. To my right was a door, to
my left, the corridor turned a sharp corner, leading to
the restroom and the interior of the shop.

I went straight to the door to Jeff's office and tugged
the penlight from my pocket. I clicked the small beam
of light on, tucked it between my teeth, and knelt to
work on the lock. When the last seized pin clicked into
place, a quiet creak of movement reached me.

I froze for an instant, and then as soundlessly as
possible, I slipped my pick and lever free from the lock
and let myself into Jeff's office. I closed and locked the

door behind me, tilting my head toward the hallway, ears pricked. The sound came again, drawing my gaze to the ceiling.

The building was similar to the hardware store where Jeff lived, a turn of the century structure with two floors. I wondered if Susan lived upstairs. Someone was moving around above me in the early morning hours. There was a sudden sigh of water in the building's pipes, another creak above, and then silence.

I crept across Jeff's office to his desk and powered up his computer. The welcome screen appeared with the password prompt, and I was stunned when I carefully typed "rose" and was granted access. I had counted on it, but it still surprised me.

The blue glow from the screen gave me enough light to work by, so I snapped off the pen light and tucked it away. I drew the camera from my pocket and ejected the memory card.

His desktop was an iMac, and the memory card slipped neatly into a port on the side of the large computer. While the contents loaded in the photo application, I created three folders on this computer labeled AMANDA, RACHEL, and EVELYN. I opened the Apple's Dock and found the Terminal application and entered a touch command to change the date. I dragged the folder labeled AMANDA into the Terminal window and pressed the return key. The folder's date was now a week before I had found the woman hanging in the woods. I repeated the same process with the folder labeled RACHEL, backdating it to last week, and then did the same with the folder bearing my name.

I dropped the two folders into the computer's Trash application and then dragged the photos from the camera into the folder labeled EVELYN. I deleted the pictures from the photo application before scrolling through the Finder window. I hid the folder bearing my name within another folder in Jeff's documents. Hidden from a cursory glance, but there when the police came to dig through his files.

I ejected the camera's memory card from the port and powered down the computer. It would not get past the FBI, but a small town police department might be fooled. To cover my tracks completely, I took the time to lock the office door and the back door behind me with my pick and lever.

First stage complete, I stripped the surgical gloves off my hands, tucked them into my pocket, and strolled casually down the alley and back out onto the street to greet the sun's rise. Adrenalin began to hum through my veins. I had set something in motion. Now I needed to stay ahead of the rolling stone as it gained momentum.

My hands were trembling as I approached the police department. I turned off course and entered the coffee shop. There was a lull, so I was able to place my order immediately upon entry. I had my peppermint hot chocolate within minutes.

I picked a seat by the window and blew on the beverage until it was cool enough to sip. I drank slowly, watching the town stir to life.

Chad Kilgore had followed me from the suburbs of Atlanta two hours north to the Chattahoochee National Forest. I had known he would. He shadowed my every step. My grandfather and I had already found the place. It was down a dirt road that branched off from the remote, two-lane state route. My grandfather was already there, waiting, his truck hidden out of sight.

Deep in the woods, I pulled to the side of the dirt road and popped the hood on my car. Chad Kilgore had been lurking in my rearview mirror since I left Atlanta, drifting farther back as I ventured onto quieter and narrower streets. It was several minutes before I heard the rumble of his engine.

I glanced into the woods, took a deep breath, and waited.

He stopped in the middle of the dirt track. His smile as he approached me made my skin crawl. "You've led me on such a merry chase, Evelyn."

"And I'm ending that chase right here, you son of a bitch," my grandfather said as he moved from behind the shelter of trees.

Chad's expression morphed from predatory to stunned confusion before the bullet my grandfather fired wiped his face blank.

Even knowing what was coming, I had still started violently at the sharp report of the World War II-era pistol. When Chad had crumpled into the dirt like a puppet whose strings had been severed, my legs weakened and I fell to my knees.

I had not realized I wept until my grandfather limped toward me, lowered himself to the ground, and enfolded me in his arms. "Hush now," he said. "It's over."

The blisters on my hands from digging his grave had taken a long time to heal.

When I finished my hot chocolate, I took the empty cup with me into the bathroom. In the stall, I dropped the memory card into the toilet and flushed it. I donned the surgical gloves again and buried the digital camera deep in the waste basket. I tucked the gloves into my empty cup and, on my way out of the coffee shop, I tossed my cup in the recycling bin.

Snow had begun to fall, and the gunmetal sky looked weighted. I took a deep breath and tucked my chin into my scarf as I traversed the distance between the coffee shop and the police station. The air was biting against the back of my throat and sharp in my lungs. It stung my cheeks, whispered into the recesses of my ears, and nipped at my lips.

The doors to the police department opened automatically ahead of me, and I stamped warmth back into my feet before I approached the desk. I was relieved to recognize the woman sitting there.

Joan smiled when she glanced up from her computer. She pressed the intercom to speak to me through the bullet proof glass. "Evelyn, what may I do for you?"

"I have a couple of questions," I said. I lowered my voice. "I'm afraid."

Her face moved and she leaned closer to the intercom. "It's absolutely horrific. I think every woman in town is afraid. And you had to find…" She shook herself. "I can't even imagine."

"I think someone is targeting me, Joan," I whispered. "I'm afraid for my life. I purchased a gun yesterday."

She nodded. "I don't blame you at all."

"I don't want to get in trouble for having it, though. Do I need to register it here with the police?"

"No, you don't need to do anything here with us. You can apply for a conceal carry permit with the sheriff's department. But you need to have lived here for six months and have a Montana driver's license."

I already knew the requirements, but I needed Joan to

remember I had been here and asked the question. "Do you offer any kind of firearm safety training course?"

"We do. The chief just decided to offer a course starting next week. He's waiving the fee for any woman who wants to take the class."

"I'd like to sign up for that, please. What day does it start?"

"Monday evening. Let me go ahead and get you registered."

I filled out the paperwork she slid through the slot to me. My fingers trembled slightly when I set pen to paper. Everything would be done by Monday evening, but it would help my case to have my name on the roster. It showed I was serious and conscientious and wanted to go about things lawfully.

I needed the odds stacked in my favor. I had every intention of surviving this confrontation and no intention of going to jail. I needed to appear innocent.

I needed to clearly be seen as a victim, even though I had no intentions of being one.

THIRTY-TWO

We can complain because rose bushes have thorns, or rejoice because thorns have roses.

-Jean-Baptiste Alphonse Karr

HECTOR

JARDINE WAS LITTLE more than a ghost town. The gold mine had closed in the nineties, and now there were only about fifty people living in the community. The outfitting companies, fishing and hunting expeditions, and vacation rentals were the only thing that kept the place on the map.

I stopped at one of the cabin rentals when I saw a group of snowmobilers readying for a day on the trails. A man broke away from the group and approached when I parked.

"Anything I can help you with, Officer?"

"I was wondering if anyone in your group saw or heard a vehicle come through the area Wednesday or Thursday night. It would have been a silver Honda Accord."

He turned and repeated my question to the group. A woman joined us. "I don't know if it was a Honda, but I woke up early the other morning and was sitting on the porch admiring the sky. We don't see the stars like this back home."

I fought the urge to prompt her to hurry along and waited for her to finish waxing poetic about Big Sky Country.

"It was maybe around four in the morning, and I heard a vehicle coming down Old Bear Creek Road. I thought it was odd because of the time of day, and because the car didn't have its headlights on."

She filled out a witness statement for me, detailing everything she could remember.

Old Bear Creek Road was a ten-mile stretch of rough mountain road that twisted deep into the wilderness. A few pack-in, pack-out campsites were located off the trail, but no one would be camping out that way this time of year. I needed to contact Park County and see if we could utilize their drones to search the area.

My cell phone rang when I reached the state road.

"An officer from Gardiner just dropped off some discs for you," Joan said at the other end of the line.

"I'll be at the station shortly."

I carried Louie in the crook of my arm, and Frank trotted at my heels as we crossed the parking lot and entered the police department fifteen minutes later.

Joan slid an envelope across the counter to me with a polite smile. "Here you are, Officer Lewis."

I caught a glimpse of the name scrawled across the top of a form on her desk. "Is this for the course the chief is offering?"

"It is. We're getting a lot of interest."

I stared thoughtfully at the form and wondered if Evelyn had purchased a gun. I collected the envelope. "Thank you, Mrs. Marsden."

In my office, Frank settled on his bed, but Louie pawed at my ankle until I picked him up and let him perch in my lap. The little dog had to keep me in his sights and had spent the last two nights curled against my side.

I slipped two discs from the envelope. One had GAS STATION written on it, the other LAUNDRY. I loaded the disc labeled LAUNDRY into my computer.

The date stamp on the recording read a week ago, so I fast forwarded and watched the accelerated motion of the street in front of the laundry in Gardiner pass from day to night again and again until I finally clicked pause. The date stamp matched what I was looking for. I carefully fast forwarded the recording until the screen darkened as night fell.

I glanced at my notes, moved the cursor on the recording until the time stamp read 20:30, and then let it play. At 21:03, headlights lit the street, and less than a minute later, a figure crossed the screen. It was a man moving down the street on foot, stride confident and unhurried.

The camera had a wide angle lens. I watched him cross the street and walk directly to a vehicle parked in front of one of the nearby inns. There was a brief flash of light as the interior light came on when he opened the door. When he pulled out of the parking spot and drove back the way he had come, I could clearly see that it was Rachel's vehicle.

I rewound the feed and watched the scene again. The image was grainy in the dark. The man stayed in the shadows and never looked directly at the camera. Even though I could not see his face, there was no doubt in my mind the identity of the man.

Noting the location of where Rachel's vehicle was parked on screen, I started the recording at the beginning. I let the feed run as I worked, glancing at the screen regularly to see if Rachel's vehicle was parked in the spot. Each time I looked, it was either empty or occupied by another vehicle.

The dress all three women had been found in bothered me. It looked like something that would have been worn decades ago, not something modern.

I brought up a second window and minimized it so I could watch the security video feed alongside it. I accessed the software program the department used for its case reports and pulled up the photo attachments on all three cases. I saved one of the photos of Amanda to my desktop and cropped the photograph until it was just a square of patterned fabric.

An image search on the internet brought up a vast array of photos and patterns. I scrolled through numerous pages until one in the bottom corner of the screen caught my eye. The pattern was not an exact match, but it was close. When I expanded the view and clicked on the link to visit the website, I was directed to an online auction site to a listing for a vintage sundress. The listing labeled Sears as the brand, the 1980s as the decade.

Movement on the screen caught my gaze, and I turned my eyes back to the security feed just as Rachel's vehicle was parked in front of the inn. I hit rewind and backed the video up a few seconds to when the car first appeared on screen. I hit play as soon as headlights lit the field of vision and noted that the time stamp read 23:57 from the night Rachel was last seen at the bookstore.

Even in the gray light of the feed, I could see how dirty the vehicle was. As if it had been driven on unpaved roads in the mountains, like the dirt track leading up to Jardine. The vehicle was parked, and then a figure exited the car. Instead of traversing the street, though, the figure ducked between buildings on the opposite side of the street and disappeared from sight.

I grabbed my notebook from my pocket, flipped to a blank page, and plotted out a timeline of events. He had grabbed Rachel sometime after the meeting at the bookstore, and at almost midnight the same night, left her car in Gardiner. The attempted kidnapping at the museum had been called in the following evening, and at 21:03, he had arrived in Gardiner, left his vehicle, and retrieved Rachel's. He was then caught on the gas station's camera heading toward Jardine at 21:07. At 04:27, Rachel's vehicle was left behind the gas station, with some return activity just out of sight of the camera twelve minutes later.

A picture was evolving in my head of the sequence of events. I needed to go back to Gardiner and find a surveillance camera that showed a different angle of the street. One that either showed Jeff's vehicle or Jeff himself clearly and undeniably.

Louie had fallen asleep curled up in my lap, and I set him on his feet on the floor as I stood and shrugged into my jacket. "Ready, boys?" I asked. Frank stretched and stood.

The phone ringing on my desk interrupted my exit, though, and I snagged the receiver.

"I can't get ahold of Yates. Any chance you can make a side trip to Livingston today?" Grover Westland, the county coroner, asked when I answered the phone.

"You found something?"

"I did. Get here as soon as you can."

I dropped Frank and Louie off at home. Frank hated

the smell of the morgue on me, and I had quickly learned Louie did not care to be left in the truck. It took me an hour to reach the main sheriff's department in Livingston. Once inside the building, I headed straight to the morgue. I knew why Frank hated the smell. It was one I could never acclimate to either. I breathed shallowly through my mouth when I entered.

Grover looked up from his desk. "Good, you're here." He moved to the mortuary cabinet and pulled open one of the drawers. "This young lady is about to go home to her family, but I wanted to show you something." He lifted the sheet and revealed the colorless, lax face of Sarah Clemens, the woman Evelyn had found at the cabins. "You're familiar with the basics of livor mortis?"

"Sure. Blood accumulating in the lowermost blood vessels after death."

"Right. We call it postmortem stain. It becomes fixed at about eight to twelve hours after death." He drew the sheet away from her entirely and patted her hand. "Pardon me, dear." He rolled her onto her side. "What do you see?"

"The staining is in her buttocks and back."

"Exactly." He laid her flat on the metal slab once more and covered her back up. "All three women have the same staining."

"Spell it out for me."

"Hector, each woman had this pattern of livor mortis. Two were hanged. This staining *should* be in their feet and legs. And come look at this." He moved across the room and flipped the switch on a display screen. The two X-rays pinned in place flared to life. "These are X-rays of Sarah and Amanda's necks."

I moved closer and studied each film. "Both are broken. Wouldn't you expect that in a hanging?"

"Only a long drop hanging breaks the neck. These women would have had to drop a distance of five to nine feet for their necks to snap. Cause of death should have been strangulation in both of these cases."

I stared at the X-rays. "These women were dead before they were hanged."

"There's more. There's residue of 2-Bromo-2-Nitro-propane-1,3-diol on each woman's face. It's a molecule called bronopol. It's found in your standard makeup wipe sold at drugstores. And each woman had overdose-level amounts of diphenhydramine in their systems."

"And that is?"

"Well, it's an antihistamine, a compound found in Benadryl. But it is also the active ingredient in over-the-counter sleep aids."

I rubbed my jaw. "He's grabbing these women, sedating them, and then recreating someone. Someone with no makeup who had her toenails painted a specific shade, wore her hair braided, and wore a specific dress." Reminded of the dress, I said, "I think the dresses may be older, from the Sears catalogs in the 1980s."

He moved to a cabinet and pulled out three evidence bags, each one with a stained but neatly folded dress inside. He offered them to me. "You're right."

The bags were already sealed, but I shifted the dress within until I could read where the tag said *SEARS THE FASHION PLACE*.

"I'll spare you the sight," Grover said, "but whoever did this removed Rachel Vickers's breasts postmortem so she would fit into that dress."

"Christ."

His face was grim. "If you haven't called the FBI yet, the department needs to. You have a serial killer on your hands." He pointed to the sheet-draped body on his table. The woman whose head had been caved in and her breasts cut off. "And he's only going to keep escalating."

THIRTY-THREE

Medical examiner's and coroner's offices in the US hold more than 40,000 sets of unidentified remains.

EVELYN

THE SNOW FELL in gentle, eddying spirals. Faye's battered Ford Explorer blocked me from view from the street as I approached my car. I glanced at my watch. I would have fifteen to twenty minutes, but I did not need to go far.

Outside of town, I would pull onto the shoulder and let my tire finish deflating. The flyer for the book club was tucked into my pocket with the Book Ends phone number on it. Ed's shop did not show up in an internet search, and I had left the card he had given me in my room. It would make sense for me to call the one number I knew in town to ask for his contact information.

I had no doubt Jeff would come. Hadn't our paths been on a collision course since he had stopped and offered me a ride? There was a poetic inevitability to it. This time, though, when we met on that lonely stretch of road, I knew who he was. And the Glock was heavy in my coat pocket.

The small black box attached to the undercarriage caught my eye as I crouched beside my car. With a tug and a twist, the strong magnets keeping it in place relin-

quished their hold. Inspecting it, I realized it was some
kind of case, and when I popped the latch, a small device lay within. An emblem like the wireless logo was
emblazoned on the device, and a green light winked
at me.

It had to be some sort of tracking device. I glanced
into the woods behind me, wondering if he lurked there
even now, waiting and watching. A chill crept over me.

I snapped the box closed and tucked it into my
pocket. Perhaps I would not need to even place a call if
he were tracking me. I retrieved the small folding knife.
I glanced at my watch again and took a deep breath before I flipped open the knife. A small nick to the base
of the valve stem was all that was needed. A soft whine
of air signaled air escaping the tire.

As I cranked my car and put it in gear, my cell phone
began to ring. I tossed the knife into my purse and
fished my phone from one of the inner pockets. When
I saw the contact I had saved into my phone, I hurried
to answer it. "Hello?"

"Hello, may I speak with Evelyn Hutto?"

"This is she."

"Oh, Evelyn! I'm sorry it's taken me so long to get
back to you. This is Roberta."

I glanced at my watch. Nineteen minutes. "Thank
you for returning my call. I take it you listened to my
message?"

"I did. Now tell me about the collection again. I
rarely accessioned private collections into the museum.
That was more Annette's territory."

Her voice was friendly and matronly. She made noncommittal noises on the other end of the line as I described the pieces.

The fresh snow made the inn's drive slick, and my tires spun briefly before I reached the top of the drive. The plows had not been down the side streets yet, so I drove slowly into town.

When I mentioned the cradleboard, I heard a slight exclamation. "Oh, *that* collection. I do remember that. I really shouldn't have accepted the donation. I knew the pieces didn't fit with our collection, but it was such a generous donation. And he was so adamant about the museum having it."

My heart quickened. "So you remember the donor?"

"Of course! He's too handsome to forget. It was Jeff Roosevelt."

I braked too hard, too suddenly at the stop sign and felt my tires lock for an instant. "Jeff Roosevelt?"

"Yes, he's that nice man who runs the bookstore in town with Susan."

I angled my wrist to see the watch face. Seventeen minutes. "Did he say anything about the collection, make any stipulations about the donation?"

"No…he just said he was getting rid of some things he had collected over the years, and he thought the museum would appreciate the gift." When I was silent for several long moments, mind racing, she spoke again. "I'm positive I had him fill out the paperwork, though. Did you check the filing cabinet in my old office? I know I was supposed to do these things digitally, but I may have forgotten to put it into the computer."

"I haven't checked the filing cabinet, but I'll do so. Thank you for calling me back about it."

"Of course, dear. I'm sorry if my forgetfulness has caused you any trouble with your cataloguing. I must have put it on a shelf and completely forgotten about it. Like I said, it wasn't something that fit with our collection. But he's hard to say no to. You'll understand if you've met him." She chuckled.

I pressed a hand to my breastbone, feeling the pounding of my heart behind the caging of bones.

I could not bring myself to exchange pleasantries, so I thanked her again and finished the call. Instead of heading out of town, I turned the car toward the museum.

The museum was open for a half day today. I snagged my badge from my purse as soon as I parked and glanced at my tire before I hurried inside. I had to be quick.

There was no filing cabinet in the office, though. I imagined I heard the steady pulse of my watch as I rushed to the repository.

An old filing cabinet stood in the corner beside a replica of a giant ground sloth no one could bear to discard. The rollers groaned in protest as I yanked the top drawer open. The hanging folders within were neatly labeled, and I pulled all three bundles labeled ACQUISITIONS free and carried them to the work table.

I glanced at my watch. Ten minutes.

A quick shuffle through the first folder revealed Roberta had filed the paperwork chronologically. I flipped through the third folder and found a section of paperwork from 2017. There were only three acquisitions from that year. The donation from Jeff Roosevelt was the second.

My fingers trembled as I flipped the pages and realized he had listed each piece in the collection, the tribal provenance, and the date he had acquired the piece. Just like any collector would. I glanced over the list. The

Arapahoe cradleboard's date was listed as 2011, the Hopi katsina as 2012. I scanned the rest of the collection and noted the dates went back fifteen years.

The list sent a shudder through me. I knew without a doubt each item corresponded with a woman who had disappeared. Hector needed to see this.

I did not have time to return the paperwork fanned across the work table to their folders and to the filing cabinet. I left them where they lay, folded the acquisition paperwork for Jeff's donation into my pocket, and hurried out to my car.

I glanced at my watch as I slipped the key into the lock. Four minutes. My tire had lost over half its air now. I hesitated. I could still carry out my plan. Now I wondered if I needed to with the evidence of Jeff's link to missing women in my pocket. But I did not know if this would be enough.

A prickling at the nape of my neck, a heightened sense of no longer being alone, was the only warning I had.

Jeff met my gaze in the reflection of my car window. "I think you're ready now, Evelyn."

My heart lurched into battering ram pace, and it took everything I had not to reach for the gun in my pocket. I calmly opened the door and slid into the driver's seat before turning my head to look up at him.

He caught the door, but I had no intentions of trying to escape. He had just made my decision for me. I should have known I would not need to draw him out.

Hadn't Chad Kilgore followed me to the woods with no provocation?

"I am," I said.

He smiled, and I had never been more frightened.

Not even when I had been locked in the dark basement and taunted by that voice coming ever-closer. Not even when I had waited on a deserted, lonely stretch of road in the woods waiting for a man I knew would relish hurting me before he killed me.

Jeff held his hand out to me. I dropped my keys into them, careful to avoid touching his palm.

Fear gave me a heightened sense of calmness, and I tracked his progress around the back of my car in the rearview mirror. He opened the door, slid into the passenger's seat, and inserted the key into the ignition.

"I want to finish telling you the story, and then you can help me with the conclusion."

"I always appreciate a good story," I whispered, throat tight. My mind raced. I could feel the pistol pressed against my thigh as I cranked the car and pulled out of the museum's parking lot. "Where do you want to go to talk?"

"I want to show you my roses." His tone was as genial as if we were neighbors talking about our gardens over a hedge fence. "Drive out of town. I'll tell you the way."

I drove slowly and cautiously. The state road was in better condition, already plowed and salted. My car began to handle oddly as I passed through town. I angled my wrist to peer at my watch.

I darted a glance at Jeff to find his gaze sharp against my face. I swallowed. "You…you wanted to tell me a story."

"I've been telling you the story since the first day we met. Have you not been paying attention?" His voice was deceptively relaxed, but in my peripheral vision, I saw his hand clench into a fist where it rested on his knee.

"I have been," I assured him. The steering on my car felt strange, and I thought I could see the dashboard bounce. "But I would like to hear it all from your perspective."

He made a noncommittal noise. "I've only tried to tell the story to Rose before. She didn't pay attention, either."

"I'm paying attention," I said. I heard the quaver in my own voice. "Who is Rose? Is she the woman I have reminded you of?"

"Have you liked her gifts I've shared with you?" He was silent for a moment, and when I glanced at him, he was staring at my throat. "You're not wearing her necklace."

"What?"

He reached out with the swiftness of a snake striking and grabbed me by the back of the neck. My hands left the steering wheel to scrabble at his wrist as he yanked me across the center console. His hand fisted in the nape of my hair, clenching so tightly it felt as if the strands were being wrenched out of my scalp. My breath was a strangled gasp. The seatbelt cut into my stomach and hips as he dragged me toward him.

The car veered dangerously, and I could see the canyon wall looming closer through the passenger's side window.

"You ungrateful bitch. You just tossed it aside, didn't you? As if it meant nothing."

"I—" I could not get the rest of the words out for

the burn in my skin and the angled wrench in my neck. Tears pricked my eyes. My heart thundered in my chest.

There was an explosion of sound and the car lurched. I reached over and yanked the wheel. The vehicle spun, and the world spun with it until it came to a violent stop.

THIRTY-FOUR

JEFF

SHE WAS HEAVIER than she looked, and my head swam with each step. After another mile, I let her fall to the ground. The freshly fallen snow cushioned her landing, but I still heard the thump of her hitting the ground. I hung my head for a moment, struggling to catch my breath.

I had been thrown against the passenger window on impact, and my brow had split as my head hit the glass. My vision was still blurred, my head throbbed in time with my heart, and my stomach roiled. A warm, wet rush of blood spilled down my cheek.

Fury and nausea were in a race to bring bile rising into the back of my throat. The ungrateful bitch had tossed my gift aside. As if it meant nothing. Just like Rose had.

Once, Rose had promised me she loved me more than anyone else. She had sworn to never leave me, vowed that she would always be true to the bond between us. But the years had passed, and she began to look at me differently. The adoration and worship were gone from her gaze. Disgust and distrust replaced the love she had once sworn would never dissipate.

So I set about showing her I had not forgotten those

vows and promises. Soon the disgust was replaced by fear. I found I liked the fear.

But fear did not equal respect, and the day I found her with him, everything changed. They were in the back of his truck, parked beside the lake well off the dirt track. I suppose she thought I would never find her, but she discounted the connection between us. I would always find her.

I had disbelieved the scene at first, certain I misunderstood. But his jeans were around his knees, her bare arms and legs wrapped tight around him. Her sighs and gasps, moans and whispered encouragement made me hard. They were not for me, though. They were breathed into his ear, not mine.

I dragged the rutting brute off of her and held his head underwater until he stopped struggling. Until he could no longer hear those sighs and gasps, moans and whimpers.

When I caught up with her, she stopped running. She turned with the sun gleaming off her hair and pushed her glasses up her nose. Behind the lenses, I saw not just terror in her eyes, but hatred.

"Please," she whispered as I approached her. A gust of wind swept through the rushes and blew her hair across her face. She trembled when I combed the locks back over her shoulders.

"You're a whore," I said, keeping my voice gentle. "You're even wearing the necklace I gave you."

She went still, and her eyes widened. "This is… I thought…"

"You are mine, Rose. You promised."

She wrenched away from me, snapping the thin gold

filigree chain from about her neck and tossing it in my face. "You're *sick*," she spat at me. "You sick fuck."

She should not have said that. And she should not have tried to run from me again.

She had wept and begged, but I reminded her numerous times that she had promised. "This is for your own good," I whispered to her.

Promises deserved to be kept. A rose would bloom for you if you tended it. That was its promise.

In the end, I had shown her that our bond could not be broken. Not even by her.

A groan at my feet startled me back to the present. I leaned down, fisted my hand in the collar of Evelyn's coat, and dragged her into the woods.

THIRTY-FIVE

Gather ye rosebuds while ye may,
Old Time is still a-flying;
And this same flower that smiles today,
Tomorrow will be dying.

-Robert Herrick

EVELYN

I ACHED EVERYWHERE, and whatever surface I was lying on moved beneath me.

Something sharp dug into my shoulder blade and raked across my back. The pain jolted me back to awareness. Everything was an indistinct blur, as if petroleum jelly had been smeared across my eyes. My hands flew to my face. My glasses were gone.

Realization struck me, and I began to struggle, reaching back over my head to claw at Jeff's hand where it was tangled in my hair and collar. He let me go, and I scrambled away from him. I was dizzy and woozy, though, and could not gain my feet quickly enough.

He caught hold of my arm and yanked me upright so quickly my neck cracked and the surrounding woods spun around me.

I squinted up at him. He held my right arm, and I

could not reach the gun in my right pocket with my left hand. "Where are you taking me?"

He did not answer me. He pulled me after him. We slid down an embankment.

"Where are we going?" I demanded again. I tried to shrug his hand off my arm, but his grip around my elbow was so tight that I was beginning to lose feeling in my fingers.

"Don't test my patience right now, Rose. You will regret it."

"Evelyn. My name is Evelyn. I'm not Rose."

I saw his face turn my way, but his features were without clarity and I could not discern his expression. "Evelyn. Rose. You both broke your promise."

"I haven't made any promises to you."

He yanked me roughly after him. I tripped over something buried in the snow, falling to my knees. He jerked me upright and kept walking. My back was wet. My jeans from the knees down were soon coated in ice, and the dampness seeped into my boots and permeated my socks.

The wind sliced through my coat, but I kept my head up and eyes peeled. Without my glasses, though, I was as good as blind. I could distinguish nothing but the stretch of white punctuated by the black and green arrows of trees. Shapes washed together into an indistinct blur as he led me deeper into the wilderness without breaking stride.

The forest thinned suddenly and deposited us on a narrow lane.

"Where are we?" I asked again when he stopped.

He rubbed his eyes, and I wondered if he had a concussion. Nausea churned in my own gut, and my head pounded with every step.

"Close," was his only response. He set off again.

I hoped walking along a semblance of a road would mean people to encounter, but there was no traffic. No drives branched off from the lane on which we walked.

We must have walked for miles. Without my glasses, with the snow blanketing the landscape, I had no sense of direction. The clouds overhead were the color of ink by the time we reached a turnoff, and the wind was sharp with the smell of snow.

"Where does this lead?" I asked when we branched off from the lane.

"You'll see," was all he said.

The trees closed in around us and snow began to fall. There was no trail that I could see. Jeff dragged me behind him as he wove between trees until the woods opened up before a sprawling ruin. As we approached, I strained my eyes to study it. Now it was little more than a leaning, sagging pile of timber, but I thought it once might have been an inn, likely from the turn of the twentieth century.

Jeff kept his grip on my arm and led me around the dilapidated structure. He stopped for a moment, fumbled in his pocket, and then pulled me after him. Without my glasses, I thought he was leading me to a mound of snow. It was not until we descended a set of steps that I realized the mound was the roof of a subterranean structure.

His hold on my elbow was tight as he worked through a complicated series of locks. He let go of me when he opened the door and swept his arm out in an invitation to enter.

I glanced at his face but it was a shadowed blur. I stepped within and caught my breath. It was a greenhouse, the interior warm, the air lush in a way that reminded me of the South. The smell of roses permeated the air, mixed with the verdant aroma of freshly turned dirt. For an instant, homesickness pierced me, and then the weight of Jeff's hand settled on my shoulder.

"Let me take your coat."

I tried to shrug his hand off. "I'm still cold," I said, though, already, sweat beaded on my brow.

"You won't be for long," he said, tugging my coat from my shoulders, pulling strands of my hair with it.

He hung our coats on a peg, punched a code into a security system keypad mounted on the threshold, and closed the door behind him. We were sealed into this false summer. The light was low, and dim lanterns lit the stone path through the maze of roses.

Many of the roses were in full bloom. I could see the smudges of colors of their petals against the dark foliage. They grew in a profusion that hugged the path and reached out to catch at my jeans and snag my hands as Jeff led me deeper into the greenhouse. I glanced back, trying to keep my coat with the gun in its pocket in sight.

My hands were numb from our long, frigid trek. I did not realize barbs had hooked my exposed skin until I felt the warm dribble of blood down my fingers. I shivered and tucked my hands close to my chest.

Some bushes were skeletal, and a number of trellises we passed under held only barren vines.

"Some of the old and climbing varieties only bloom in the spring and fall," Jeff said. "My hybrids are repeat bloomers, though." There was pride in his voice, and a level of devotion that sounded closer to obsession.

"Impressive," I allowed. "But I don't understand why you wanted to show me this."

The stone path passed under one last trellis before we reached the center of the greenhouse. There, separated from the other roses, stood a single plant. I was close enough to make out one oversized blushing pink bloom on one thin spindle of a stem.

"This is why," he said, approaching the lone bush. He reached out and cupped the rose with a caressing touch most reserved for a lover. "I had to show you Rose. So you would understand."

When I squinted past him, I saw the dark depression in the ground where a trench ran through the center of the greenhouse. A shovel lay in the dirt next to it. I glanced behind me. I could not see the entrance to the greenhouse or my coat with the gun in its pocket through the maze of roses.

"Who was Rose?"

"She was everything." The worshipful tone in his voice made the hair on the nape of my neck stand on end, as did the smile he turned to me.

That smile faded swiftly, though, as he studied me. "Where are your glasses?"

The question was abrupt and agitated. I backed away as he stalked toward me. "I don't know."

I flinched when he reached toward my face. He touched the bridge of my nose and let his finger linger there for a moment. "This is wrong. You need your glasses."

I did not know what his sudden obsession with my

glasses stemmed from, but I nodded. "I do. I can't see without them. Let's go back."

He stared down at me for a long moment before shaking his head. "You don't need to see to dig." He caught my elbow and pulled me toward the trench. "Dig, and I'll tell you the story."

A shovel was a weapon, I reminded myself, as I picked up the tool. "I found the collection you donated to the museum."

He made a noncommittal noise. "I knew you were clever."

"Why did you give away your trophies?" I pushed the blade of the shovel into the soil.

"Fate," he said softly. "It was meant to be, you and I. And I was out of room on my shelves."

There was no dignity in digging one's own grave. I knew that was what I was digging, and I was soon sweating. "To make room for more? What did you take from the woman at the cabin? From Amanda and Rachel?"

"I didn't need anything from them. They were just to get your attention."

I stopped digging and stared at him, sickened. "You have my attention."

He smiled. "Good. Keep digging, and I want you to listen."

I pushed my sleeves up to my elbows. My hands burned and wept blood where the thorns had snagged my skin. My stomach and head protested each movement as I tossed a shovel full of dirt to the side.

The more Jeff spoke, the more certain I was that he was completely unhinged. He talked of roses and promises, and I could not tell if he spoke of an individual woman or of the bushes that surrounded us.

A small bit of paleness in the rich black earth caught my attention. I squinted as I leaned over and picked it up. I held it close to my face to study it. Realization struck me so suddenly I dropped it. It was a bone, a slight digit from a finger or perhaps a toe.

The horror I had been pushing aside flooded me. I glanced around the greenhouse in dawning realization.

"Who is buried here?"

I could see he turned to me, but I could not see his expression. "I told you. Rose. I couldn't leave her behind. She would have hated being left in Kansas."

My knees weakened. I stooped, picked up the bone, and held it out to him. "Is...is it just Rose who is here?"

"They are all roses now." He plucked the bone from me and rolled it between his fingers. "You really haven't been paying attention. That disappoints me."

They were here. Christ. They were right here, the women connected to the pieces of art, hidden beneath the dirt with roots twining around their bones and roses growing from their hearts.

I was certain of it when Jeff moved to kneel beside the rose bush in the center of the greenhouse. He used his fingers to make a depression in the soft dirt, tucked the tiny bone in the hole, and covered it back up, smoothing the soil back into place with careful strokes.

I could not stand in this grave of my own making any longer. I lurched over the lip of the hole and stumbled to a nearby wrought iron bench. I sat down hard, still gripping the shovel. "I am now." My words were rushed. "I am paying attention now. I want to understand."

He was quiet for several long moments, crouched beside the rose bush. "Then you have to understand that Rose was the one who awakened it inside me."

"Awakened what inside you?"

"Don't play dumb, Evelyn. It doesn't suit you. We all have it lurking within us. For some, it never stirs. Others quell it." He took a deep breath and let it out with a sigh. "And for some of us, we embrace it. Mine slept for a long time after Rose. She was my first, and it all leads back to her. I thought that was the end of it consuming me. The others..." He stood and crossed to kneel in front of me. "They were just to keep it in check and keep it sated. It didn't howl and gnash at me the same way it did with Rose." He met my gaze and smiled a smile that chilled me to the core. "Until I saw you on the road that day."

I swallowed. "Because I reminded you of Rose?"

"Because you made me realize it was not gone. It was simply waiting for perfection again."

I shrank away from him as he leaned toward me. He ran his hand through my hair and pulled a long lock toward his face. I bit my lips to keep a whimper from escaping and clenched my hands around the handle of the shovel. He stroked my hair along his cheek and breathed in deeply.

Nausea coiled in my stomach, and fear quaked through me. I closed my eyes and turned my face away. His fingers tightened suddenly before he dropped the strands as if they were on fire and leaned away from me. I darted a glance at him to find fury twisting across his face.

"Don't turn away from me."

"I—"

His hand cracked across my cheek so quickly I did

not even have time to brace for it. I was still catching my breath and blinking away the shocking sting when he caught my chin and rubbed my smarting cheek with his palm.

"Just like Rose," he whispered.

I stared into his eyes, willing back the tears that threatened to blur my vision. I had thought it was the startling blue of his eyes that made it difficult to hold his gaze. Now, though, I realized it was the utter lack of emotion in his eyes. They were completely flat, like the glass of a doll's eyes that reflected my own image back at me.

"She didn't keep her promises either."

I swallowed. "Who was she?"

"My other half."

"Why did you kill her?" I whispered.

His mouth tightened, and I gripped the handle of the shovel.

"Was she repulsed by you?"

Something moved in his face. Something ugly and warped and twisted that lurked beneath that breathtakingly handsome facade. "Shut up." He stood and paced away from me.

"Did she laugh at you?"

His fists clenched. "I said shut *up*."

"She laughed at you," I said. And then I did the same. My laugh felt sharp like a knife, so hard and forced it hurt my throat.

It garnered exactly the reaction I was aiming for. Jeff took a lunging step toward me.

I stood and swung the shovel. I put all of my strength into the swing, and when the flat side of the shovel connected with the side of his head, the blow reverberated through me.

He met my gaze for a split second, eyes wide with shock, and then he fell.

I was running before he even hit the ground. I tossed the shovel aside, leapt over the bench, and bolted. I could not find the stone path. The greenhouse was a labyrinth in my blindness and in the dimness. I forded into the roses, and the vines snagged around my legs. It seemed as if they reached out and clung to me beseechingly with skeletal hands, begging me not to leave them in this harrowing grave.

A sob caught in my throat as I fought through them, but their grip was tenacious. I tripped and fell. Thorns latched onto my skin and sliced at my face, throat, and hands as I struggled to disentangle myself. The barbs pierced my hands as I fought their grip.

My blood spilled into the dirt.

I heard a groan, a shuffle of movement behind me. I wrenched free, scrambled to my feet, and shoved through the thicket of floral tombs. I put my hands up before my face to try to fend off the lancing barbs that struck me. I staggered when I tore through the grip of roses and they shoved me onto the stone path.

"Come now, Evelyn," Jeff called suddenly. "You know it's pointless to resist what's between us."

I pressed my hands to my mouth to hold back a whimper as I spun, squinting and trying to discern where his voice was coming from.

Come out, come out, wherever you are.

"Rose tried to resist. She learned the futility." His voice turned low and coaxing. "I'm not going to hurt you."

I spotted the blurry recess of the entrance to the greenhouse and raced toward it. My coat was a beacon. I yanked it off the peg and thrust my hand into my pocket, but my skin was slick with blood. My palm slid over the grip of the pistol.

My fingers slipped over the handle of the door. I could hear Jeff behind me, steps stumbling, breathing erratic.

Come out, come out, wherever you are.

The handle turned, and I flung the door open. I felt a snag at the back of my blouse, but I jerked away.

I scrambled up the steps and ran, not slowing when my ankle rolled under me and pain shot up my leg. My feet had wings, even in the deepening snow, and I made it to where the trees seemed to form a tunnel over the trail we had tracked through the woods before he was on me. He tackled me from behind, driving me face-first into the snow. I put my hands out to stop my fall and felt a sickening snap in my left wrist when I hit the ground.

I thought I would suffocate, pressed into the blanket of snow with his weight crushing me and my wrist screaming as it broke. But then his weight was gone and he was yanking me over onto my back.

He crouched over me. Even without my glasses, vision swimming with pain, I could see the wildness in his face. He jerked me up, fist clenched in the front of my blouse, until we were face to face.

My coat. The gun in the pocket. It had fallen just out of reach.

"You don't run from me!" He screamed the words, spittle flying to land against my cheeks. He shook me so hard my neck cracked.

I scrambled to reach the hem of my coat. My finger-tips brushed the fabric, but it was too far out of reach.

"You do *not* run from me."

His hands slid up and wrapped around my throat. When I fought him, he drove me flat on my back in the snow. I punched at him with my left hand, my vision going dark with the pain, as he scrabbled to lock his fingers around my neck.

I struggled, managing to shift enough to draw my knee up between us. I had little leverage and space, but I kicked him as hard as I could in the groin. He fell back with a shriek, and I lunged the last few inches of distance to my coat.

Then he was over me again, but the distraction had given me all the opportunity I needed. I squeezed the trigger.

The gun bucked in my pocket as it fired. Jeff flinched back, and I squeezed the trigger again. And again and again. After six times, there was a click. The gun fell hot and silent in the confines of my pocket.

Jeff and I stared at one another. I thought I had hit him, but he stood frozen above me. After a long moment, he swayed and crashed to his knees. I scurried backward, and he pitched forward to sprawl in the snow.

My breath left me on a sob. I realized the soft, animal-like whimpers I heard were my own. I rolled to my hands and knees. The pressure on my left wrist made me vomit.

When my stomach was empty, I tucked my left arm against my chest, the pain a sharp drumbeat radiating through me. I gulped the frigid air and struggled to slow my breathing. I trembled violently, from the pain, the cold, and the aftermath of the adrenalin. A glance back at the hulking darkness of the ruins sent a deeper chill through me. I struggled to gain my feet.

I threaded my right arm into my coat, but a wave of nausea swamped me again when I tried to insert my left arm into the sleeve. I gave up and clutched the lapels together as I stumbled through the woods.

The cover of the trees eased when I reached the narrow lane and revealed the snow storm that had settled over the mountains. The snow fell in sheets, as heavy as a downpour, softer than rain and far more foreboding. When I glanced back into the shadow of the trees, I was spurred to keep moving.

I headed back in the direction Jeff had brought me. The drive had to lead somewhere.

My hair was soon soaked from the snow, and my teeth chattered so hard it had set the pounding in my head to cacophony proportions. My arm was a constant throb. My face stung so badly from the cold that it felt like any movement would crack my skin wide open. I could no longer see the lane before me through the fall of snow.

I realized I had ventured from the old track when I floundered into snow knee-deep, but no matter which direction I turned, I could not find the road again. Frustration and fear tore at me.

I threw my head back and screamed. The snow was like a blanket, though, muffling the cry even as it left my mouth. It dampened all sound until all I could hear was the fall of flakes past my ears, the strumming of my heart, and my sawing breath.

The realization was loud, though. So loud it was deafening and so heavy I staggered at its weight. It did not matter that I had escaped the grave I had been digging. It did not matter that I had killed Jeff before he had managed to kill me. I was going to die tonight.

I laughed, and it sounded like a sob.

"That is pretty fucking unfair," I whispered. Then I laughed again, because I had long known life was a far cry from fair.

I slogged through the snow with my head down, pressing on against the storm and the despair. There was no sensation of falling. I was upright one instant, stumbling through the snow, and the next I was face down in the powder.

I managed to gather the energy to roll onto my back, but the snow was a deep, soft cradle. I sighed as I settled deeply into its embrace. I was not shivering any longer. A sliver of concern pierced me, and then it slipped away with the drowsiness that weighed me down. I could not feel my hands or feet, but at least the jagged edge of cold that bit down to the bone had subsided.

I took a breath and inhaled the fine layer of snow that had settled on my face. I coughed, and the sound jolted me. I struggled to my knees and then floundered unsteadily to my feet.

When I fell again, I could not get back up. The most movement I could make was rolling to my back to stare at the endless expanse of sky above me. There was a break in the snow, I realized belatedly. The last light of the sun winked over the mountains and extinguished, leaving behind a stained, cold winter's sky that would soon be black.

I did not realize I cried until the tears froze and the track of skin between the corners of my eyes and my ears began to burn. The grip of sleep was too strong to resist, and soon I did not even feel the snow that was burying me.

THIRTY-SIX

In 2017, there were 260,977 cases of missing females under the age of 21 and 61,888 of missing females over the age of 21.

HECTOR

THE ANCIENT RED car had crashed in almost the exact spot where my wife's vehicle had been found on the empty, snow-skirted road fifteen years ago.

There were black marks on the road from burnt rubber, and the little Civic had plowed straight down the embankment into a snow drift. Both the driver's side and the passenger's doors were flung open. The battery had long-since died. There was blood against the glass of the passenger's side window, and the airbag on the driver's side had exploded.

"What the hell happened here?" I asked Ashton and Cooper.

"Someone called dispatch about an abandoned car," Ashton said.

The front left tire was ragged and shorn from a blowout. "Where are the occupants?"

"Good question," Cooper said.

A groan of brakes brought my attention to the road. Ed hopped down from his rusty tow truck and picked his way carefully down the embankment. "This is Ev'lyn's car," he said. "She alright?"

"I don't know."

Something in my voice brought all three men's gaze to me. I fished my phone out of my pocket and pulled up the tracking app. I tapped on the tracker attached to Jeff's vehicle, and the emblem on the screen pinpointed a location right in the heart of Raven's Gap.

I dialed Book Ends. Susan answered after several rings.

"Susan, it's Hector," I said. "Is Jeff there?"

"No, he was supposed to be working the front today while I hosted the book club meeting, but he never showed and didn't answer his phone when I called. Is something wrong?"

"Call me back if he shows up," I said, and hung up the phone.

I knelt beside the front left tire. The blowout had ripped the rubber to shreds. I reached under the car, feeling for the tracking device, but it was gone. I climbed the embankment, and the other three men trailed after me.

"Hector?" Ed asked, but I held up a hand.

I searched the road and the shoulder, but the device was nowhere to be found. I pulled the app back up on my phone and selected the tracker linked to Evelyn's vehicle. The pin dropped on the screen some ten miles northeast of where we stood.

"Ashton, call Peters. I want the car processed as if it were a crime scene. Cooper, you're coming with me."

"What the fuck is going on?" Cooper asked.

I met Ed's concerned gaze. *The sacrificial lamb.*

William's words rang in my head. "We need to find Evelyn."

The snow fell in torrents, and my range of vision narrowed to just a few feet in front of my hood. Fifteen years and now he was in my grasp. I just had to find him in time.

The ping on the map in the tracking application led me past Gardiner to a spot where the Yellowstone River curved north in an oxbow. An old track angled off of the state road and crossed the curve of the river over a narrow single-lane bridge that was frequently washed out in the spring thaw. The bridge and lane were rarely used any longer. When they were, the traffic was mainly on foot.

Cooper flashed his lights behind me as he followed me into the pull-out. I parked, and through the blinding snow, I saw a dark shape leave the vehicle behind me and jog toward my truck. I unlocked the door.

"This is madness," Cooper said, as he threw himself into the truck. "We're way out of jurisdiction."

"Call the sheriff's department. They can meet us out here."

"What do you think we're going to find?"

I grabbed the remote and lowered the plow on the front of my truck.

Justice. That's what I wanted to find.

I glanced at the app on my phone. The tracker that should have been on Evelyn's vehicle was about five miles down the track. It was stationary now.

I squinted through the windshield and crept across the rickety bridge slowly. Cooper gripped the *oh shit* handle and let out a relieved breath when we reached the far side of the river.

I passed my phone to Cooper. "Tell me when we're approaching the location marked here."

It was slow going, but the plow cleared the way. By the time Cooper signaled that we should be closing in on the location, the whiteout had abated from a swirling blizzard to a steady fall of snow.

I pulled to the side of the track. The snow was no longer blinding, but it deafened the landscape into muffled silence.

Cooper passed my phone back to me and I studied the dot on the screen before trekking farther down the lane. I had not gone fifty yards before the app indicated I had reached the tracker's location. I veered into the woods and heard the crunch of Cooper's steps behind me and his heavy breathing.

Anticipation tightened like a noose around my throat.

"I think this is the old LaBelle Hot Springs Resort," Cooper said, when the woods thinned and the dark shadow of derelict timber buildings could be seen through the snow. "We used to come out here when—"

He would have tripped over the mound in the snow had I not reached out and grabbed his shoulder. Guilt and hope were the double edge of the knife in my gut as I knelt and brushed the snow aside.

"Shit," Cooper breathed, and cued the radio to connect with dispatch.

I had expected to find Evelyn dead at Jeff's hands. I had counted on it. A woman's murder would not sit easily on my conscience, but on the other side of the scale was finally bringing my wife and daughter's killer to justice. The need for vengeance outweighed the guilt. I had made a promise to my girls, and I intended to keep it.

But it was Jeff who lay sprawled facedown, blood pooled in the snow beneath him. I stripped off my gloves and pressed my fingers to his throat. No pulse.

I sat back on my heels and rubbed a hand over my jaw. Not even relief made it through my shock.

"Well, Evelyn, I'll be damned," I whispered.

I stood and scuffed my foot through the snow surrounding Jeff's body until I kicked something small and plastic. I slipped the tracking device into my pocket.

"Hector!" Cooper called. He lifted a hand and gestured for me to join him around the fallen ruins of the old turn of the century resort. "You're going to want to see this."

I followed him around the remains into a sunken greenhouse filled with roses and the gray light of twilight. He led me along a stone path to the center of the greenhouse where a single bush with a single rose in bloom stood out from the others. A trench was laid through the center of the greenhouse. In the middle of the trench, a hole had been dug. I glanced around and spotted a shovel lying beside a nearby bench. A smear of blood stained the metal.

"What the hell happened here?"

"There's more," Cooper said. He knelt by the solitary rose bush and pointed into the dirt.

I crouched beside him and brushed away the layer of dirt to expose the bones of a human hand. "If Yates hasn't called the FBI yet, he needs to."

FRANK FOUND HER three hours into our search.

I stripped off my gloves and swept the snow away.

Frank paced around us, whining, and Cooper radioed in our location.

I pressed my fingers against her throat. Her lips were blue, her face completely devoid of color save for the livid scratches on her face and throat. There was no flicker of movement, no signs of life or movement of her chest, but I felt a faint tremor of a pulse.

I stripped off my coat and wrapped it around Evelyn. She was limp, and her skin was icy to the touch. I yanked off my cap and pulled it over her head. Her hair was stiff and frozen, the strands crusted with snow. My eyes dropped to her bare hands, and my stomach sank. I gingerly slipped my gloves over her fingers before bundling her into my arms.

"Evelyn, I have you." I thought I saw her eyelashes flutter. "You're safe now."

I left Frank with Cooper with instructions for him to take the poodle to Maggie. I rode in the Medevac chopper they landed on the old mining road to fly her to Bozeman and paced the hallways as they worked to stabilize her. A nurse found me several hours later.

"You can come sit with her now," she said. "She's not out of the woods yet, but the doctors are feeling more confident than they did when she was brought in."

She led me into the Intensive Care Unit and directed me into the second room. Evelyn was swaddled in blankets. Even her head was covered. Only her face, neck, and one arm were exposed. A nasal tube oxygen line was hooked around her still face, and her right arm was riddled with IV lines and monitors. Two lines had been placed in her neck. My stomach lurched at the sight of the machine pulling her blood from one line and pumping it back into her body through the other.

"Her kidneys have shut down?" I asked.

"No, no," the nurse assured me. "We use the hemodialysis machine to warm the blood in extreme cases of hypothermia like this one. She has this vascular catheter along with a pleural and peritoneal catheter." At my blank look, she said, "In addition to warming her blood, we're doing warm saltwater solutions around her lungs and in her abdominal cavity to warm up her body."

The beeping of the machines monitoring her vitals was erratic. "Her heartbeat is irregular?"

The nurse nodded. "That's not unusual in patients with severe hypothermia. She went into cardiac arrest when we first started working on her, and it is still a danger. But I promise you, we're being very careful and we're monitoring her continuously." She checked the dialysis machine and the bags of fluid hanging on the pole at Evelyn's bedside. "Are you here to arrest her when she wakes up?"

I thought I saw a flicker of muscle movement in Evelyn's fingertips, but when I glanced at her face, it was still. "No." I was here to thank her.

"I'll be at the desk just outside if you need anything."

I sat in the chair at her bedside, tipped my chin to my chest, and let exhaustion pull me under. I woke to the sound of shallow, rasping breath and lurched upright. I took one look at Evelyn's face as she struggled for breath and lunged from the chair.

"Nurse!"

It was the same woman who had attended her earlier

who came running at my shout. "I've paged the doctor. I'm going to have to ask you to step outside."

Over the next days, Evelyn's body struggled to fight the pneumonia that settled in her lungs.

Maggie showed up at the hospital the first morning. "Go on home, Hector. You have work to do, and the dogs are waiting for you."

"What are you going to do?" I asked as she pulled up a chair close to Evelyn's bedside.

She enfolded the younger woman's bandaged hand in her own. "Sit with her. She shouldn't be alone right now."

Back in Raven's Gap, I waited for updates on Evelyn's condition. When pneumonia finally loosened its grip after days of antibiotics through a PICC line and breathing treatments, she was taken into surgery. She underwent a subsequent surgery the next day.

The FBI sent a team to help us process the greenhouse. The composting trench was a graveyard. Each rose bush was being dug up, every piece of soil examined. Thus far, the body count was over ten.

A search of his computer at work found a folder of photographs of the inn with Evelyn coming and going. There were files on Amanda and Rachel as well, and the technicians were still trying to retrieve the contents.

In the alleyway beside the hardware store, in the stairwell, and in his loft apartment, there were numerous cameras set up to record every angle of entry into his home. Motion detectors and half-buried electrical lines were found surrounding the greenhouse.

I pushed open the door to the apartment and studied the interior from the threshold. It was one large open space with exposed ducts and copper pipes, brick walls, and plank flooring. It was immaculate. Not a thing out of place, not a dish in the sink, not a crumb on the counter. The shower in the bathroom was dry, and there was not a wrinkle in his bed.

I donned a pair of black nitrile gloves and moved to the bookcases lining the far wall. Frank paced around the room sniffing in corners before he settled into a sprawl on the floor. Louie trotted at his heels and then curled up against him with a sigh.

I searched for hours. The evidence team had already been through the place with a fine-tooth comb. If there was anything in the apartment that hinted at something out of the ordinary, they would have found it. According to their reports, only the files hidden on his computer at the bookstore and the greenhouse showed his true nature.

Most of his books were first edition classics and gardening books on roses. I pulled one after the other off the shelf and flipped through them. An hour after I started on the books, I cracked the spine of a Faulkner tome and the pages slid aside to reveal a photograph tucked within.

I studied the photo with dawning realization. A boy and girl in their early teens sat on a porch swing. The girl grinned into the camera, all youthful beauty and enthusiasm. She wore a coat with polka dots over a flower print dress, and her hair was caught in two braids. The photographer had captured her just as she pushed her glasses up her nose. The boy stared at the girl beside him, face unsmiling. His gaze was fixed and held all the worship of a prepubescent boy.

I flipped the photo over, and on the back was a woman's fine print. The first word was smudged, but the others read *& Rose, 1986.*

IT TOOK ME a week of searching the National Crime Information Center files to find Rose Jeffers, listed as missing from Cawker City, Kansas since 1990. She had disappeared at the age of eighteen, last seen leaving her parents' farmhouse in the company of her boyfriend, who had also never been seen again.

I called Cawker City, a minuscule dot on the map, and when I finally caught one of the few police officers on the phone, I was given Mary Ann Jeffer's number.

When I explained who I was and why I was calling, the tremulous voice on the other end of the line said, "Someone finally believes me? Please, come over. I'll put a kettle on."

I gently informed her that it was a fifteen-hour drive and that she could wait to put the kettle on until the next afternoon.

I drove down through Colorado to avoid Nebraska. Kansas reminded me uncomfortably of the place where I had been born and left to raise myself. Windswept and empty, swallowed up by the sky. Forgotten middle America where the people perpetually squinted against the sun and lived and died within a narrow radius of plains. The endless openness had always left a knot in my throat. I had never been out on a boat in the ocean before, but I imagined that featureless stretch of barrenness was just as haunting.

Places like this whittled people down to bone and sinew and bitterness. My mother had been a prime example.

I reached the outskirts of Cawker City and followed the directions down a dirt county road until I reached a T in the road. In the northwest corner of the T, the house stood just as Mary Ann Jeffers had told me.

The windmill leaned precariously. The roof of the silo had fallen in on itself. The house was in desperate need of repairs and a paint job. Snow dusted a neat yard, though. The flowerbeds around the house would be a profusion of color come spring. There were cushions in the swing, and the porch was swept clean.

The woman who answered the door was worn and withered with age. Her eyes were bright, and her smile was kind.

"You're the police officer who called me."

"I am. Thank you for agreeing to talk with me."

She glanced past me and eyed the figures staring at her from the cab of my truck. "Bring your dogs on in. I love dogs."

Frank and Louie were only too happy to oblige as she ushered me into her home.

She led me into a sitting room that was clean and bright and decorated with an overwhelming profusion of floral patterns. "Make yourself comfortable," she invited, and then shuffled from the room.

I stood awkwardly beside the blue sofa with glaringly pink flowers, but Louie hopped up onto the cushions and curled up against a green pillow with yellow flowers embroidered on it. Frank stood in the doorway, tail wagging. When I shifted to peer around the corner, I found him watching Mary Ann Jeffers load a tray with a tea kettle, saucers and cups, and a tin of cookies.

The saucers and cups rattled as she struggled to lift the tray, and I moved to take it from her.

"Oh, thank you, dear. That is very kind of you."

I placed the tray on the coffee table and politely drank the heavily sweetened tea she poured for me. Even the saucer and delicate cup that my hands dwarfed had flowers on them.

Louie moved to her lap, and Frank rested his head on her knees. I pretended not to see her sneak them both a cookie.

"After I spoke with you on the phone, I pulled out all of my old albums."

She nodded to a box beside a purple chair with white flowers on it. I placed the box at her feet and sat beside her as she retrieved a photo album. She wiped the dust away. The knuckles of her hand were gnarled, the skin crinkled like tissue paper over fine bones. There was a tremor in those bones as she turned the cover and angled the oversized book so I could see.

I had not come for tea or to see baby pictures, to see the photographic evidence of a little girl aging from infant to teen. But I sat patiently for the next hour and made noncommittal noises over the albums.

Many of the photographs were torn in half, someone clearly and ruthlessly cut out of the picture. I noted that when the little girl was around seven or eight, she began to wear glasses. In most of the pictures she was laughing, bright-eyed and gap-toothed, sweet and innocent. In many of the pictures after she began to wear glasses, the camera caught her pushing her glasses up her nose.

"My Rosie was the sweetest thing," she said softly. "She never met a person who didn't fall in love with her, never met an animal that didn't start following her around. She was just...sunshine. Sunshine and smiles." Her voice was soft, and her fingers stroked over the pretty face behind the sleeve of plastic. She looked up and met my gaze. "The police never believed me. Do you finally believe me?"

"Tell me why the photographs are torn," I said, keeping my voice gentle.

She bowed her head and let out an uneven breath. "Where Rosie was light, he was...darkness. Shadow. He loved Rosie to a point where I... I worried. It was obsession. It wasn't natural."

I handed her the photograph I had found in Jeff's apartment. She covered her mouth with her hand as she studied the picture. "I tried to tell them," she whispered.

"Tell me about him now," I encouraged her.

"To everyone else, he seemed like such a good boy. So polite. So friendly. Such a handsome little boy. No one believed me."

"I believe you."

She shook her head and covered her eyes. Her next breath caught wetly and raggedly in her chest.

I took her hand and enfolded it between mine, waiting to speak until she composed herself and met my gaze. She wore glasses herself, and her eyes were damp behind the lenses.

"I believe you. I've seen the bones. Everyone will believe you now. The evidence is there."

She searched my face. "Is he dead?"

"Yes."

Her eyes slid closed, and it was not grief that made her face sag but relief. "Good," she said. "Good." She stroked Frank's topknot and met his limpid gaze. "I know that should not be my reaction. But it is. I'm glad."

And then she began to tell me what she had tried to tell everyone all those years ago.

THIRTY-SEVEN

You may break, you may shatter the vase, if you will,
But the scent of the roses will hang round it still.

-Thomas Moore

EVELYN

I WOKE SLOWLY, and it took a long moment before I realized I was in my new room on the first floor of the inn. Last night, I had been discharged from the hospital. When I turned my head, I could see the sunlight filtering around the edges of the tightly drawn curtains. The river sighed and warbled as it rushed past.

There was a heavy, cottony feeling in my head and a sore tightness in my chest. My hand felt heavy and numb. I lifted my left arm and studied my casted wrist and my hand swaddled in bandages. The sight still made my breath catch in my throat. The gauze left my thumb and first finger exposed. It was stunted on my middle finger and then wrapped flat to my palm where my ring finger and pinky should have been.

I drew my right hand from underneath the blankets and held it up to the early morning light. I turned it back and forth, reassured by the whole appendage marred only by deep but healing scratches. I flexed my hand, curled it into a fist, and then straightened and wiggled my fingers.

I turned my gaze back to my left hand. I no longer felt the wrench of emotion when I looked at my damaged hand.

Maggie, the owner of the diner, had been sitting at my bedside in the hospital when I first gained consciousness.

"By the time the search and rescue team found you, you were severely hypothermic and had frostbite." I turned my head on the pillow and squinted at the blurry figure at my bedside. I flinched away when she leaned toward me before I realized it was Maggie. She pressed the remote to raise the head of my bed and stood to ease a pair of glasses onto my face. "Faye found this extra pair in your room at the inn. I hope you don't mind that we went through your things."

They were an old pair of glasses, not my current prescription. Even so, I sucked in a shuddering breath as the room came into focus. My chin trembled in relief at finally being able to see again, and I closed my eyes against the overwhelming flood of emotion. When I opened my eyes and saw my hand, saw that Maggie held it in her own and I could not even feel it, I had cried in earnest.

"I had frostbite?" I finally asked, voice a rasp around the weight in my chest. A rough cough rattled through me.

"It was most severe in your fingers and toes. Doctors tried to save your middle finger, but the gangrene persisted and they had to take part of it. You've lost two toes on your right foot." Her voice had been matter of fact but gentle. "And part of your right ear."

Shock reverberated through me. I lifted my unscathed hand to feel the bandage covering my ear, and I stared at the outline of my feet under the sheet. I could see the bulk of bandages on the right.

Now when I looked at my hand, when I felt the shorn remains of my ear, I remembered the certainty I had felt in the midst of the whiteout, the realization that I would die. And that was enough.

The next week was grueling. Maggie and Faye took turns driving me to physical therapy. The last remnants of pneumonia were hard to shake. The sensation began to return to my hands and feet, bringing with it a prickling awareness that pieces of me were missing.

I remembered the small finger bone I had found in the greenhouse, and I shuddered. I could learn to cope with fewer digits, with the blisters from my altered stride, with the balance issues and the ache in the arch of my foot weighed against that fate.

I was questioned by the FBI. They had taken over the case. I repeated my story to them, from beginning to end, from the moment on the road mere weeks ago to the women I had found to the private collection at the museum to the horror of his greenhouse and the aftermath. I found the papers detailing the donation to the museum still folded in my pocket and gave them to the agents.

Hector and his poodle, Frank, with Rachel's little dog in tow, came to the inn at the end of the week. Hector sat across from me in the great room. I grew chilled easily these days, and when he saw me shiver, he stoked the fire burning in the hearth.

"Thank you," I said. "For finding me."

Frank hopped carefully onto the sofa alongside my stretched out legs and curled up against me.

Hector dipped his head toward the poodle. "Thank him."

I threaded the fingers of my right hand into Frank's curls. "Is this the end of it, then? For you?"

I remembered the woman's Mona Lisa smile in the banner in Ed's shop. The little girl's grin.

"It's just the beginning." His gaze lingered on my face with an expression I could not quite make out. "There have been fifty-six remains found. The forensics team is working on identifying them, but it will be a long process."

They are all roses now. I shivered. "And Rose? He told me it had all begun with a woman named Rose. Have you found out who she was?"

He leaned forward and rested his elbows on his knees. His face moved as he rubbed the back of his neck. For the first time, I saw a chink in that harsh, still façade. He looked weary.

"His real name was Russell Jeffers. Rose was his sister. His twin."

My other half.

I dreamt of roses that night, their vines skeletal hands that reached out to me beseechingly and begged me not to forget them where they lay.

EPILOGUE

The Rose is without an explanation;
She blooms, because She blooms.

-Angelus Silesius

HECTOR

Two Months Later

"I WANTED TO be the one to tell you," Grover said when I answered the phone. The coroner continued before I could say anything. "I wanted you to hear it from me and not read it in a report."

"You found them." Thank fuck. I could finally bring my girls home, where they belonged, where I should have cherished them.

The silence on the other end of the line went on for too long. "I wish I could tell you that. But the DNA matches came back with nothing, even on the Jane Does." He sighed. "Their remains were not recovered at the greenhouse. I wish like hell I had answers for you. But they weren't there, Hector."

I sank onto the edge of my bed. My legs would not hold me up any longer. Frank jumped up on the bed beside me and curled up with his chin on my knee.

Given a serial killer's reliance on patterns, if Winona

and Emma were not found among the remains in the greenhouse, it was unlikely Jeff Roosevelt had killed them. The realization carved me open with a dull, serrated knife.

My instincts about the man had been right. I had used an innocent woman as a pawn to prove just that. But now the belief I had held for fifteen years that I knew who was responsible for the disappearance of my girls vanished. Fifteen years of certainty were burned to ash in an instant.

Pressure built behind my eyes, and I tilted my head back.

The web was still tacked to my ceiling. Maps with Winona's usual route in and out of town highlighted, memories of things she had said that might be a link scrawled on Post-It notes, receipts, photos printed from the CCTV camera footage around town in the weeks leading up to that one day. Tacks were shoved into the map at the locations she visited regularly. I had not pinned the photograph of Jeff Roosevelt back in place.

The blank spot in the center the labyrinth of clues stared back at me.

*   *   *   *   *

"Current institutional practices allow missing and murdered American Indian women to disappear not once, but three times—in life, in the media, and in the data."

-Missing and Murdered Indigenous Women and Girls, a case study by the Urban Indian Health Institute

AUTHOR NOTE

I was plotting this story when Mollie Tibbetts went out for a run near her home in Brooklyn, Iowa, one evening in July of 2018 and never returned home. The case gripped me. I checked the news obsessively every day to see if she had been found until word of her body being discovered was released on August 21st.

I did not know Mollie. I cannot fathom the grief those who loved her feel. But I was still devastated to read that press release, even though I knew it was coming.

I was devastated, because all women have the potential to be Mollie. We leave our homes and venture into a world that we know is never completely safe, not for our mothers, our daughters, our sisters, or ourselves. We women never expect to be victims. We women never go jogging or hiking or out for a drink or on vacation expecting to not come home. But regardless of how strong and smart and prepared we are, we women are acutely aware of our vulnerability, of the weight of statistics against us. We may well go out for a run one evening and, like Mollie, never return.

Because we have all been Mollie. We have all been young and beautiful, tender-hearted and filled with hope for our futures. We have all felt safe and secure. And we have all had to learn that one day, we could potentially become a headline.

But the stark truth is not all women who go missing

make it to the headlines. The undeniable fact is that it is missing *white* women who are given the spotlight in our news coverage. In a recent case study, the Urban Indian Health Institute identified 506 unique cases of missing and murdered American Indian and Alaska Native women and girls across seventy-one selected cities. The number is likely much higher, but there is no comprehensive data collection system regarding the number of missing and murdered women in Indian country.

The National Crime Information Center reported that, in 2016, there were 5,712 reports of missing American Indian and Alaska Native women and girls, though the US Department of Justice's federal missing persons database only logged 116 cases. That is a staggering, paltry number, any way you look at it. It means that in a single year, 5,596 women not only went missing, but they were also allowed to fall through the cracks, disappearing not just from life but from the data as well. If you want more gut-wrenching numbers to illustrate how unacceptable this is, it means that over the course of 365 days, fifteen women went missing every single day, and there is no record of their disappearance in our federal databases. Not only are they gone, but the country has forgotten about them.

Native women living on tribal lands in America are murdered at an extremely high rate—in some communities, more than ten times the national average. The Center for Disease Control and Prevention has reported that murder is the third-leading cause of death among American Indian and Alaska Native women.

There is an epidemic of violence and abduction against Indigenous women, a harrowing normality of mothers, daughters, sisters, and friends being gone one day, never to be seen again. There are no resources put to use to find them, no widespread media coverage, and no remembrance of those lives in our data.

The Violence Against Women Act has a specific section addressing safety for Native women. Congress needs to reauthorize, expand, and improve the VAWA. In 1978, the Supreme Court case Oliphant v. Suquamish stripped tribes of the right to arrest and prosecute non-Indians who commit crimes on Indian land. There were some amendments added to VAMA that would allow tribal courts to prosecute non-Indians who sexually assault tribal members, but the bill has languished, and more needs to be done. There needs to be a restructuring of how law enforcement in and outside Indian country communicates, and law offices in Indian country need funding and resources to help combat this data gap.

Savanna's Act aims to bring justice for missing and murdered Native American women. The legislation would improve data collection on tribal victims, remove barriers for tribal law enforcement, and create guidelines for responding when someone's reported missing. The bill would improve tribal access to federal databases for tracking missing tribal persons, require the Department of Justice to consult with tribes while developing guidelines, mandate reporting statistics regarding missing and murdered Native Americans to Congress, and streamline coordination between tribes and law enforcement agencies with training and technical assistance in putting the guidelines in force. The bill stalled in the U.S. House in December 2018 but was reintroduced in 2019 along with the *Not Invisible Act*.

I do not think there is a simple solution to the epidemic of violence and invisibility Native American women face. It is a complex situation steeped in racism, injustice, and infrastructure failure.

Perhaps the first step toward change is a nationwide awareness of this tragedy. I hope this story has shone a light on the horror Indigenous women face on a daily basis. My book is fiction, but for the women who are living this, it is a heinous, appalling fact.

These women should not be invisible. And they should not be forgotten.

ABOUT THE AUTHOR

Meghan Holloway found her first Nancy Drew mystery in a sun-dappled attic at the age of eight and subsequently fell in love with the grip and tautness of a well-told mystery. She flew an airplane before she learned how to drive a car, did her undergrad work in Creative Writing in the sweltering South, and finished a Masters of Library and Information Science in the blustery North. She spent a summer and fall in Maine picking peaches and apples, traveled the world for a few years, and did a stint fighting crime in the records section of a police department.

She now lives in the foothills of the Appalachians with her standard poodle and spends her days as a scientist with the requisite glasses but minus the lab coat. She is the author of *Once More Unto the Breach*, available now from Polis Books. Follow her at @AMeghanHolloway.

Get 4 FREE REWARDS!

We'll send you 2 FREE Books plus 2 FREE Mystery Gifts.

BRENDA JACKSON — *Follow Your Heart*

ROBYN CARR — *The Country Guesthouse*

RICK MOFINA — *SEARCH FOR HER*

B.J. DANIELS — *FROM the SHADOWS*

FREE Value Over **$20**

Both the **Romance** and **Suspense** collections feature compelling novels written by many of today's bestselling authors.

YES! Please send me 2 FREE novels from the Essential Romance or Essential Suspense Collection and my 2 FREE gifts (gifts are worth about $10 retail). After receiving them, if I don't wish to receive any more books, I can return the shipping statement marked "cancel." If I don't cancel, I will receive 4 brand-new novels every month and be billed just $7.24 each in the U.S. or $7.49 each in Canada. That's a savings of up to 28% off the cover price. It's quite a bargain! Shipping and handling is just 50¢ per book in the U.S. and $1.25 per book in Canada.* I understand that accepting the 2 free books and gifts places me under no obligation to buy anything. I can always return a shipment and cancel at any time. The free books and gifts are mine to keep no matter what I decide.

Choose one: ☐ **Essential Romance**
(194/394 MDN GQ6M)

☐ **Essential Suspense**
(191/391 MDN GQ6M)

Name (please print)

Address _____ Apt. #

City _____ State/Province _____ Zip/Postal Code

Email: Please check this box ☐ if you would like to receive newsletters and promotional emails from Harlequin Enterprises ULC and its affiliates. You can unsubscribe anytime.

Mail to the Harlequin Reader Service:
IN U.S.A.: P.O. Box 1341, Buffalo, NY 14240-8531
IN CANADA: P.O. Box 603, Fort Erie, Ontario L2A 5X3

Want to try 2 free books from another series! Call 1-800-873-8635 or visit www.ReaderService.com.

Get 4 FREE REWARDS!

We'll send you 2 FREE Books plus 2 FREE Mystery Gifts.

Love Inspired Suspense books showcase how courage and optimism unite in stories of faith and love in the face of danger.

FREE
Value Over
$20

Visit
ReaderService.com
Today!

As a valued member of the Harlequin Reader Service, you'll find these benefits and more at ReaderService.com:

- Try 2 free books from any series
- Access risk-free special offers
- View your account history & manage payments
- Browse the latest Bonus Bucks catalog

Don't miss out!

If you want to stay up-to-date on the latest at the Harlequin Reader Service and enjoy more content, make sure you've signed up for our monthly News & Notes email newsletter. Sign up online at ReaderService.com or by calling Customer Service at 1-800-873-8635.

RS20